The leash whipped out of Chantal Livingstone's hand and streaked along the sidewalk in the dog's wake. "Oh, no," she whispered, breaking into a run herself. "If anything happens to this dog, my job is history."

Ahead, the cat leaped onto a window ledge. Brandy lunged after it and began barking frantically, balancing on her sturdy back legs, her big front paws against the wall, straining to reach the hissing cat.

Chantal retrieved the leash and pulled. Useless. Brandy outweighed her by thirty pounds.

Then a man appeared behind Brandy. He grabbed her collar, gave a quick pull, and the dog landed flat on all four paws, panting loudly but no longer barking.

Chantal exhaled slowly, then focused on the man. Certain she knew who he was, she glanced toward the curb and saw a dark blue van with skis strapped on the roof. Yup, it had to be—the dog handler, Denver Brooke.

"Ms. Livingstone, I presume," he said dryly. "And I suppose this furry cat chaser must be our star."

Chantal sighed. "I'm afraid so."

ABOUT THE AUTHOR

"I want to give a special thanks to all my readers who have written to me," says Dawn Stewardson. "I really enjoy hearing their comments. And I always write back. Sometimes it may take a while, because it takes so long for your letters to actually reach me, but I absolutely *always* reply."

Dawn lives in Toronto with her husband, John, her two dogs, Rutherford and Julie, and her cat, Yeats. Letters to Dawn Stewardson may be sent c/o Harlequin Reader Service, P.O. Box 1397, Buffalo, NY 14240

Books by Dawn Stewardson

HARLEQUIN SUPERROMANCE
329–VANISHING ACT
355–DEEP SECRETS
383–BLUE MOON
405–PRIZE PASSAGE
409–HEARTBEAT
432–THREE'S COMPANY
477–MOON SHADOW
498–ACROSS THE MISTY

HARLEQUIN INTRIGUE
80–PERIL IN PARADISE
90–NO RHYME OR REASON

Don't miss any of our special offers. Write to us at the following address for information on our newest releases.

Harlequin Reader Service
P.O. Box 1397, Buffalo, NY 14240
Canadian address: P.O. Box 603,
Fort Erie, Ont. L2A 5X3

COLD NOSES, WARM KISSES

Dawn Stewardson

Harlequin Books

TORONTO • NEW YORK • LONDON
AMSTERDAM • PARIS • SYDNEY • HAMBURG
STOCKHOLM • ATHENS • TOKYO • MILAN
MADRID • WARSAW • BUDAPEST • AUCKLAND

Published October 1992

ISBN 0-373-70521-2

COLD NOSES, WARM KISSES

This one's for my readers,
especially to those of you who wrote to tell
me how much you enjoyed reading about Rutherford,
the heroine's dog in my Superromance,
Three's Company.

And for John always.

doing that with me - she said to

CHAPTER ONE

Two THINGS SOMETIMES caused a tiny dull throbbing directly behind Chantal's temples. One was drinking Bristow Fine Champagne. The other was dealing with Nolton Bristow, owner and CEO of the company that produced it. This morning, only the man was causing the throbbing.

"I want this ad campaign kept strictly hush-hush," Nolton said. "I haven't even let Marlene in on it."

Chantal was tempted to say she doubted Nolton's wife got off on spying for his competitors. Instead, she said, "I won't breathe a word until Jay gets back from Mexico. Then I'll talk to him about the idea and—"

"We can't wait for Jay to get back," Nolton said. "I want the commercials shot by the end of January, latest."

"Nolton, I—"

"I know, I know," he interrupted again. "That doesn't give you much time to get the shoot site checked out. So you'd better call that dog guy's agent right now."

"Nolton, the idea of spending several days in your chalet, alone with some man I've never even met, makes me very, very uneasy."

"Just tell him things are strictly business between the two of you, Chantal. You've never had any problem doing that with me," he added pointedly.

Reluctantly, she reached for the phone, recognizing defeat when she was facing it.

"Too bad tomorrow's Christmas day," Nolton muttered as she dialed. "But see if he can leave the day after, huh? I'll send Brandy over to your place about seven in the morning."

Chantal nodded, doing her best to ignore the way the dull throbbing in her head had escalated into a rat-a-tat-tat that would do a jackhammer proud.

"Rachel," she said when the agent picked up, putting what she hoped was enough enthusiasm in her voice to fool Nolton. "Rachel, it's Chantal Livingstone. About the shoot with that Saint Bernard breeder..."

"Denver Brooke," Rachel supplied.

"Right. Listen, Rachel, my client has just come up with the most fantastic idea you've ever heard...."

"RACHEL," DENVER SAID, "That's the most ridiculous idea I've ever heard." He tipped his ancient recliner back as far as the telephone cord allowed, resting his cowboy boots on the scarred surface of the desk, listening to what the people at Jay Clawson Advertising had decided they wanted.

"You know I'm primarily a breeder," he said when she was through. "I only train my own dogs."

"I explained that to Chantal, Denver. She got backed into a corner on this, though. The client still wants you, specifically, because you know Saint Bernards so well. But he's suddenly insistent they use *his* dog in the commercials."

"Has it been trained *at all?*"

There was a pause at the other end before Rachel said, "I don't believe so."

Denver rubbed his jaw. He was crazy for having the slightest thing to do with Madison Avenue. "Rachel, for me to train a dog well enough to use it in a commercial could take months—if it could be done at all. I think you'd better tell your Ms. Livingstone that either we use McGee or it's not a go."

"I suspect that would mean it's not a go, Denver. Look, before you say no, consider the money again, okay?"

He crossed one boot over the other and considered the money again. Rachel was a good agent. She'd convinced the ad agency to pop for twice his normal daily fee by telling them that being away from the kennel would cost him.

And his bank account could certainly use a boost. If its balance got much lower, he'd be sharing the dogs' kibble for dinner.

"Denver?" Rachel pressed. "Look, I didn't realize their using a strange dog was going to be a major deal for you. I told Chantal we were on, that I'd just phone her back to confirm you could leave on the twenty-sixth. So how about you decide one way or the other, then call her yourself. We're closing early today...you know...Christmas Eve and all?"

He grabbed a pencil, wrote down the number Rachel rattled off, wished her Merry Christmas and hung up.

McGee clambered to his feet and laid his massive head in Denver's lap.

"What do you think, fellow?" Denver said, scratching behind the dog's ear. "Think we can convince this Chantal Livingstone their idea's a dumb one?"

The dog yawned.

"Yeah, that's how I feel, too. But I guess we'd better give her a call and see what we can work out. I've gotten kind of used to eating people food."

CHANTAL WAS HALF WATCHING along the street and half watching her suitcase. No one was really likely to try stealing it from her front steps this early in the morning. The addicts generally got later starts to their days. But you never knew in Manhattan.

The frosty air had just started her shivering when a yellow cab turned off Amsterdam onto West Eighty-fifth.

She gazed at it heading toward her, hoping it was Brandy arriving first. Having to wait would hardly improve Denver Brooke's negative attitude.

And she didn't imagine it had improved any when he'd called Nolton with his questions about Brandy. Nolton probably hadn't known even half the answers. She wouldn't have been surprised if Denver had phoned back to tell her their deal was off.

Of course, calling it a "deal" was using the term loosely. "Absolutely no guarantees," he'd told her. "I can't promise you a thing when I've never even seen the dog."

She'd said she understood. "You'll just do what you can with her." No, it certainly wasn't much of a deal. But it was Denver's parting shot that had really made her wince.

He'd said, "This whole idea is insane, you know."

She knew. Only too well. The idea of a city slicker like her traipsing off to the boonies with a gigantic dog and a complete stranger... being stuck in Nolton's chalet with some man...

"You have absolutely nothing to worry about," Rachel had told her reassuringly. "Denver's a real nice guy. You know we'd never send you even a marginal weirdo."

Well, maybe he wasn't a weirdo, marginal or otherwise. And she hadn't spent her entire life in New York without learning how to take care of herself. But what kind of name was Denver Brooke? Sounded like a cowboy's. A cowboy who bred dogs in Jersey, though?

The cab slowed as it neared her, then jerked to a halt, an enormous black man sitting in front, an enormous brown-and-white dog sitting in back.

Chantal eyed the dog, suddenly not at all sure she wanted it here first. She wasn't exactly afraid of dogs, but she hadn't realized Saint Bernards were *quite* so huge. The top of Brandy's head was grazing the roof of the cab.

She reminded herself the dog was gentle as a lamb. Nolton had said so. Of course, Nolton was hardly renowned for George Washington-type honesty, but it was simply a matter of standing here with Brandy for a few minutes. Until Denver Brooke arrived. Then he could take over.

The driver threw open his door and glared at her. "You the one who's expecting this beast?"

When she nodded he shoved himself out of the taxi, grabbing a small gym bag from the passenger's seat and tossing it to her. "I'm supposed to tell you the dog's papers and tags and stuff's in there. But do the world a favor, huh, lady? Next time this thing's going somewhere, let it walk."

"She was bad?"

"She howled. All the way from East Sixty-third and Park to the corner of West Eighty-second. And between howls she drooled. Man, I gotta towel down my back seat now."

Chantal apologized, digging in her pocket for a tip, even though she knew Nolton had already taken care of the driver at the other end.

He seemed slightly mollified by the ten-dollar bill she handed him and opened his back door.

Brandy looked out at the cabbie. The cabbie looked over at Chantal. She asked if Brandy had a leash on.

The man reached inside the cab, grabbed the end of a leather lead and handed it to Chantal.

She cleared her throat. "Let's go, Brandy."

The dog didn't move a muscle. The man told her she had to sound as though she meant it.

Chantal repeated herself, trying to sound as if she meant it, tugging on the leash for emphasis.

Brandy lay down on the back seat and drooled onto her huge front paws.

The driver said, "Look, lady, I gotta radio pickup to make. You wanna move it?"

"I'm trying to move it," Chantal told him, dropping the gym bag and yanking on the leash with both hands.

The driver swore, stomped around the car and opened the other back door. "Okay, lady. You pull, I push."

They did. Brandy dug her paws into the seat and howled loudly enough to wake every resident of the Upper West Side.

"Lady, you want I should just go ahead and shoot this thing, or what?"

Chantal gazed through the car at the man, wondering whether he actually had a gun. Probably. And he'd probably be happy to use it. "Wait a minute," she said quickly. "I'll have her out of your cab in just a minute.

She dashed into her town house and raced back out with a salami chub. "Here, Brandy," she called, waving the meat.

"Get closer," the driver snapped. "Wind's blowing the wrong way. She can't smell it from there."

Chantal got closer. Brandy's big black nose twitched and she wriggled off the seat onto the sidewalk.

Chantal tossed the salami down, no point risking her hand, then picked up the gym bag and the end of the leash, while Brandy devoured six sandwiches' worth of meat in two seconds.

"Have a nice day," the cabbie called, squealing away from the curb.

"Very funny," Chantal muttered, her gaze following the taxi down West Eighty-fifth, hoping she'd see a van coming toward her.

A dark blue van, Denver Brooke had said. He'd be driving a dark blue van. But there was nothing moving on the street except the departing taxi and a neighbor who regularly walked his German shepherd along the block. She'd always thought it was a very large dog, but compared to Brandy it was a pygmy.

She watched them approaching, saw the shepherd see Brandy, felt Brandy's leash grow instantly taut. "You be good," Chantal said, looking down and tightening her grasp.

The man caught her eye when she looked back up. "Christmas present?" The first time he'd ever spoken to her.

"No. No, I'm just sort of looking after her for a couple of days."

Suddenly Brandy lurched at the shepherd, practically jerking Chantal off her feet, and the two dogs began circling each other, tails wagging furiously, leads tangling.

"Good thing yours is a female," the neighbor said, unwrapping a leash from around his legs. "Otherwise we might have a fight on our hands."

"Good thing," Chantal agreed, thankful for small mercies. She glanced up the street again, this time *praying* she'd see that van.

"Come on, Butch," the man said, pulling his dog away.

Only they didn't exactly move *away*, because Brandy simply lumbered along beside Butch. Chantal braced herself and yanked on the leash. If Brandy felt the tug, she ignored it and dragged Chantal past the next house.

The neighbor glanced back at her, smirking. "Looks like you're coming for a walk."

And that was when the damned cat materialized.

Brandy's nose twitched. Then she leapt a foot in the air and came down running.

The gym bag went flying. The leash whipped out of Chantal's hand and streaked along the sidewalk in Brandy's wake.

"Oh, Lord," she whispered, breaking into a run herself. If anything happened to Nolton's dog, her job was history. And the heavy morning traffic on Columbus was only half a block away.

Ahead, the cat raced up a staircase and onto a window ledge. Brandy screamed to a halt beneath it and began barking frantically. She was balancing on her sturdy hind legs, big front paws against the wall, straining to reach the hissing cat. It swiped a paw through the air, almost connecting with the dog's nose.

The front door of the brownstone burst open, and a woman in curlers and a housecoat began screaming at

Brandy. Or maybe she was screaming at Chantal. Maybe even at the cat. It wasn't clear because she was screaming in a foreign language.

Chantal retrieved the leash and pulled with all her might. Useless. The dog outweighed her by at least fifty pounds. Brandy continued barking, the cat continued hissing, the woman continued screaming.

And then a man appeared behind Brandy. He grabbed her collar, gave a quick pull, and the dog was flat on four paws, panting and whimpering but no longer barking. Disaster averted.

Chantal exhaled slowly, then focused on the man, certain she knew who he was.

She'd give him tall. Not especially dark, though. His eyes were a warm brown, as was his too-long hair. And as for handsome...well, rugged was more accurate. And entirely too rough trade for her taste.

A five o'clock shadow darkened his jaw—and it was only seven-thirty in the morning. Scruffy jeans molded his long legs and hid most of a pair of—she'd just known it—a pair of cowboy boots. And something that looked as if it might be a genuine, worn-out World War II flight jacket covered a faded work-shirt stretched across his broad chest.

She glanced over to the curb, seeing what she expected. A dark blue van with a New Jersey license. And skis strapped on the roof. Terrific. This Jersey cowboy figured he was going on vacation. She looked back at him, told herself to make the best of things, and smiled.

"Ms. Livingstone, I presume," he said dryly.

DENVER FOLLOWED CHANTAL back toward her house. She stopped to pick up a gym bag from the sidewalk, then gave Denver a little shrug. "Dropped it during the excitement," she explained.

Denver nodded, thinking she was lucky to find it still there.

"I just have to run in and get the camera," she said, tossing the gym bag on top of a suitcase and opening her front door. "I almost forgot it, and if I had, we'd have been camera shopping in Quebec. Our director expects me to come back with enough potential shoot sites for him to plan six commercials around."

Denver pushed Brandy's rear end into a sit, then watched Chantal heading up the stairs. She had one of the cutest little behinds he'd seen in a long while.

When she disappeared from view, he turned his attention to the town house. Someone had done a first-class job of transforming twenties construction into nineties livability.

The curving oak staircase practically floated up to the second floor, and the side of the hallway opposite it was mirrored, making the space seem far wider than it actually was. Ahead, at the rear of the house, enough of the kitchen was visible that he could see the back wall was mostly glass. It overlooked a tiny city garden.

He glanced at the stairs again as Chantal started back down, a video camera slung over her shoulder. "I was just admiring your place," he said. "You do any of the work yourself?"

She laughed, shaking her head. "I'm allergic to dust, starts me sneezing nonstop."

"Ah . . . you aren't allergic to dogs, are you?" For a horrible second he thought she was going to tell him she was.

"I don't think so," she finally said. "But all I'm sure about are dust and freshly mowed grass. I've never actually been around a dog for long enough to tell."

He nodded, hoping she wasn't about to discover allergy number three. Her sneezing nonstop, from here to Quebec, wouldn't add much to the trip.

"I'll take these," he said, stepping outside and picking up both her suitcase and the gym bag with his free hand.

She locked the front door, and they started for the van. A few feet along, Brandy tried to bolt after a squirrel.

Denver jerked her sharply back. Just as he'd assumed, using Brandy for the commercials probably wasn't an option. The dog seemed like a washout.

The lady, though...well, this trip might not turn out to be quite the nightmare he'd been anticipating. He wasn't forgetting she was in advertising, which meant her middle name certainly wouldn't be Sincerity. But at least, going on first impressions, she wasn't going to be obnoxious company.

In fact, after he'd bailed her out of that scene with the cat, the way she'd looked straight at him with those big blue eyes and merely said, "Thank you, I don't know a thing about dogs," well, that had been kind of cute. Especially when he'd expected her to launch into a litany of excuses for not being able to handle the situation, starting with one about her only being five-three or four and the dog being a lot heavier than her.

He glanced down at her again as they walked. Twenty-eight or nine. And nice-looking, with a neat nose and slim little figure. And shoulder-length tawny hair that he'd guess didn't come out of a bottle.

Not that she was his type. Not at all. He liked his women a little disheveled, not looking as if they'd stepped directly off a page of *Vogue* when they'd actually been chasing after a dog.

And her clothes were completely wrong for where they were going. But those Fifth Avenue suede pants and bomber jacket were probably as low on the fashion scale as she owned.

He just hoped she at least had some extra sweaters in her case. And a pair of serious boots. Without three-inch heels. And with warm linings.

About five yards from Denver's van, Chantal realized it wasn't empty. And given the way Brandy suddenly began dancing, the dog had spotted the apparition at the same moment.

Only it wasn't really an apparition. It was another Saint Bernard. Sitting in the driver's seat, staring through the windshield at them, one huge front paw draped casually over the steering wheel.

Chantal stopped dead and looked at Denver, knowing without asking what he was up to, not liking it.

She'd told him when they'd talked on Christmas Eve that they definitely couldn't use his dog. But he was apparently one of those men who figured being male automatically put him in charge.

Lord, having to work with that type of man was bad enough. Now she was going to be trapped with one twenty-four hours a day.

"That's McGee," he said. "But don't worry, I won't let him drive . . . at least not until we're out of Manhattan traffic," he added, giving her an annoying, aren't-I-just-too-cute-for-words smile.

Chantal began walking again, counting to ten before glancing at him once more and saying, "Look, I thought I'd made myself clear. The whole point is to use *Brandy* in these commercials. And the reason you're coming along while I check out the site, is so you can see how she reacts in the snow, and so you'll have a couple of solid days to work with her."

Denver shrugged. "And I thought I'd made *myself* clear. No guarantees. So I brought McGee along," he added, stopping at the van, "just in case."

"Just in case what?"

"Oh, just in case you wanted to see how much better a pro performs than a rank amateur. McGee's already done more than a dozen commercials. He's perfectly trained. And he's intelligent."

"I don't think Brandy's actually *dumb,*" Chantal said, the words slipping out in a surge of defensiveness. A ridiculous surge, considering she'd first laid eyes on the dog half an hour ago. And considering that, right this moment, Brandy was bouncing up and down on the sidewalk like an enormous furry ball, clearly dying to make McGee's acquaintance.

"Well, at any rate," Denver went on, "I figured that if I can't do anything with Brandy, you could plot out whatever you're plotting out with McGee."

Chantal said, "I see." And she did. Denver was going to have no qualms about telling her how to do her job. And he figured it would be easier to sell her on using McGee than give Brandy a crash course in basic training. And, dammit, he was probably right. But selling her and selling Nolton Bristow were two different things.

What Nolton wanted, Nolton got. At least, that was the rule at Jay Clawson Advertising.

If it weren't, she wouldn't have to be making this ridiculous trip. At least not accompanied by this cowboy. Mr. Denver would be sitting back in his kennel right now, with his perfectly trained dog.

He slid open the passenger-side door of his van and motioned to McGee. The dog immediately climbed out of the driver's seat, retreated to the open carpeted space behind it and settled down beside an enormous bag of dog food.

Denver let Brandy scramble inside, and she scooted back to where the other dog was lying, her large behind wriggling, giving a funny little leap when she reached him.

McGee simply looked at her. The two of them filled the van's entire cargo area with their bulk.

"Brandy, sit," Denver ordered.

The dog gave another playful jump, her attention solely on McGee.

"Just thought I'd try," Denver said. "But I suspect this is going to be a long trip."

Chantal refrained from saying she'd been suspecting that since the second Nolton suggested it.

Denver put her suitcase behind the seat, and she climbed in. The van smelled decidedly of dog. Behind them, Brandy began making whining noises and worrying at McGee's ear. Chantal watched for a minute, mentally weighing her options.

From the looks of things, having another dog along was only going to distract Brandy. But Denver had mentioned on the phone that his kennel was someplace down past Somerville. So was she going to insist he take McGee back there? Go a good seventy miles out of their way? During the morning rush hour? When they already had maybe a nine-hour drive ahead of them to reach Nolton's chalet?

Hardly. She might be darned annoyed, but she wasn't an idiot. They'd just have to keep McGee locked up or something.

Denver climbed into the driver's seat and began poking through the gym bag Nolton had sent along, saying he was checking for a rabies certificate. "We don't want to drive all the way to Canada and be turned back at the border. And when I called your Mr. Bristow, he didn't sound too sure about anything."

"That's because he only bought Brandy three days ago."

"Oh?" Denver said, looking over. "I guess that explains why the name on this registration paper isn't Brandy."

Chantal nodded. "That's just what Nolton decided to call her."

"So...he buys a dog three days ago...and insists you use her in his commercials...even though she's not trained?"

Chantal said it was a long story, that she'd explain once they got going.

"Then let's get going." Denver started the van.

The instant the motor revved to life, Brandy began to howl. The air inside the van vibrated with sound, the wailing so loud it hurt Chantal's ears.

Denver looked across at her. "Please tell me she won't do that for long."

"She won't do that for long," Chantal said, leaving it there, not volunteering about the drooling.

BRANDY WOUND DOWN her howling shortly after they'd crossed the Triborough Bridge and were on the Bruckner Expressway, heading for the New England Thruway, not really *all* that long after Chantal had begun thinking that maybe she should have let the cabbie use his gun.

She glanced into the back, checking the drool situation again. Earlier, there'd been puddles of it. Now they'd pretty much soaked the carpet, and the stains were mingling with older ones.

Denver asked what she was looking at. She glanced at him guiltily and said, "I think Brandy drooled a little on the carpet."

"Saint Bernards all drool," he told her, his eyes on the road again. "Don't worry about it."

She nodded, looking back once more. She suspected dogs must have redeeming qualities. Otherwise, so many people wouldn't have them. But she hadn't yet determined what they were.

While she watched, Brandy circled a couple of times, then flopped down beside McGee and closed her eyes. If Chantal didn't know which was lying where, she wouldn't be able to tell them apart.

"So," Denver said, "you want to fill me in about this little adventure? Tell me why it's so important to use that howling mutt back there in this ad campaign? And why you're using mountains in Quebec for the shoot instead of the Poconos or the Catskills? Snowy mountains all look alike, you know."

Chantal ignored his sarcasm and told him yes, she knew. "As I said, it's a long story."

"That's okay. It's a long way to Quebec."

She smiled a little, despite herself. The Jersey cowboy's dry sense of humor had come as a surprise.

"So?" he pressed.

"Well...let's see..." she said, staring out at the traffic on the expressway, wondering if anyone else out there was driving all the way to Canada today. "I'm not sure exactly where to start."

"How about with Brandy? When Rachel first talked to me about this job, we were going to use McGee. The next thing I heard, your client was hot on using his own dog. Then you tell me he just bought her. So what's the deal?"

"The deal is that Nolton Bristow is Jay Clawson Advertising's most important client. Which means when he says, 'Jump,' we jump. And Nolton was suddenly inspired to play Lee Iacocca. Which also explains why we have to use his ski chalet as our shoot site."

Denver's gaze briefly flickered to her. "Thanks, you've made everything perfectly clear."

That sarcasm, Chantal thought, was likely to become more than a little wearing. "I'd better back up the explanation a little," she said. "Do you know who Nolton Bristow is?"

"Haven't got a clue."

"Well, he's the Bristow of Bristow Fine Spirits. And the commercials the agency is going to be shooting are for the launch campaign of a new product, Bristow VSOP Brandy."

Denver glanced across at her once more, his expression saying that she had to be kidding. "You aren't going to tell me your commercials will have a Saint Bernard running through snow-covered mountains, with a brandy keg around its neck . . . are you?"

"I'm afraid so. I know it's hardly original, but it was Nolton's idea."

"And he actually figures it's a good one?"

"So good it's classified."

"It's what?"

Chantal smiled again. She shouldn't poke fun at Nolton, but sometimes it was impossible to resist. "Nolton occasionally gets ideas he thinks are so good that he swears us to secrecy about them. He worries somebody might steal one of them. Jay Clawson and I call those his classified ideas."

"In other words," Denver said, grinning, "Nolton Bristow is paranoid city."

"Well, since he's our major account, and also a friend of Jay's, we prefer to call him security conscious."

"But you're supposed to be keeping the details of this highly original ad campaign quiet."

"Completely."

Denver said he appreciated Chantal letting him in on the classified secret before she'd actually had to.

"You should," she told him, "because it's something that only *I* know about. I mean, Jay knows about using a Saint Bernard with a keg in the mountains. But Jay's in Mexico on vacation, and Nolton just hit me with the Lee Iacocca angle on Christmas Eve. He said he hasn't even told his wife about it, wants to keep it entirely hush-hush for as long as possible."

"Ah, yes... the Lee Iacocca angle," Denver said. "I was hoping we'd be getting back to that."

"Nolton's idea," Chantal explained, "is to personalize the launch campaign by featuring himself in it. You know the ads that had Lee Iacocca talking about cars?"

Denver nodded.

"Well, we're going to try to get the same sort of results by introducing Nolton as the man behind Bristow Brandy. Just the way Lee sold people on domestic cars instead of imports, Nolton will sell them on American brandy instead of imported."

"You think that'll work?"

"It's not a bad hook. Kind of compensates for the lack of originality. Besides, Nolton's a good-looking man, so consumers will have an attractive face to put with the Bristow name. And hopefully, at point of sale, they'll remember the company's American and buy domestic."

"But why," Denver asked, "does it matter which dog you use?"

"Oh, right. The dog's part of personalizing the campaign. So is the setting. We're going to use *Nolton's* dog. And *Nolton's* chalet. The commercials will make it clear they're his."

"So that's his reason for buying the dog. And calling her Brandy."

"Exactly."

Denver shook his head, his expression saying how low his opinion was of that.

About as low as hers, Chantal thought guiltily. But she didn't have much choice about going along with Nolton's whims. She liked working for Jay Clawson Advertising.

"Apparently Nolton was glancing through the want ads," she elaborated, "and seeing one for a Saint Bernard was what sparked his Lee Iacocca idea. So he bought her."

"From ... ?"

"Some young couple in the Bronx."

"When I was checking through those papers in Nolton's bag, I noticed from her registration that she's fifteen months old."

Chantal didn't see the relevance of that until he went on.

"Which probably means," he explained, "she was a last year's Christmas puppy that outgrew her welcome. And what," he added, his gaze flickering across the van once more, "is going to happen to her when Nolton's ad campaign is done?"

Chantal looked into the back at the sleeping dogs, trying to imagine how Brandy would settle into life in the Bristows' Park Avenue penthouse. It was a difficult thing to imagine.

"Geez," Denver muttered, "no wonder the poor dog doesn't seem too bright. At this point, she can't even know what her name's supposed to be. Some people just don't think, do they? Or they just don't care."

"Nolton Bristow *is* an impulsive man," Chantal admitted. "But his wife, Marlene, is awfully nice. So maybe Brandy will work out just fine with them."

Denver stared straight ahead through the windshield and said, "Or maybe she won't."

Chantal glanced back again, eyeing Brandy uneasily, not wanting to think Denver might be right.

CHAPTER TWO

MARLENE BRISTOW GLANCED anxiously at Nolton, hoping he'd save the scene she knew was coming until after their son had made good his escape.

"So, I'll see you two again in a couple of months," Kip said, giving her a quick kiss on the cheek, then playfully punching Nolton's arm. "Take care."

"And you enjoy Maine, dear. And drive carefully," Marlene added, hugging him tightly, telling herself once more that everything would work out.

"The heir to the Bristow millions," Nolton snapped as Kip closed the door behind himself. "And that's how he walks around. We send him off to an Ivy League college, and within four months he looks like he belongs in the Bowery. I ordered him at Thanksgiving to get his hair cut, Marlene. By the next time we see him he'll probably be wearing it in a ponytail."

"He's only nineteen, Nolt. And he's never lived away from home before. Can't you try to go a little easier on him?"

"Dammit, Marlene, appearances are important. I've told you that a million times."

She didn't say a word. But she'd bet that, in their twenty years of marriage, she'd heard the phrase at least *two* million times, and she'd long ago given up arguing that other things were more important.

"Kip reflects on me," Nolton persisted. "And I don't want people thinking I approve of the way he looks. We should have sent him to West Point. They'd have made sure his hair stayed the right length."

"Nolt, just give him awhile, okay?"

Nolton said that what he should give Kip was a good, swift kick.

Marlene said they had time for another coffee before she had to leave.

"You really keen on going this year?" Nolton asked, glancing at the Vuitton case waiting by the door.

"Not exactly keen. But you know I always gain five pounds between Thanksgiving and Christmas. And you know that every time I do, you start making comments about not wanting me to turn into a blimp on you. A few days at the spa is the easiest way to lose weight." She turned and headed through the penthouse to the kitchen, trying to convince herself she had to go through with this right now. She'd promised. And it was the best time to... No. There wasn't going to be a *best* time. Not ever. And how could she hit Nolt with both things at once? She just wasn't sure she had it in her. But she so wanted to get everything out in the open and over with.

She poured the coffee, skim milk for Nolt, low-cal sweetener for her, and carried the mugs into the solarium overlooking Park Avenue.

"I don't know where Kip thinks he gets off," Nolton muttered, trailing after her and slumping into a chair. "I mean blithely announcing when he arrived that he'd be leaving again on the twenty-sixth."

She tried to smile. It only made her feel more hypocritical. She was just so sick of lying, but Kip's news had sent her reeling and she needed to rebuild her courage.

So instead of addressing what she knew had to be brought into the open, she said, "Nolt, remember when you were nineteen? If your girlfriend's parents had invited you to spend some of the holidays with them, what would you have done?"

"Girlfriend," Nolton said. "That's another thing. He's supposed to be getting an education at that damned college, not making out with girls."

Marlene murmured something inane about all work and no play.

"Who is this Cathy, anyway?" he demanded. "All Kip did when I asked for details was mumble."

"She's no one, Nolt. Don't dwell on it."

"But I figured he'd be spending the entire holiday here. I figured you'd go to your stupid spa and Kip and I could maybe do a few things together. Hell, it's probably just as well he left, though. Someone I know might have seen him with me, and the way he looks... But what am I supposed to do all week? I told the staff I wouldn't be in, so I can't even go to the office. I wouldn't want them thinking I'm indecisive."

"I guess you shouldn't have been quite so quick about Brandy, Nolt."

"What's that supposed to mean?" he demanded.

She eyed him uncertainly. He was watching her with extremely suspicious eyes. "All I meant," she said slowly, "was that if you hadn't bundled her off first thing this morning, to stay at that trainer's kennel, she'd have been here to keep you company."

He merely shrugged, pointedly shifting his gaze away, a sure sign he was keeping secrets again. And if they were about Brandy, she wanted to know exactly what they were, because the poor dog was going to end up being another complication in this whole mess.

"Nolt?" she said.

"What?"

"Is there something I don't know about Brandy?"

"I told you, Marlene. I want to get her trained as quickly as possible."

"Yes, I know what you told me. But is there something you didn't tell me?"

"Nothing important. It's just that when I talked about the trainer's kennel, that's not exactly...well, listen, let's drop the subject for now."

"Nolton, you never tell me anything. And now you've brought this enormous dog in here without a word to me beforehand. So if you've something up your sleeve, I'd really like to hear about it."

"Look, Marlene, you're going to be chatting with all kinds of rich biddies at the spa. Rich biddies with husbands who run businesses themselves. And I wouldn't want you to mention anything that...well, look, just don't say anything about Brandy at all. And when you get back I'll tell you this idea I've had. But forget about it for now, understand?"

She nodded, and he clearly relaxed a little.

"You know," he said a minute later, "maybe what I'll do this week is charter a plane and fly down south, join Jay for a few days of sun and surf. He told me he was going away alone this year."

Marlene glanced over the top of her coffee. "Did he mention exactly where he was going?"

"Mexico someplace."

"Mexico's a big country, Nolt."

"Well, his secretary might know exactly where he's gone. I'll be damned if I'm going to sit here alone, twiddling my thumbs for days on end."

IN THE BACK OF THE VAN, Brandy and McGee were a communal heap, a single sleeping pile of fur. Chantal suspected she'd envy them that fur before long.

The outside temperature had been steadily dropping as they'd driven north. And Canada was serious snow— snowbanks piled along the sides of the highway and thick white blankets covering the mountains.

"So," Denver said, glancing over, "how much farther?"

She looked down at Nolton's hand-drawn map, saying it couldn't be very much farther at all, and Denver merely nodded.

His being content to rely on her as navigator had been a pleasant surprise. Maybe she'd initially misjudged him a little. Maybe she didn't really have to worry about him trying to take charge of every aspect of their expedition.

He slipped another cassette into the tape deck, and strains of Beethoven's Fifth filled the van.

That she and the Jersey cowboy had the same taste in music had been another pleasant surprise. They'd hardly talked during the trip, had simply listened to tapes.

She sat watching him for a minute as he drove, thinking he'd fit right into one of those westerns where men were men and words were minimal.

He was in the age-range of the few men she occasionally dated —early to mid-thirties. But that was the only similarity. If he were the kind of man she was used to, a fast-tracking, fast-talking Manhattan type, she'd have heard his entire life story by now. But she barely knew a thing about Denver Brooke.

Of course, she didn't care to. Oh, she was still a little curious about his name. But aside from that...well, she preferred good conversationalists. He was entirely too much the strong silent type for her taste.

And anyway, given they'd be alone together for the next few days, it made sense to keep in mind that remark Nolton had made—about her making it clear to Denver that this was strictly business. She wanted that *perfectly* clear.

They passed a gas station Nolton had marked on the map, and she looked down at it again. "Denver, there'll be a road on the left soon, leading to someplace called St. Leonard. Nolton has a grocery store marked at the turnoff, so we should probably stop."

"Let's make it a quick stop. I don't want to be trying to find his place in the dark."

Chantal nodded, glancing out into the gathering gray dusk, then focusing on the map once more. "The road to the chalet is just past the store, immediately after we pass a highway sign saying Trois-Rivières, 50 Kilometers."

"Traw what?" Denver said.

"I think it must mean Three Rivers."

Denver shook his head. "Why would someone like Nolton have a chalet in a French-speaking province?"

"Good skiing?" Chantal said.

He grinned a little at that, then turned his attention back to the road.

Actually, she thought, watching a French-language billboard whizz by, she wasn't too keen on that aspect, either. Chantal might have originally been a French name, but her French vocabulary pretty much consisted of *oui, non,* and *bonjour.*

She realized she was watching Denver again. This time, her gaze drifted south from his rugged profile, and she decided he likely *was* strong as well as silent.

Broad shoulders and chest. Those scruffy jeans stretched tautly, delineating muscles in his thighs. She had a suspicion that women who were into the primitive male would find him attractive.

Primitive... right—good word for him. Maybe a little animal magnetism there. Maybe more than a little. Or maybe it was just that being surrounded by the great outdoors lent his type something. He probably looked like hell in a suit and tie, though. And she lived in a suit-and-tie world.

Only another mile or so along, they spotted the road to St. Leonard and pulled off the highway. The weathered little grocery store looked as if it had been standing there forever.

The dogs scrambled to their feet when the van stopped, but Denver glanced into the back and told them they wouldn't be getting out this time.

McGee sat down. Brandy remained standing and began to drool.

Chantal got out and began to shiver. This trip had taken them from cold to colder to coldest.

Inside, the store was every bit as quaint as its exterior had promised. Worn wooden floor with well-trod center paths in the aisles. An old fashioned hanging scale and a cash register that would fetch an outrageous price in an Upper East Side antique shop. What signs there were, were all in French.

"*Bonjour,*" a man greeted them from behind the counter.

"*Bonjour,*" Chantal repeated.

Denver mumbled something that sounded like bonbon. "Not exactly your Lexington Avenue deli," he added quietly to Chantal, picking up one of the little wire shopping baskets and steering her down an aisle.

He started to load their basket with prepackaged cold cuts and cheese.

"I take it we aren't going to cook," Chantal said.

"After that long a drive? Even opening these packages will be an effort. Let's just grab some fruit and bread and get going."

The old cash register keys clanged loudly when the shopkeeper rang up their items. Chantal absently glanced at the stack of newspapers on the end of the counter. A picture of a cute little boy, about ten, was splashed across the front page—beneath a headline that read *Le Fils de Claude Gagnon Est Enlevé!* Whatever that meant.

As the man started bagging, she slipped a couple of twenties onto the counter, telling Denver the groceries were on Jay Clawson.

The shopkeeper stared at the bills for a moment, then spoke to her in French.

"Pardon?" she said, realizing the pointlessness of the word as it popped out. She wasn't going to understand him a second time around, either.

He repeated himself.

Denver said, "Oh geez, I'll bet he's telling us he doesn't take American money."

"That is not it," a woman's voice offered in French-accented English.

Chantal turned. The store's one other customer was walking over, smiling. About thirty, with long, untamed dark hair, she wore skintight orange ski pants and an open ski jacket that revealed a centerfold figure.

She said, "He is just telling you what is the exchange rate he gives on American currency, saying you would maybe prefer to pay with the Canadian dollars."

"No, the exchange rate is fine," Chantal said. "Please tell him it's fine."

The woman spoke to the man, then glanced back at Chantal. On the way by, though, her dark eyes lingered on Denver.

Right, Chantal thought. Suspicion confirmed. If you went for the primitive type, Denver Brooke was one you'd go for.

"You are staying near here?" the woman asked as the shopkeeper handed Chantal her change.

She said yes, they were staying at the Bristows' chalet.

"That is not so far from my place," the woman said. "My name is Pierrette Pelletier. If you run into any problems," she added, looking straight at Denver, "just call me. The Bristows have my number."

Chantal felt pretty sure *she* had Pierrette's number, too.

Denver grinned at the woman—an extremely broad grin, Chantal noted—then said "Thanks" and introduced himself. "And this is Chantal Livingstone," he added.

Pierrette Pelletier's eyes registered the different last name, then flickered to Chantal's naked ring finger, and she smiled an even more friendly smile. "Well, if you are here for a while," she said, looking at Denver once more, "*I* might call *you.*"

And ask you to come up and see me sometime, Chantal silently added. Then she watched Denver watch Pierrette Pelletier wiggle her way back to where she'd left her shopping basket.

"Nice," he murmured, picking up their bags of groceries.

"Very," Chantal said.

"Friendly, I meant."

"I knew what you meant," she said, starting for the door with him, glancing at him as surreptitiously as she could, wondering if she might have been just a tiny bit hasty in judging him as *entirely* too much the strong silent type for her taste.

JAY FLUNG OPEN THE DOOR and wrapped his arms around Marlene, saying, "God, woman, where have you been? I thought you'd be here hours ago."

"Oh, Jay, I'm sorry. I...I've been sitting having coffee in some doughnut shop all afternoon. I had to be alone for a while to think."

"It's okay," he said, holding her. "You're here now. It's just that I've been worried sick about what was happening at your place."

She pressed her face against his chest, hugging him tightly, unable to speak.

"Hey," he finally said, "come on inside. We've got the rest of our lives to hold each other now."

He grabbed her suitcase from the hall, followed her into the living room, and sank onto the couch beside her.

The early evening dusk, trailing lazily through his living room windows, was softening his sharp features, and she reached out to trace them with her fingertips, assuring herself he wasn't a figment of her imagination. Sometimes, when they were apart, she thought he must be, because he made her so happy it seemed he had to be part of a dream.

He took her hand, saying, "Tell me how it went. Was it as awful as you expected?"

She swallowed hard. "I didn't tell him, Jay. I couldn't."

Slowly, he drew back and gazed at her. "You've changed your mind?" he murmured, his voice barely audible.

"Oh, no! Oh, no, it isn't that at all." She shook her head, wishing with all her heart she'd been braver. This should have been the first day of the rest of her life...of her life with Jay. That had been their plan. She was supposed to have told Nolt she wasn't really going to the spa at all, that she was leaving him. But somehow... No, not somehow. She hadn't told him because she was so weak. Nolt knew as well as she did their marriage was a sham. But if she'd told him she and Jay were in love...

"Then what is it?" Jay asked, taking her other hand in his as well and gazing into her eyes. "What went wrong?"

"It's...oh, Jay, nothing worked out the way we expected. Instead of Kip spending the rest of his vacation at the penthouse, instead of him being there with Nolt for the next week..." She took a deep breath, then backtracked and started the explanation from when Kip had come into her room and blurted out his story.

"So," she concluded five minutes later, "you can imagine how Nolt's going to take the news about Kip. And I just...I just couldn't tell him about it, then turn around and tell him about us and...and I ended up not telling him anything at all."

"And he thinks you've gone to your spa again," Jay said.

She nodded miserably.

Jay shoved himself up from the couch and began pacing the room, slowly shaking his head, not saying a word. But it wasn't hard for her to imagine what he was thinking.

Twenty-three years she'd been married to Nolt, and only the first few had been even a bit happy. But she'd never said a word to anyone, not until a little over a year ago, when she and Jay had been talking at a party and he'd passed some comment that made her realize he knew.

Then, she'd unexpectedly wanted to talk about it. And just as unexpectedly, Jay had told her how he felt about her. Jay, whom she'd adored, but had never let herself think of as anything more than a good friend, claimed to have always been in love with her.

All that time and she hadn't known. All that time and they'd wasted it. But once things started coming out into the open, it wasn't long before she admitted to herself that she loved Jay, too.

And for the past year, she'd been so madly in love with him she hadn't been able to think straight. Now, though, he was thinking she didn't really love him.

The phone began ringing and she tensed.

"Don't jump," Jay said, glancing over at her. "You know the service will take it. And as far as they're concerned, I'm in Mexico."

"Sorry. I just can't…I guess I'm just not cut out for this, Jay. I must be a throwback to the Victorian era, because every time I'm here and that phone rings I think it's Nolton and I feel guilty."

Jay waited until the ringing stopped, then said, "Marlene, how many times do I have to tell you there's no reason to feel guilty? This isn't some tawdry affair. Hell, maybe this doesn't even count as an affair at all. We're probably the only people in Manhattan who've been in love with each other for this long without sleeping together."

She shook her head, her throat tightening. "I'm sorry, Jay. I wish I didn't have these hang-ups. Oh, I love you so much, but even though Nolt cheats on me I could never have felt right about...not while I was still living with him. And I meant it to be all over with him by now. I really did."

"Marlene...Marlene you said as soon as Kip left for college. I understood your wanting to hold off while he was living at home, but he left four months ago. If you'd told Nolt then, everything would have been settled by now."

"But I didn't. I know what I said and I tried to but I didn't. Every time I opened my mouth, I started thinking how terrible he'd feel. His wife and his best friend. It's just such an awful, hurtful cliché."

Jay sat down beside her again and took her hands once more. "Marlene, you know Nolton and I haven't really been best friends for years. He's changed so much that...well, I don't have to tell *you* what he's like. But if it hadn't been for you, our friendship would have ended entirely, a long time ago."

"But your agency...his account..."

"We've been through that, too, over and over again. So Bristow Fine Spirits is a major account and I'll lose it. So what? Look, the only thing I really care about is you."

She buried her face in the warmth of Jay's shoulder, wishing she could simply stay here with him without hurting anyone by doing so.

"I've loved you forever," he murmured. "You know I have. It broke my heart when you married Nolton. I stood there beside him, his best man, hating him because he was the one who'd found you and not me.

"But you know what scares me?" he added after a minute.

She shook her head against him.

"The thought that you might never leave Nolton. That you still love him."

She drew back and gazed at Jay. "That isn't true. It isn't true at all. I haven't been in love with Nolt for years. And he doesn't really love me anymore, either. I've become just another one of his possessions."

"Then I guess...I guess maybe what scares me is that you won't leave Nolt because you don't love me enough."

"Oh, Jay," she murmured, "I love you more than anything. You have to believe that."

He took a deep breath and slowly shook his head. "You have to make me believe it. We've reached the point that you have to show me."

"Jay, I do show you, don't I?"

"It isn't enough, Marlene. I want to be married to you. I want to be able to take you places in public, and I want to make love to you when we're alone together. I've tried to be patient, but I can't stand another twenty years with you as Nolton Bristow's wife."

"It won't be another twenty years, Jay. It won't even be another one year. I'm going to make the break. Soon. We've got this week at least, and then I'll tell Nolton it's over. But with Kip complicating things, I just needed a little more courage."

"I think you made a mistake, Marlene, offering to talk to Nolt for Kip. He's a big boy. He shouldn't put something like that on you."

"Maybe you're right. Oh, undoubtedly you're right. But don't blame Kip. He didn't put it on me, I volunteered. Jay, he tried to talk to Nolt himself but just couldn't. You know that piercing look Nolt uses. He had Kip pinned like a butterfly, and Kip started babbling nonsense, and before I could even think, I dragged him off and said I'd talk to his father about it. And oh, Jay, Nolton isn't going to take it well."

She paused, smiling ruefully. "Did I actually say he isn't going to take it well? Jay, he'll go positively berserk. You know how much he hates not being in charge of family decisions."

"It's hardly a *family* decision, Marlene."

"Oh, I know it isn't really. But Nolt's so used to controlling everyone. Especially Kip and me."

The phone started ringing once more and she tensed again.

Jay sat up and took her by the shoulders. "Let's get out of here for a few days. Out of my apartment, out of Manhattan. Let's go someplace where we can be absolutely alone, with no interruptions, and let's make some firm decisions. Let's decide for sure when you're going to tell Nolton about Kip. And when we're going to tell Nolton about us. And how soon we can get married and where we'll go on our honeymoon and—"

Marlene put her fingers to his lips. "All right. Let's go someplace where we can be absolutely alone, discuss everything in entirely different surroundings. I like that idea. But stop talking now, before you get to the part about deciding how many children we should have. I'm not sure I'm up to starting another family."

Jay gathered her into his arms. "I don't want any children, love. I don't want to have teenagers when I'm in my sixties. All I want is us to be together for the rest of our lives."

She nuzzled his neck and murmured that's all she wanted, too. "I thought," she added, smiling as he be-

gan nibbling his way down her throat, "we'd just decided we were going to go away someplace."

"We will," he said, kissing her ear. "But maybe we
won't go until tomorrow...or the next day. Right now,
let's just sit here for a bit longer and consider where we
want to go."

CHAPTER THREE

DENVER DECIDED it must have been growing darker at double speed while they were in the grocery store. By the time they hit Highway 55 again, the last of the cloudy day had slipped entirely into cloudy night, with no visible stars and only the faintest haze to suggest there was actually a moon in the black sky.

He turned right, onto the first road he saw past the sign for Trois-Rivières, hoping to hell Nolton's map was accurate, because the road wasn't marked. It also wasn't very wide or very well plowed. There was probably more snow packed onto the surface than piled along the sides.

The map indicated they'd pass an empty cabin about halfway to the chalet, but the headlights were picking up nothing except evergreens and snow. Even the surrounding mountains had been obliterated by the night.

He was just asking Chantal if she knew how far Nolton's place was from the highway when a sharp blast— the unmistakable roar of a rifle—cut him off mid-word and started his heart pounding.

He slammed on the brakes, swearing at his stupidity when the van began sliding out of control. He steered into the skid, pumping the brakes, praying they wouldn't end up in a ditch, vaguely aware of the dogs being thumped against one side of the van, of Chantal grabbing her armrest, of the way his heart was racing.

A second shot exploded. Close. So close. But Denver couldn't even try to see where the shooting was coming from. All his attention was focused on trying to control the van.

He felt the steering come back and yanked the wheel to the left. The van shuddered, over-corrected, and lurched across the narrow road. He jerked the steering wheel in the other direction, not as far, trying to regain control, and finally managed to weave to a stop, still safely upright and on the road.

He shifted into neutral and looked over at Chantal. She was ghostly pale in the dim light of the dash, staring at him with large frightened eyes.

"Sorry about that," he said.

"You...you did fine. I thought we were going to tip over for sure."

"I grew up in Colorado. Learned how to drive in snow. But I should never have hit the brakes in the first place. It was just that—" He bit back the word *gunshot*. She was pure city. Maybe she hadn't realized.

"Those were shots, weren't they?" she said.

"Uh-huh, that's what they were, all right."

Behind them, the dogs were whining—unhurt, but upset by the excitement. He spoke reassuringly to them for a minute, then turned back to Chantal. "Must have been a hunter," he tried, thinking she might buy that.

She didn't. "People don't hunt in the dark, do they?"

He merely shrugged. She was city but she wasn't stupid.

"Denver...you don't think it might have been someone shooting at *us,* do you?"

"No." That was precisely what he'd been wondering, but there was no point in getting her more upset than she already was. "I mean, why would someone shoot at us?" he added. "It doesn't make any sense."

She gave him a nervous little smile. "I don't know. But if I'd wanted to be randomly shot at, without it making any sense, I could have stayed in Manhattan."

He simply stared at her for a moment, then began laughing. New Yorkers weren't exactly renowned for their sense of humor, but this one certainly wasn't turning out to be what he'd expected.

"Let's get out of here," he finally said, shoving the gearshift back into drive.

He drove slowly now, glancing from one side to the other, still seeing nothing but evergreens and snow.

"Look," Chantal said, pointing off to the left, "there's the cabin Nolton marked on his map."

Denver looked. The cabin was barely visible from the road, but it was there, light gleaming faintly from the windows—very faintly, but definitely light. He started to say it wasn't empty, but Chantal beat him to it.

He glanced over at her. She was wearing a frightened expression again, so he said, "Maybe it's not supposed to be empty anymore. Maybe someone's moved in since the last time Nolton was up here. Could be a hundred different explanations."

"Could be that whoever was doing the shooting is living there," she said.

Denver accelerated a little, thinking she might be right, still wondering if it was possible the shooter had been intentionally shooting at *them*.

If he had been, it really wouldn't make any sense. Chantal had said this excursion was part of Nolton Bristow's classified secret plan. Aside from the two of them, Nolton was the sole person who knew they were coming here. And why would someone shoot at total strangers?

Chantal stared ahead into the night, until the headlights picked up a driveway. It was posted with a sign reading Bristow, and she breathed a little more easily. Just beyond the drive, a split-rail fence marked the road's dead end.

They turned and followed the winding drive up to the chalet—an enormous place built of giant logs. A balcony stretched across the width of the second storey and the right-hand side extended out into a three-car garage.

"Nolton wanted you to be sure to use the garage," she said. "He told me your engine would freeze up if you parked outside."

Denver nodded. "We'll get our things into the chalet first, though." He pulled to a stop in front of the door and cut the engine, leaving the headlights on to light their way in.

The quiet was overwhelming. She hadn't known you could hear silence. And if it weren't for the headlights, the night would have swallowed them. To either side of the beams of light, the chalet was almost invisible, merely a huge, dark shape in the midst of its own little forest of fir trees.

It made her think about the children's story of Hansel and Gretel. She didn't actually expect they'd find a witch living in the chalet, of course, but this utter isolation made her nervous. She was used to bright lights, big city.

Oh, she'd admit it wasn't exactly safe in New York, but she knew what evils lurked there. And knew how to watch out for them. Whereas here in the wilderness . . . well, the sooner they got inside and turned on the lights, the better.

Denver glanced across at her. "Not much like night-time in the Big Apple, is it?"

"Not much? I think we could safely go as far as to say not anything. I've never been to a place this dark and quiet in my life."

"And cold. Don't forget cold," he said, opening the van door to the frigid air. "Come on, you're going to freeze in those clothes you're wearing. Let's get in where it's warm."

They unloaded the dogs, Denver quickly snapping a lead on Brandy. "We're going to have to keep a close watch on her," he said. "She's just dying to make a mad dash for freedom."

Chantal dug the key out of her purse and unlocked the front door. No rush of warmth greeted them. In fact, it felt almost as cold inside as out.

"Hey," Denver muttered, stepping inside after her, "your Nolton sure believes in keeping the thermostat turned down. Can you find a light switch?"

She was already feeling along the wall. "Got it," she said, flicking on the lights.

Only they didn't come on. She jiggled the switch up and down. Nothing but tiny clicking sounds. "Denver?" she said anxiously.

"McGee, sit," he said, then found Chantal's hand and gave her the leash. "Hold onto Brandy while I check whether it's just the one switch that's a problem."

Slowly, he made his way across the room, a barely visible figure in the darkness. A quiet click told her he was trying a lamp. The unrelieved darkness told her it wasn't just the one switch that was a problem.

"Well, that explains why it's so cold," he said. "The power must be off. That probably happens fairly often out here."

Chantal tried to decide whether no heat was worse than no light. She was already cold from head to toe. "There were lights on in that cabin we passed," she reminded him.

"They were awfully faint. Could have been oil lamps or something. Look, there's got to be a flashlight around. Probably in the kitchen. You stay there and I'll see what I can find."

While she waited, Brandy edged closer and pressed against her legs . . . a solid, warm body . . . kind of reassuring.

She stroked the soft fur on the dog's head, deciding she'd just discovered one of the redeeming qualities dogs had. "What's the matter, Brandy?" she murmured. "Are you afraid of the dark, too?"

And then a welcome beam of light played across the room and Denver said, "We're not really in such bad shape. I checked the phone and it's okay, so we're not cut off from the world. And I found a box of these as well as the flashlight." He played the light on the half-dozen fat, flat-bottomed candles he was holding. "Hell," he added with a grin, "I even came across a case of Bristow Fine Champagne. And it's so cold in here we don't have to worry about putting it on ice."

He shone the flashlight slowly across the living room. Two heavy leather couches, a couple of overstuffed chairs on either side of a huge stone fireplace, a polished wooden floor, a gigantic polar bear rug lying in front of the fireplace, and a pile of wood stacked beside it.

"Here," he said, handing Chantal the candles and a book of matches. "Why don't you light these while I go turn off the headlights. Then I'll start a fire. We can at least get the living room warm."

She lit the candles, putting two on each end table and the final two on the coffee table, then stood watching Denver.

He'd come back in, tossed his battered flight jacket onto a chair, and was crouched down arranging wood in the fireplace. The flickering candlelight highlighted the dark angles of his profile and added golden streaks to his brown hair.

When she'd first seen him this morning, she hadn't thought he was particularly attractive. She remembered that clearly...so why couldn't she remember what she'd found objectionable? She certainly saw nothing to object to now.

He glanced at her. "Fire's ready to light. Want the honor?"

She shook her head. "Go ahead, I got to do the candles."

He struck a match and leaned closer to the wood, his shirt stretching across his broad shoulders and his jeans clinging tightly to his hips.

No, definitely nothing to object to. Physically, that was. But a dog breeder from Jersey was definitely not for her.

The fire caught and quickly began to crackle, sending a delicate scent of wood smoke into the air and a yellow glow dancing across the white bearskin.

Denver rose and turned to her. "This isn't going to be too bad, after all. Actually, it's kind of nice, isn't it?"

Actually, it was kind of unbelievable. Candlelight, a bearskin rug in front of a crackling fire, champagne waiting in the kitchen—even if it *was* Bristow Fine Champagne.

She reminded herself it made sense to keep things strictly business, but there was something about the Jersey cowboy...no, more likely it was just this setting that was affecting her strangely.

Saying it was romantic would be vastly under-describing it. If she didn't know better, she'd think this was a setup. All that was missing was moonlight.

She glanced over to the window on the back wall, and sure enough, the moon was just peeking between clouds. Silver moonbeams were racing down to play on the forest of evergreens and sparkle on the snow. Absolutely gorgeous. "Look outside, Denver," she said.

Then, just as he looked, a man's face appeared at the window.

AS SUDDENLY AS IT had appeared, the face at the window vanished.

For an instant, they stood in shocked silence. Then Denver grabbed his jacket and wheeled toward the door, yelling, "McGee, come!"

"Denver, wait," Chantal said, her heart in her throat. "It's okay. I've got McGee."

"Denver, what if *he's* got a rifle?"

That stopped him. He stood rubbing his jaw while McGee waited quietly at the door and Brandy pranced around in front of it.

"Should we call the police?" Chantal finally asked.

"I doubt they'd be concerned. Looking in a window isn't exactly a felony."

"But after those shots...?"

Denver shook his head. "There's nothing to say the two are related. And hell, there's nothing to say the cops around here even speak English.'' He strode back across the room, peered out into the darkness, then picked up the flashlight.

"Denver?" she said anxiously. "You aren't going out there?"

"Not yet. First, I'm going to have a look around inside and see whether Nolton keeps a gun here."

Chantal glanced around the enormous living room. The crackling fire sounded sinister now. And ominous black shadows were dancing on the walls, in time with the leaping flames. Suddenly, Denver having come along on this trip didn't seem like such a bad idea at all. "I'll go with you," she said. "Help you look."

They didn't have to go farther than the kitchen. They opened one of the drawers and found a handgun inside. The sight of it made her feel both better and worse. It looked so... deadly. Shiny but cold in the flashlight's beam. The letters and numbers etched on the metal made it seem even more real.

Denver leaned over her shoulder and picked it up. She followed it with her eyes and a little shiver seized her as he fiddled with the cylinder.

"It's loaded?" she asked, the words shaky when they came out.

"Don't worry. The safety's on."

"What are you going to do with it?"

He didn't answer, simply stuck the barrel into the waistband of his jeans, against the small of his back.

It clearly wasn't the first time he'd done that, which also made her feel both better and worse. She said, "I hadn't realized dog breeders knew about guns."

"I haven't always been a dog breeder," he replied.

That did nothing to lower her anxiety level. What *had* he been? Maybe... well, it might be best if she didn't think about possible maybes. But she was definitely back to being uncertain whether or not she was glad he was along.

He handed her the flashlight, saying, "Why don't you see if you can find an after-hours number for the electric company and try calling them? I'll go out to the van, get the groceries and our things, then move it into the garage."

Chantal followed him into the living room and beamed a path of light to the door. "Take McGee with you, Denver."

He gave her a look that said she was being absurd but motioned to the dog.

"And be careful," she murmured, holding tightly to Brandy's collar.

He glanced back. "Chantal, I'm going twenty feet to the van, not all the way to Outer Mongolia. And whoever that guy was, by now he's probably miles from here."

She nodded, wishing *she* were miles from here. Four hundred or so miles, safe in her town house on West Eighty-fifth instead of in the middle of Nowhere, Quebec, with a virtual stranger.

The door closed behind Denver, and she resisted the urge to watch through the window to make sure he was all right. She *was* being absurd. So she was just going to stop worrying. All that had happened was that some silly man had looked in their window. Of course, there'd been those shots on the road.

She tried to force the recollection of them from her mind and headed to the kitchen.

There was a little book of numbers by the phone, and, when she found no electric anything under *E*, she began searching from the beginning, pausing on the *P*

page at the name Pierrette Pelletier. A few entries below it were the words Power Off, and a number scrib-
bled beside them.

Chantal dialed it, got a recording in French and sat
listening to it, stroking Brandy's head and feeling dumb.
She finally hung up after the tape was silent for a minute, then began repeating its message without an inter-
vening word of English.

For about two seconds she considered the idea of
calling Pierrette, then rejected it. Maybe...if it got *really* cold. But the fireplace was warming up the living
room. And surely the power would come back on soon.

"What's your guess, Brandy?" Chantal said. "Think
anybody knows we're out here freezing in the dark?
Think somebody's doing something about it?"

Brandy simply gazed up at her, making her smile. She
was probably imagining it, but the gaze seemed to be
one of pure adoration. Then the dog quietly drooled
onto her suede pants.

DENVER POURED MORE Bristow Fine Champagne into
Chantal's glass, extremely aware of the alluring scent of
her perfume. He'd noticed it earlier, in the van, but
somehow it had grown increasingly intoxicating as the
evening had worn on.

He retreated to his own side of the polar bear rug and
relaxed against one of the big leather cushions he'd
moved from the couches to the floor. The area directly
in front of the fireplace was almost a comfortable temperature.

He sat ostensibly watching the fire, but actually
watching Chantal in its flickering light.

Before dinner, she'd changed from her suede outfit
into pants he suspected were real cashmere, and a pale

yellow sweater covered in beaded designs. She was still overdressed for a ski chalet but at least looked warmer. And less Fifth Avenue perfect. Her hair being a bit messed up helped. And her makeup had worn off. She was almost...he decided he couldn't go as far as disheveled, but she was a darned sight more appealing than she'd been earlier.

Not that he wanted to start finding her too appealing. He'd be a complete idiot to let that happen. They'd be spending the next couple of days together, a few more when they came back up for the actual shoot. But then they'd be going their separate ways again. And the last thing he needed was to end up thinking about her after that.

He forced his eyes from her and glanced over to check on Brandy. He didn't want that dog wandering all over the Bristows' chalet.

Even the best of Saint Bernards could never qualify as dainty. And Brandy certainly wasn't a best-of-breed when it came to behaving. But right now she was safely asleep beside McGee. Tomorrow, he'd have to see whether she was entirely hopeless or if there was anything at all he could do with her.

"Your name," Chantal said, her voice startling him, "comes from growing up in Colorado, right?"

It took his brain a moment to register what she'd said. A second moment to realize she'd been sitting there thinking about him. A third to realize he liked that idea, and a fourth to wonder how the hell she knew he'd grown up in Colorado. He asked.

"You said so. Earlier. You said you knew how to drive in snow because you grew up in Colorado. So Denver is a nickname, isn't it?" she pressed, her big blue eyes gazing across the two feet between them.

He nodded. "The marines gave me my education. And marines are big on nicknames."

"The marines," she repeated.

"Yeah, you know. They put you through the military academy. Then you give them the next few years of your life. By the time I got out, I'd been Denver for so long I could scarcely remember my real name."

"Which is?"

He grinned at her. "Which is best forgotten, anyway."

"Best Forgotten Anyway? That's an awfully strange name. I can can see why you'd prefer Denver."

He laughed. Cute. Very cute. Possibly... possibly he shouldn't be quite so concerned about finding her appealing. After all, it had been a long time since he'd found any woman even the slightest bit appealing. And if they could have some fun for a couple of days, see where things might lead with no strings attached, what would be the harm?

"And in the marines is where you learned about guns," she said.

That made him laugh again. "What did you think? That I'd been a Mafia hit man?"

"No, I just thought... I didn't think anything. I was simply curious."

The champagne, he decided, had been a darned good idea, if he wanted to see where things might lead, that was. Because she hadn't seemed the least bit interested in anything about him until they'd begun drinking it.

"So... you left the marines and started a kennel?"

"Not right away."

"Oh? What did you do in between?"

He shrugged. "This and that. Look, do I get a turn in here or is this interrogation entirely one-sided?"

She considered that, then asked him what he'd like to know about her.

He glanced at the empty champagne bottle, sitting next to the half-empty one, wondering if that second bottle had been quite as good an idea as the first. Maybe not. Because if he was *really* thinking in terms of a couple of days, no strings attached, why did he want to know what he wanted to know?

He answered his own question by reminding himself that he wasn't totally unscrupulous. If *he* were involved with a woman, he wouldn't want some other guy coming on to her. He drank a little more champagne, then plunged ahead. "Do you have a someone in your life?"

Chantal gazed at him while he sat regretting the question. If she told him she did, he'd feel obliged to back off.

"You sound," she finally said, "decidedly like my mother."

He grinned at her again. "Your mother has a deep voice?"

She ignored that. "I do not," she said, enunciating precisely, "have a particular someone at the moment."

Since she didn't follow up by asking whether or not he did, he volunteered that he didn't.

"But you have a kennel," she said.

"Ah...yes."

"I've never known anyone who had a kennel. How did you get into that?"

"I just needed to...just wanted a change. And I have a knack with animals. I find it easy to train just about anything. Probably because my parents always had a lot of pets. At any rate, starting a kennel just seemed natural."

Chantal nodded slowly, as if he'd said something extremely wise, and he edged the half-empty champagne bottle farther away. They'd both had enough.

"And what about you?" he said. "How did you get into advertising?"

"My father. I followed in his footsteps because he liked his job so much. And he told me it was a good field for a woman, that there wasn't much discrimination."

"And you've found that's true?"

She shrugged. "My father's a wonderful man. He tends to see things from a male point of view, though."

Denver laughed. "Well, that's hardly surprising."

"But you didn't finish telling me about your kennel," Chantal said. "How many dogs do you have?"

"Four. McGee, Julie, Lily and Tara."

"Just four?" She looked over at Brandy and McGee, still sleeping peacefully. "Four is only two more than we have here."

He thought about complimenting her on her addition, then thought better of it. "I'm into quality, not quantity. They're all champions."

"Julie, Lily and Tara," she said. "You have three females but just one male."

"Uh-huh."

"That's not fair."

"I'm a breeder, Chantal. I only need one male. And the dogs don't care."

She looked at him as if she didn't believe that. "And where do you keep them?"

"Usually, they're all in the house with me. Or outside. I've got a few acres. And the property's fenced, so I don't use runs. And when there's a litter, I just turn the kitchen into a nursery."

Chantal glanced at the dogs again. "They must have big puppies."

"It's a big kitchen."

"And that's all you do?" she said. "Just have puppies, I mean?"

"Yeah, that's basically *all* I do," he said, not quite able to keep the sharp edge out of his voice. But why couldn't he? He'd known the question was coming. And he'd known, before they'd even met, precisely what a Madison Avenue fashion plate would think of a man who did nothing but keep a few dogs.

So why in hell had he been thinking what he'd been thinking and getting all friendly with her? The second bottle of champagne hadn't been a good idea at all. And neither had his thought that they might mix a little pleasure with their business. Because strings had a habit of suddenly appearing in no-strings relationships. And there was no way he'd ever risk becoming involved with a dyed-in-the-wool Madison Avenue type.

She was eyeing him uncertainly. "Denver, if I sounded insulting, I didn't mean to. I just...well, I don't know anything about the breeding business. And all I meant was that I didn't realize you could make a living at it with as few as four dogs."

She seemed so honestly concerned she'd hurt his feelings that he regretted snapping at her. "I breed each of my females once a year," he offered. "The pups sell for a good price and Saint Bernards have large litters. Plus I do the odd commercial. McGee and I even did a movie last year. And I spend a fair amount of time at dog shows, showing for people who want champions but don't have the time or patience it takes."

"And who looks after the dogs when you're not there?"

"There are a couple of teenagers down the road from my place. They're usually available on weekends. And their mother will come by if I need someone during the day. But this timing was good for the boys. With it being Christmas vacation, they've moved right in until I get back."

Over in the corner, McGee clambered to his feet, Brandy right beside him.

Denver pushed himself up. "I'll take the dogs out. Then I guess we'd better find some blankets and turn these couches into beds. The upstairs will still be freezing. I'll be a few minutes...if you want to change down here where it's warm, I mean."

Chantal smiled at him. "Thanks. I think I'll do that."

Denver put a leash on Brandy and took her and McGee out into the crisp night. He walked them down the driveway a bit, the cold air clearing his head.

His thoughts had been getting far too heavy in there. He wasn't at the slightest risk of actually falling for a woman in just a few days. And as far as a little pleasure was concerned . . . well, Chantal didn't strike him as the sort who casually fooled around.

He'd been wrong about women before, though. Not that he'd push. At least, not hard enough to make her uncomfortable. But if she happened to be willing...

"Come on, guys," he said to the dogs, turning back, absently wondering what would have happened if he'd met Chantal a few years ago. Would anything serious have developed between them? Back when he wouldn't have seen any problem in getting involved with her type?

He shook his head. No point in thinking about what might have happened if. He'd never regret his decision. And a woman like her would never understand it.

CHAPTER FOUR

CHANTAL WOKE WITH A START, feeling cold and not knowing where she was. She glanced over and saw the remnants of a fire sputtering quietly in a fireplace.

Nolton's chalet. Nolton's chalet after too much Bristow Fine Champagne. Her mouth was dry, and there was a tiny dull throbbing behind her temples. Lord, and she was responsible for advertising that stuff.

But she didn't think the headache or the cold had wakened her. And then she heard the noise again and realized what had. Someone was upstairs, moving stealthily about.

She pulled the blankets tightly around her neck and sat up, staring through the darkness at the other couch, hoping it was empty, that Denver had gone up to the bathroom.

No such luck. He was lying there, fast asleep in the dim glow from the fireplace, one bare arm sprawled across his chest, the other trailing down the side of the couch onto the floor.

"Denver," she whispered.

"Denver," she tried again. He still didn't move. Any louder and whoever was up there might hear her. She crept off the couch, shivering as she pushed the blankets down.

Her robe had vanished into the night, and she felt around the floor for it with her foot, extremely aware of how short her nightshirt was, reminded why she hadn't been entirely sure that sleeping in the same room as Denver was a good idea.

Finding the robe proved impossible, so she finally just scurried across the bearskin, almost falling when she tripped on the heap of Denver's jeans.

"Wake up," she hissed into his ear.

That got a snoring noise out of him, but nothing more.

From upstairs came a muffled shuffling.

She grabbed his shoulders and shook him. "Denver! Wake up!"

"Mmmmmhh?" he said, wrapping one arm around her and pulling her down on top of him. "Chantal," he murmured sleepily, starting to cuddle her in beside him. "What a delightful surprise."

She pounded her fist against his naked shoulder so hard she felt the impact all the way to her elbow.

Denver said, "Ouch," and finally opened his eyes. "What the hell are you doing?"

"I'm trying to tell you," she told him, squirming free of his arm, "that there's somebody upstairs. In the chalet. Walking around."

They listened. There wasn't a sound from above them.

"You sure?" Denver whispered.

"Positive."

He started to shove the blankets off, then stopped. "Ah . . . how do you feel about men who sleep raw?"

"Denver!" she hissed, grabbing his jeans from the floor and heaving them at his head. "Just get these on and find the flashlight and that gun before whoever's up there decides to come down."

Too late! Whoever it was started thumping down the stairs.

Chantal whirled toward the staircase in panic, unable to see a thing across the room. Behind her, Denver cleared his throat.

"Shh!" she whispered frantically, "he'll hear you."

"She," Denver said.

"What?"

"*She'll* hear me. Brandy will. That's a dog coming down the stairs and McGee's standing over by the door."

Chantal focused on the dark staircase again and managed to make out a dog's shape, lumbering down the final steps.

Brandy wandered over to Chantal and snuffled her bare leg with an extremely cold and wet nose, transforming her feeling of relief into one of discomfort. "Do they always do that?" she demanded, turning back to Denver. "Oh, sorry," she added quickly, seeing he was still zipping his jeans.

"Do what?" he said, snapping the waist closed. "Wander around in the night or nuzzle people?"

"Both, I guess."

"Depends on the dog. They all have different personalities. Listen," he said, then was silent for a moment. "I think I hear the furnace. The power must have come on while we were asleep." He reached across to the end table, tried the lamp, and soft light flooded one side of the room.

Then he turned back to face her, all broad shoulders and bare chest. Heavy stubble on his face and thick dark chest hair tapering to a vee, inviting her eyes downward to where that vee disappeared into his jeans.

And muscles. Serious muscles. Lord, he probably wrestled in his spare time. Maybe he *would* look like hell in a suit and tie, but the way he looked in tight jeans and nothing else made her knees a little weak. Even his bare feet were sexy.

She realized she was blatantly staring at him about the same instant she realized he was blatantly staring at her. About the same instant she remembered that all she was wearing was a thigh-length silk nightshirt. About the same instant she noticed it was suffering from a severe case of static cling.

She glanced down, spotted her robe on the floor and grabbed for it. "It's still cold in here," she mumbled, slipping it on.

"Spoilsport," Denver said, grinning at her.

She swallowed uncomfortably, trying to ignore the gleam in his dark eyes.

"It's nice and warm in bed," he said, grinning even more broadly.

"Not funny, Denver."

He shrugged, glancing at his watch. "Can't blame a fellow for trying. But it's almost seven. It'll be getting light any time now. You want me to scout around for shoot sites with you after breakfast?"

"I think you'd better get started with Brandy, instead. A couple of long days' work, and I'm sure you'll have her in great shape."

"Can't do that," Denver said. "Dogs don't have long attention spans. The most I can do in a day is two or three hour-long sessions."

Chantal eyed him suspiciously. Was that the truth or a volley in his campaign to use McGee? "Well," she said, "we've got to shoot those commercials by the end of January, latest."

"We can always use McGee."

Bingo! she thought. "Denver, you were hired to train Brandy, not to tell me how to do my job."

He gazed at her as if trying to decide whether to be insulted, then grinned.

She didn't smile in return. She'd rather he were insulted. At least, then, he might give his idea a rest.

He gestured toward the front door, where the two dogs were sitting side by side, both looking hopeful that it was walk time. "Chantal, tell me which one's Brandy."

She glanced at them and said that Brandy was the one who acted like a fool and McGee was the well-behaved one.

Denver said, "No, I mean right now. Look at them and tell me which one is Brandy."

She looked. "I can't tell them apart just by appearance."

"Exactly. And do you think Nolton would be able to? You have to know a dog pretty well to distinguish it from others of the same breed."

"But Nolton *will* know Brandy. If we don't shoot until the end of January, she'll have lived with him for a month."

"Don't be too sure about that. When I called him, he said something about maybe I could board her for a few weeks, keep working with her until after the shoot. You know, Chantal, I wouldn't be surprised if Brandy was history as soon as the commercials are shot."

"You really think so?"

"I got that sense, talking to him."

Chantal looked over at the dogs again, feeling badly but not sure which one of them she was feeling badly for. "Try with Brandy," she finally said firmly. "That's what our deal was."

He nodded. "Okay, I'll give it a shot, but don't get your hopes up. Why don't I take them out, then work with Brandy a bit while you get dressed and make breakfast. After that, we can all tag along when you go searching for your perfect settings. I don't think you should be wandering around out there on your own."

He didn't have to add, *not after the reception we got last night.* Chantal knew exactly what he meant.

"WHAT?" CHANTAL SAID. She'd come downstairs thinking they were the height of efficient organization. After breakfast, they'd each selected one of the guest bedrooms to use, moved their things upstairs and gotten ready for the site-scouting expedition. And it was still early.

But Denver's expression definitely wasn't crying out, 'efficient organization.' The way he was looking at her, he obviously figured something was wrong.

He said, "Chantal, have you done much walking in snow?"

"Does Central Park count?"

He shook his head. "I almost froze when I was out with the dogs. You've got to wear warmer clothes. And you can't wear those ridiculous high-heeled boots."

"They're not ridiculous. They're fashionable," she said, glaring pointedly at his scruffy cowboy boots.

"On the sidewalks of New York, they might be fashionable. In the ski hills of Quebec, they're ridiculous."

"Denver, they're the only boots I have. And these are the warmest clothes I have."

"Well, they won't do."

She upped the voltage of her glare. Trying to tell her what to do when it came to the dogs was one thing. She could live with that because he *did* know more than she did there. But telling her how to dress smacked of that downright male arrogance she'd seen in him when they first met.

"Look," he went on, apparently oblivious to her annoyance, "the closet in the master bedroom is jam-packed with women's clothes. I noticed that when we were looking for the blankets last night."

"I can't wear Marlene's clothes. Not without asking her, at least."

"So phone her."

"I can't. She goes to a spa between Christmas and New Years."

"Fine. If she's lounging at a spa, the last thing she'll care about is you wearing her clothes. I just hope her boots fit you."

"Denver..."

"Hurry up and change, Chantal. I'm getting hot in here."

She hurried up and changed into a ski outfit. She didn't like Denver telling her what to do. Not one little bit. But maybe...well, he did seem to know what he was talking about when it came to a few things besides the dogs. Out here in never-never land, that was. In Manhattan, he'd probably get hit by a cab if he tried to cross a street.

It only took two extra pair of socks to make Marlene's boots fit, and she trudged back downstairs ready to go. "Satisfied?" she said. "I feel as if I'm ready for an Arctic expedition."

"Good. Then maybe you won't get frostbite." Denver opened the front door to cheery sunshine and they started off, McGee walking sedately, Brandy straining on her leash.

Denver snapped her sharply back to his side, saying, "Brandy, heel!"

"Doesn't that hurt her neck?" Chantal asked. "Jerking her like that?"

"Just enough to get her attention."

They headed into the stand of evergreens behind the chalet. It had snowed during the night, smoothly blanketing the ground and decorating tree branches. The snow clung like powder to their boots and turned the dogs' legs from brown to white.

"A winter wonderland," Chantal murmured, thinking of the gray slush that passed for snow on the streets of New York.

"Uh-huh," Denver said. "But unfortunately, the snowfall covered any tracks that were out here. I was hoping we'd be able to tell where our visitor came from last night. Or where he went."

She simply nodded, not wanting to talk about the face at their window. In the bright light of day, last night seemed blessedly long ago and far away.

They were out of the trees and halfway up the first hill before she even thought about the video camera. "Oh, rats," she muttered to herself.

Denver asked what was wrong.

"I forgot the camera. Left it sitting on my bedside table."

Denver shoved Brandy's rear end into the snow with a firm sit command, handed Chantal the lead, and told McGee to stay. "Don't go anywhere," he added to Chantal, starting back the way they'd come.

She gazed around. Mountains in the distance. Hills and trees and snow everywhere she looked. She cer-

tainly wasn't going anywhere. Getting lost was probably awfully easy to do around here. Those hills and trees
were all alike.

She watched Denver disappear into the stand of
evergreens and was turning to survey the landscape
again when a movement caught her eye. She focused on
the spot, certain she'd seen something. But now all was
solid white. White snow . . . and then she managed to
make out a shape. Over where she'd seen motion, almost invisible, sat a huge white rabbit. Stark still in the
snow. Staring at them with unblinking eyes.

A dreadful, ominous feeling swept her, and she
glanced at the dogs. They were both sitting quietly.

Please, Brandy, she said silently. *Please don't see the
rabbit. Please let's not have a rerun of the cat incident.*
But if they did, she wasn't even going to try to hang on
to the leash. She wasn't about to be dragged through the
snow and ice and risk ripping Marlene's clothes.

McGee's nose twitched. Then Brandy's. In unison,
both massive heads swiveled toward the rabbit. But
Brandy didn't stop there. She roared into motion,
howling as she went.

The rabbit leapt to life and raced up the hill, Brandy
in hot pursuit.

Chantal glanced at McGee as the lead whipped out of
her hands. He whined at her but didn't move.

She looked back at Brandy, disappearing over the
hilltop, and swore. What should she do? Go after the
dog or wait for Denver? "Come on, McGee," she said,
deciding he undoubtedly had enough brains that he
wouldn't get lost. "Let's try to at least keep her in sight.

"McGee, heel!" she added as an afterthought. And
surprisingly enough, the dog began to trot along right
beside her.

Running was far harder than walking. Uphill much harder than level ground. Every few steps, one of her feet crunched through the crisp layer beneath the few inches of fresh snow, almost tripping her. By the time they reached the crest of the hill, her heart was pounding and her throat hurt.

Brandy was visible in the distance, still going full tilt as Chantal and McGee slipped and slid down the slope. At the bottom, they hit a flat stretch that made progress easier.

Brandy had disappeared from sight now, but had left a clear trail. They hurried along it until the muscles in Chantal's thighs were aching and her lungs burning.

She finally stopped, considering turning back, thinking maybe they should be going after Brandy in the van. Then she spotted the dog up ahead.

Its snout was buried in the snow, and its bushy tail was swishing back and forth a mile a minute. No doubt the rabbit had vanished, Alice-in-Wonderland-like, into a hole.

Chantal started forward once more, then stopped again, seeing something that was almost hidden from view by a windbreak of trees.

Ahead on the left, about halfway to where Brandy was standing, sat the cabin. The empty cabin that wasn't empty at all. Last night there'd been lights on inside it. Today, smoke was curling from the chimney.

Chantal rested her hand on the reassuring breadth of McGee's back, stood catching her breath for a moment, then quietly called to Brandy.

No reaction. That tail just kept swishing away.

"Damned dog," she whispered to McGee, starting forward again, eyeing the cabin uneasily as they drew nearer.

Except for the smoke there was no sign of life, but she wasn't taking any chances. She and McGee skirted the very edge of the clearing, where a dense stand of trees swept around it.

They were almost directly in line with the front door, about twenty feet from the cabin, when the door opened and Chantal's heart stopped.

In the doorway stood a man. A man holding a rifle. The man who'd been at their window last night.

CHANTAL'S GAZE FROZE on the man in the doorway. Her heart was pounding, and each ragged breath formed a little icy cloud before her face. She tried to smile, but her lips wouldn't cooperate.

Even bathed in cheery sunshine, he looked mean enough to have walked straight out of a segment of "America's Most Wanted." Somewhere between fifty-five and sixty, he wore jeans, a plaid shirt and a scowl on his face that was making her shake with fright. Or maybe it was the way he was gripping his rifle, as if he'd like nothing better than to use her for target practice, that made her tremble.

"Qu'est-ce que vous voulez?" he snapped, jerking his gun in her direction.

She managed a strangled, "Ahhhhh...." while deciding what he'd most likely asked her. About what she was doing here, maybe?

"My dog," she said, pointing at Brandy. Her snout was still buried in the snow. "My dog ran after a rabbit and I was chasing her."

The man glanced at Brandy, then back at Chantal, McGee sitting beside her. *"Prenez vos chiens et partez, s'il vous plaît! Ils sont trop dangereux pour mon petit-fils."*

She tried a second, "Ahhhhh...." reasoning that the first one hadn't gotten her shot, but this time she didn't even have a guess about what he'd said.

"Chantal?" Denver called from behind her.

She whirled around.

Denver simply stared at Chantal for a moment, feeling the craziest flood of relief that she was fine. But of course she was. McGee was with her. And Brandy was just across the clearing. They were all perfectly okay, and he'd been acting like a lunatic, charging along the trail they'd left, imagining ridiculous things, the video camera slamming against his chest as he ran.

He casually adjusted the camera and wiped the perspiration from his forehead. "You're all right," he said as his breathing slowed a little.

"I'm not sure," she whispered, telling him with her eyes to look left, past the stand of trees.

He did, murmuring, "Oh, geez," when he saw the whole picture. The sight of that rifle knotted his stomach and set his brain to marine mode. He had to handle this the right way. The man could be serious danger.

Denver straightened his shoulders and called across the clearing. "There's no need for that gun. We'll just collect the dog and get going."

The man rattled off something in French and shifted his rifle.

Denver swore quietly, told Chantal not to move, then started for Brandy, forcing himself to walk at a slow, even pace.

Chantal held her breath, her gaze flickering back and forth between the cabin and Denver, until he'd reached the dog and retrieved the end of her leash.

"That's it," he said, giving the man a friendly wave and yanking Brandy so hard she yipped. "Sorry we disturbed you."

They were almost back to Chantal when a child's voice drew her attention to the cabin once more. Just inside the doorway, a skinny, dark-haired boy was jabbering excitedly and trying to squeeze out past the man.

"Tiens-toi!" he snapped, grabbing the child's shoulder and propelling him back inside. *"Tiens-toi là!"* he added, slamming the door behind them.

Chantal's gaze remained on the closed door, relief that the man was gone mingling with a peculiar feeling about the boy.

"Let's get the hell out of here," Denver said, taking her arm. "Let's get the hell out of here before that guy decides he needs more fresh air."

"Anyone ever tell you that you come up with absolutely brilliant suggestions?" she said as Denver hustled her from the clearing into the trees.

He rewarded her with a grin that started her feeling a little less anxious. Once they'd put some distance between themselves and that man, she'd be just fine.

But Denver went into his strong silent routine on the way back to the chalet, and there was nothing to take her mind off how frightened she'd been.

"He was the man from last night, wasn't he?" she finally said. "It wasn't just someone who looked like him, was it?" she added, hurrying a little faster. Between Marlene's too-large boots and Denver's long legs, keeping up with him was difficult.

"I'd say it was the same guy, all right," he said.

"Well then...Denver, does any of this make sense to you? Those shots on the road? His looking in our window? Standing there today as if he'd be delighted to shoot me?''

"Chantal, none of it makes the slightest sense. But at least we're okay. And maybe there's even a logical explanation for everything. Maybe if we spoke French or he spoke English, we'd all be laughing about this right now."

Chantal doubted it. The man didn't strike her as having a sense of humor. "But there's something else that's not quite right. I can't imagine that man is the boy's father. Their ages don't work. And what are they doing in a cabin that's supposed to be empty?"

"I don't have any answers, Chantal. You'd be a lot further ahead if you'd brought a detective along on this trip, instead of a dog breeder."

She glanced up at him. Back at that cabin, she'd been darned glad it was him she had along. Still was, if she were honest about it. He might not be Sherlock Holmes, but being with him made her feel a lot better than she felt with most men.

He caught her eyeing him and gave her a disconcerting look, as if he could tell what she was thinking, and she scrambled for something to say.

"Look over there, Denver. See the way that line of trees is sweeping down the hill? The contrast of sunlight and shadows on the snow? That might make a good backdrop for one of the commercials. I'll just take a quick shot of it. Then at least I'll have done *some* work this morning."

Denver handed her the camera. "I'll stay here and keep Brandy out of your way."

Chantal crunched through the snow until she had a good perspective on the trees and shot a minute or so of tape. "Denver?" she called back to him. "Would you mind playing movie star with the dogs for a minute? About halfway up the hill? I need movement to see how the angles work.''

Denver muttered something about Actors' Equity probably having rules against this sort of thing, but strode up the hill with McGee and Brandy.

"Action!" Chantal shouted when he stopped and stood looking down at her.

She framed them in her viewfinder, clicked on the power switch and shot Denver playing monster with the dogs. McGee clearly knew the game and backed through the snow on his belly, growling ferociously as Denver stalked him. Brandy, still on her leash, bounced along beside them, kicking up huge sprays of snow with each bounce.

Chantal edged to the left, wondering if Nolton would consider trying this game for an actual shoot. Surely even Nolton Bristow could convince people he was a real human being if they saw him acting like a kid.

Brandy began twirling madly around in circles, tying herself up with the leash, making Chantal laugh. The dog was a total goof, but her goofiness was heart-warming. Even Denver forgot about his monster role and stood laughing.

He had, Chantal thought, the deepest, warmest laugh imaginable. Just hearing it made her smile. She clicked off the camera and called up the hill to him. "Aren't you going to untangle the poor thing?''

He grinned. "Put the camera down first.''

"What?''

"Put the camera down.''

She set it onto the snow. When she glanced back up, Denver had formed a snowball and was pitching it at her.

"You rat!" she yelled, ducking to keep it from hitting her in the face, taking a quick step to maintain her balance.

But something caught her foot and she pitched sideways, pain seizing her as she hit the ground. The fall itself hadn't hurt, but her ankle . . . the pain was bringing tears to her eyes.

An instant later Denver was kneeling beside her, asking if she was all right.

"My ankle," she whispered.

"Don't move," he said. "Just lie still while I check it."

She tried to prop herself up on her elbows to see what he was doing, but a dog snuggled its warm length against her, pressing so closely that she could barely breathe, let alone move.

"You caught your toe under a root," Denver was saying. "I have to take your boot off to see how bad it is."

When she cried out at a sudden stab of pain, the dog whined sympathy into her ear. She'd just discovered, she realized, another redeeming quality about dogs.

"Sorry," Denver said, "but it's off, now. Geez, how many pairs of socks are you wearing?"

"Three."

"I'm going to have to take a couple of these off, too, Chantal. I can't feel anything through them."

She gritted her teeth while he peeled the socks down, then bit back a sob as he gently twisted her ankle. The movement made it hurt something fierce.

Finally, he turned back to look at her. "Good news. Nothing's broken."

"Great," she managed. "I was afraid I'd have to miss the prom tonight."

Denver didn't smile. "Chantal, I'm really sorry. That snowball was a dumb idea."

"No, it wasn't. If I'd thought of it first, I'd have thrown one at you. Besides, my ankle's not hurting too badly. Only throbbing a bit."

"Well, let's get you home. Brandy, move!" he said, shoving the dog away from her.

"That's Brandy?" Chantal said. "I just assumed it was McGee."

"Nope, it's Brandy. She has strong Saint Bernard instincts, wanted to keep you warm."

"Good girl," Chantal whispered to the dog, giving her a quick, heartfelt hug. "Maybe there's hope for you yet."

Denver called McGee over and tied the end of Brandy's leash to the other dog's collar. "Way you go, McGee," he said, gesturing in the direction of the chalet and swatting Brandy's rump to start her off.

He picked up the camera, then turned his attention back to Chantal. "Put your arms around my neck. If you try to walk, you'll feel a lot more than a bit of throbbing."

It took a second for her to realize what he meant. When she did, she told him he couldn't possibly carry her.

"Of course I can," he said. "I can carry two hundred pounds of Saint Bernard, so I can certainly manage you. Just watch you don't bang your ankle against me."

"But..."

There was no point in arguing further because Denver simply scooped her up and started off.

"This would be easier if you put your arms around my neck and leaned into me," he said after they'd gone a few yards.

Tentatively, Chantal put her arms around his neck and leaned into him. He felt big, warm and secure and smelled of cold wool and a unique male scent that made her want to breathe deeply against him.

Yes, being with him *definitely* made her feel a lot better than she felt with most men. And the way he was holding her almost made her forget the pain in her ankle. Because his holding her made her feel something else entirely, something she knew she was foolish to be feeling for a man with whom she had absolutely nothing in common.

But the something felt so darned good that she wouldn't worry about it just right now.

CHAPTER FIVE

"CHANTAL..." DENVER paused, telling himself to keep a lid on his frustration. But this discussion was ludicrous. And it had been going on all afternoon.

"Chantal," he repeated a touch more calmly, "be reasonable. We've got an armed maniac for a next-door neighbor and you can't walk. Now those strike me as two first-rate reasons for getting the hell out of here."

She gazed at him thoughtfully, no doubt trying to come up with yet another ridiculous argument for not leaving, and he rubbed his jaw, wondering if she was actually the most stubborn woman in the universe or only the most stubborn one he'd ever met. Staying up here any longer would be positively insane. How could she possibly not see that? And how could she sit there on the couch, her ankle so swollen he'd used two pillows to elevate it, and claim it barely hurt?

"Denver, how many times do I have to tell you?" she said placidly. "I'll be walking just fine by tomorrow. I'm a really quick healer. You'll see."

Hah! What he'd see was that Chantal wouldn't be up to scouting sites again for days. And when it came to his staying because of that dog...

"And you'll work miracles with Brandy," she said.

He stared at her, wondering if she did mind-reading as a sideline.

"I just know you'll have her trained in no time. You said yourself that she has good instincts."

"What I said was she has good Saint Bernard instincts. Rescue instincts. Not acting instincts. Chantal, you told me you have to shoot the commercials by the end of January. And I've seen enough of her to be sure there's no way I could have her adequately trained by then."

"I'm not certain I believe that," Chantal said so quietly he maybe hadn't heard correctly.

"What?" he demanded.

"I said I'm not certain I believe you couldn't have her adequately trained. From day one... no, from before day one, from the first moment I talked to you on the phone, you've wanted to use McGee rather than spend time training Brandy. If you didn't want to do the job we hired you for, why did you take it?"

While she was speaking, Denver could feel his blood pressure rising a point a second. "I told you," he snapped when she finished, "that I'd try with her. No guarantees, I said, remember? No promises, remember? Well I've tried and—"

"Big try," Chantal interrupted. "Half an hour before breakfast this morning."

"Dammit, Chantal, I'm the dog expert here. And I'm telling you that Nolton's just going to have to resign himself to using McGee."

"Dammit, yourself, Denver. I'm the advertising expert here. And I'm telling you that Nolton wants to use his own dog and Nolton's the client. So we're not giving up after half an hour."

"Typical! Just typical Mad Avenue! What the hell do you think? That your client's God? That I can bend reality to suit his whims? And reality, Chantal, is that

Brandy is one dumb dog and your Mr. Nolton Bristow is straight out of luck."

Chantal didn't say another word to him, just leaned over to where Brandy was sitting beside her and gave the dog a hug. "You're not dumb," she whispered loudly enough that Denver could hear. "I don't think you're dumb, I think you're the best dog I've ever met."

"For God's sake, Chantal! She can't even sit on command, let alone understand English!"

That remark earned him a glare. "Fine," Chantal eventually said. "If you can't train her, you can't train her. In which case, there's no point in your staying here any longer, is there?"

"Exactly. That's exactly my point," he said, regaining his own composure now that she was seeing reason. "So let's get the hell out of here, huh?"

"Not me, Denver. If you can't do your job, you go on back home. But I have no choice about staying here a little longer. I can't go back with only one potential shoot site on tape. Jay and Nolton would—"

"For Pete's sake!" he shouted, not believing she could be so stubborn. "Both Jay and Nolton would understand that you couldn't go hiking around the hills on a bad ankle."

"No, you're only half right," she said in an infuriatingly calm tone. "Jay would be okay with it but not Nolton. And if Nolton's unhappy he'll make darned sure Jay is unhappy, too. And it would be my fault, because I wouldn't have done my job."

"Chantal, that doesn't make sense."

"Yes, it does. It makes perfect sense. Denver, you asked me last night if I found advertising types discriminated against women. Well, they do. I've had to work darned hard to get where I am."

"I'm sure you have, but—"

"And my job's very important to me. I don't take chances on blowing it."

"Oh, come off it! We're talking about sites for some dumb commercials." He bit back the rest of what he'd been going to say. The look on her face told him he'd just stepped over the line again.

He thought she might really explode this time, but she surprised him. "Denver, let me explain. Three years ago, Jay took a big chance by entrusting me with the Bristow account. And I'll admit that managing it involves doing a lot of things I'm not crazy about. But I do my best to keep Nolton happy with our agency. And right now, that means staying here until I've got those shots."

"Fine. If that's the way it has to be, just give me the camera and I'll go out and shoot every inch of scenery in sight. Then we can get going. Okay?"

"No, not okay. You know it isn't that simple. I need a variety of specific sites. I'd estimated taking at least two solid days to find them. And that was before this ankle. But...well, since you're certain we won't be able to use Brandy, there's no reason *you* have to stay any longer. I can easily...well, I can get back somehow."

"Dammit, Chantal! You know I wouldn't leave you up here in weirdo land on your own."

She gave him an annoying little shrug. "You don't have to feel responsible for me. That wasn't part of the deal. And I'd still have Brandy here. She'd protect me if there was any problem."

He glanced at the dog. If Brandy ever protected anyone it would undoubtedly be by accident. She'd be far more likely to sit on Chantal's bad ankle than protect her.

He tried to imagine Chantal hobbling around on her own, then said, "We've been arguing about this so damned long, it's gotten too late to head back today, anyway. I'm going out to get some more groceries. We can discuss this again when I get back, maybe figure out a compromise."

"Maybe," she agreed, smiling at him, pretending she was actually open to compromise. But he knew darned well she wasn't. She was determined to stay until she had half the scenery in Quebec on tape. If he left tomorrow, it would be only he and McGee going home.

He gestured at the stack of magazines he'd brought down from the master bedroom. "Those'll give you enough to read while I'm gone?"

"Denver, they'd give me enough to read if you were gone for a month."

"Well, I'll only be about half an hour. So stay put until I get back."

"Aye, aye, sir," she said, giving a mock salute as he grabbed his jacket and headed out.

The frosty air didn't do as much to cool him down as he'd hoped. He fumed all the way to the grocery store, caught himself muttering out loud over the vegetables and was still in a funk when he got back into the van and roared onto the highway once more. There shouldn't be even the slightest question about leaving.

Chantal's logic was completely illogical, but maybe she'd been right about one thing. Maybe he *shouldn't* feel responsible for her. That *wasn't* part of the deal.

He slowed as he reached the narrow road leading to the chalet. When they'd first arrived, driving in the darkness, he hadn't noticed there were signs posted just off the highway - one forbidding trespassing, the other saying this was a private road. That probably explained why it was poorly plowed.

A private road...just the Bristow chalet and the cabin with that rifle-toting madman in it. Could he really leave Chantal alone up here with a neighbor like that? Not likely. Not even remotely likely.

But he shouldn't stay. Something was happening between him and Chantal that he hadn't expected and that he definitely didn't want. Because if he'd set out intentionally looking for a woman who'd be incompatible with him, he couldn't have found a better one than her. They lived completely different lives in totally different worlds. So the sooner he got back to his world, and away from her, the better.

He came to a decision. He was going to call her bluff. Odds were that she was just putting on a brave front about staying up here alone. So as soon as he got to the chalet, he'd tell her he'd definitely decided to head back to Jersey in the morning. Tell her that if she wanted to come along, fine. Or if she wanted to stay on her own, until she got a hundred sites on tape, that would be fine, too. But he'd be out of here first thing.

DENVER OPENED THE DOOR leading from the garage into the laundry room and headed through it and down the hall. When he reached the living room he stopped dead, a rush of uneasiness sweeping him.

Neither Chantal nor the dogs were in sight. And the stack of magazines had slithered from the couch to the floor.

The uneasiness escalated when he heard a male voice in the kitchen.

Quietly, he put down the carton of groceries and headed quickly across the room, pausing in the kitchen doorway. The voice was coming from the television set on the kitchen counter.

Chantal was sitting at the end of the table, her ankle propped up on a chair seat, a dog lying on either side of her, and the TV remote in her hand.

Both McGee and Brandy gazed up at him and wagged their tails but Chantal seemed hypnotized by the screen.

He watched it for a minute, trying to figure out why. She had on a news broadcast. In French. Then she clicked through a couple of channels and stopped at another newscast.

"Chantal?" he finally said.

She turned and looked at him, eyes wide and luminous. "Denver! Oh, I'm so glad you're back. You're just not going to believe this."

"I'm not going to believe what?"

Chantal swallowed hard and he realized she was near tears.

"Chantal? What is it?"

"Oh, Denver, it's that little boy we saw this morning. In the cabin. I think . . . I think he's a kidnapping victim."

"You think what?"

"I think that man with the rifle kidnapped him and is hiding him in the cabin."

Denver just stood staring at her, wondering what on earth had prompted such a bizarre idea.

She wiped her eyes and swallowed again. "Don't look at me as if I'm loony tunes. Everything adds up. It explains why the cabin that's supposed to be empty isn't. And why the man came peering in our window."

"Why?" Denver asked.

"Because," she said, looking at him as if he were a little dense, "he didn't expect anyone would be here and wanted to see who was. And it explains why he was so upset when I appeared practically on his doorstep this morning. And the boy...you saw how he tried to get out of the cabin while we were there. Denver, I think that poor little boy's been kidnapped."

"Chantal, you're adding two and two and getting sixty-three. I really don't—"

"No, Denver. I thought I'd watch a little TV because I was bored, and when I turned it on, the picture of a little boy was on the screen. And it looked just like the boy from this morning. And then I realized I'd seen the picture before. When we stopped at the grocery store, on our way here, it was splashed across the front page of a newspaper. Right under the headline."

"And the headline said he'd been kidnapped," Denver concluded.

Chantal shook her head. "I didn't have the foggiest notion what it said. It was in French. But I think that must be what they're talking about. I channel-surfed a little, and he was a news story on one of the other channels, too."

"And the story was about him being kidnapped."

She gazed at him for a moment, this time as if he were *more* than a little dense.

"Denver, I'm *assuming* the story was that he's been kidnapped. The television's all French, too. We only get four channels and every one is French."

"Hell," he muttered, "we might as well be in France as Quebec. But, look, are you absolutely sure the boy in the cabin is the boy in the news?"

"I...well, not absolutely. It looks like him, but I'm not a hundred percent certain. I've been flicking back and forth, hoping to catch more on the story. Maybe I should go back to the first channel—see if they do a re-cap."

"No," Denver said. "Stick with this one until it's almost the half hour."

They focused on the set, and not three minutes later, the announcer assumed a concerned expression, began speaking in a worried voice, and a boy's photograph replaced the newsroom shot.

Denver eyed it intently. It did look something like the boy they'd seen. A skinny child, about ten, with dark hair.

"Gagnon." Chantal repeated the name quietly as the announcer read his copy. "That has to be his last name. On the other channel, they were saying things about two people named Gagnon—a René and a Claude. But that's all I could understand."

"And that guy at the cabin didn't call the kid by name, did he?"

"No, not that I heard. But what do you think, Denver? Is it him?"

He gazed at the picture for another second, still trying to decide. "I don't know," he finally said. "You're right. It could be. But I'm not certain, either. I only saw him for a couple of seconds. And there are probably thousands of ten-year-old boys who look alike."

"So... so we should call the police, right?" Chantal said anxiously. "Even though we're not positive. Oh, Denver, if we're right... that poor little boy."

Denver nodded slowly. "I just wish we were sure it's the same kid. And that we've got the story figured straight. I mean, we're going to look like idiots if there hasn't even been a kidnapping."

"What else could it be?"

"I don't know. Maybe he's dying of some rare disease and they're asking for bone marrow donors or something. You're positive there isn't an English-language channel?"

"I've been through every number twice, and all I got was either French or static."

"Then I guess we call the police."

Chantal sat watching as he checked Nolton's book for a number, feeling a million times better now that they were reporting their suspicions. If that actually was the little Gagnon boy in the cabin, he'd be rescued.

Beside her chair, Brandy yawned, then sat up and rested her head on Chantal's lap. She scratched behind the dog's ear, the way Denver did, pleased with herself for figuring out how to tell the dogs apart. Yesterday, she'd realized that McGee was a little larger. But that difference didn't help much unless they were standing side by side.

When Denver had gone out, though, she'd studied the two of them carefully and discovered a difference in their markings. The white fur of McGee's chest extended into a collar that ran completely around his neck. It was pretty much hidden by brown fur, but it was there, while Brandy had only a spot of white on the nape of her neck.

Denver began speaking into the phone, giving his name, and she turned her attention back to him.

"I'm staying at a chalet off Highway 55, not far from the turnoff to St. Leonard," he said, then paused, frowning.

"English," he said. "Does anyone there speak English?" He shook his head at Chantal and murmured this might not be as easy as they'd assumed.

"No, no français," he said into the receiver. "Doesn't *anyone* there speak English?"

He listened for another minute, then simply hung up, saying, "This is nuts. What the hell do we do now? Drive around the province trying to find a damned police station? Then use sign language?"

Chantal glanced at Nolton's phone book. "You could call that woman we met at the store, that Pierrette Pelletier."

Denver's frown was replaced by a grin. "Anyone ever tell you that you come up with absolutely brilliant suggestions?" he said.

"ALLO?" A WOMAN'S VOICE answered the phone.

"Is that Ms. Pelletier?" Denver asked.

"Yes, I am speaking."

He gave Chantal a thumbs-up sign. "Ms. Pelletier, this is Denver Brooke. You probably don't remember me, but we met in the grocery store and—"

"But of course I remember you," she purred, her voice suddenly forty-degrees warmer.

"Oh. Oh, well, good."

"And my name, it is Pierrette."

"Uh-huh. Pierrette it is, then. Listen, Pierrette, you're going to think this is an awfully strange question, but we saw something on the news that...well, we aren't positive what the story was and thought maybe you could tell us."

"Mais oui, of course. If I have seen it."

"It was something about a little boy. I think his last name is Gagnon. His photograph's been in the paper as well as on TV, and we think they're saying he's been kidnapped. Is that right?"

The silence at the other end lasted so long Denver started wondering if the connection had been broken. Then Pierrette cleared her throat and spoke again. "Yes...yes, the child was kidnapped...several days ago...in Montreal."

"Did we have the story straight?" Chantal whispered. "Was he kidnapped?"

"Yes. In Montreal," Denver whispered back, wondering why Pierrette's voice had lost the forty degrees of warmth. But she'd begun speaking again, so he concentrated on what she was saying.

"His father is Claude Gagnon, a wealthy businessman. And there is, of course, a...how do you say...a ransom demand. But why are you asking about this?"

"Because we saw a little boy this morning. One who looked like the Gagnon child. I tried calling the police but didn't get anywhere speaking English. Then we decided maybe we should make sure we didn't have the story figured wrong before we went any further."

"You saw the child this morning? Where?"

"There's an old cabin on the road to the Bristow chalet."

"Yes, I know it."

"Well, the boy was there. With a man who was maybe fifty-five or so. A man with a rifle."

There was another pause, this one shorter, then Pierrette said, "I think I am understanding. Denver, what did the man look like?"

He gave her a brief description.

"Oui," she said. "Yes, that is Maurice Charlebois. The cabin, it is his. He seldom uses it, but there must be a reason for him to be there with this boy. And it cannot be little René Gagnon. I cannot think Maurice is a kidnapper."

"Do you know him well, Pierrette?"

"No...not well."

"Then I wonder if you'd do me a favor and call the police for us? Ask them to check that cabin? Just in case?"

"Denver...this is not a good idea. Believe me. I have lived here some years, and the child you saw with Maurice will not be René Gagnon, and—"

"Pierrette, it's not only that we saw the boy this morning. There've been peculiar things happening since the moment we got here." He told her about the shots on the road and Maurice's face at their window.

"Mais oui," she said quietly when he'd finished his story. "Yes, I can see why you would have a worry. But to call the police...listen to me for a minute. I must explain to you how it is."

Chantal sat, watching Denver, waiting impatiently for him to hang up. She didn't have the slightest idea what Pierrette Pelletier was going on about, but she was certainly going on at great length.

"I really don't think you should do that," Denver finally said.

Chantal whispered, "Don't think she should do what?" but he waved her off.

"Okay," he said. "If you're that determined, I'll go with you."

"Go where with her?" Chantal demanded.

"Well..." he said into the phone, ignoring Chantal, "yes, I can see your point. All right. All right. We'll see you in an hour or so."

"What?" Chantal said the instant he put down the receiver. "What's happening?"

"Pierrette is going to the cabin to check things out."

"By herself? Is she crazy?"

"I wouldn't be at all surprised. A lot of what she was saying sounded kind of strange. But apparently that wacko with the rifle owns the cabin. Only, according to her, he isn't wacko, just a little standoffish."

"*A little standoffish?* What is she? The reigning queen of understatement?"

Denver grinned a worried-looking grin. "That was my phrase, not hers. She kept slipping into French, but I gathered that's what she meant. And she says it can't possibly be the Gagnon boy, that there has to be a logical explanation for everything. So she's going to hop on her snowmobile, zip over to the cabin...and find out what it is."

"Denver, it'll be pitch black outside soon."

"She said it's perfectly safe around here."

Chantal shot him an oh-sure look and he shrugged. "Well, anyway, she said it won't take her long to get there cross-country. Then she'll stop here on her way home and tell us what's what."

"But, Denver—"

"How was I supposed to stop her?" he said. "And you heard me offer to go along, but she wasn't having any of that, said she'd be just fine. Said if a stranger arrived it would only upset the guy."

"Well...given his reaction to me this morning, she's probably right on that point. But, Denver, why would she want to get involved? Why didn't she simply call the police like you asked her to?"

"Because she doesn't think there's a chance this Maurice is a kidnapper. And apparently the local police are a modern version of the Keystone Kops—not too sharp and more than a little excitable. And it would be a major coup for them to solve a Montreal kidnapping. So she figures they might go in with guns blazing. And she said she's not taking a chance on being responsible for someone getting killed.''

"I suppose that makes sense," Chantal said slowly. "So what do we do now?"

"You just sit there and keep your ankle up. I'll throw together something for us to eat. Then I guess we wait."

She swallowed uneasily. "And hope we don't hear any shots from the cabin?"

Denver walked over to the counter, opened a drawer, and pulled out Nolton's handgun. "And hope we don't hear any shots from the cabin," he repeated quietly.

DENVER HAD JUST LIT an after-dinner fire when they heard the faint noise of an engine. "That sounds like a snowmobile," he said. "She must be all right."

Chantal nodded, banishing her horror-movie fantasies about what could have happened to Pierrette.

"Let's see what she's got to say," he added, slipping Nolton's gun into the drawer of an end table as he started for the door.

Brandy and McGee trailed along behind Denver, and Chantal gazed after them, feeling left out. She really *was* sure her ankle would be a lot better tomorrow. For the moment, though, getting back from the kitchen had been more than enough exercise. But if Denver simply stood at the door and talked to that woman, she'd kill him.

He didn't. He politely ushered Pierrette into the living room and gestured her to the chair nearest the fire. She looked as if she'd be glad of its warmth. Her cheeks were almost as pink as her raspberry snowmobile suit.

She said hello to Chantal, then began patting the dogs, gushing about how gorgeous they were until Denver impatiently cleared his throat.

"Do not look so worried, Denver," she said, clasping her hands over her knees and smiling up at him. "It is exactly how I supposed. For everything, Maurice Charlebois has the explanation. The boy is his grandson. They are having...how do you say...a wilderness holiday at the cabin."

"You're certain that's the truth?" Chantal asked. "You talked to the little boy? Not just the man?"

"*Oui, absolument.* The boy is called Jean-Paul, and he goes to the School of the Sacred Heart in Trois-Rivières. But he is here until the New Year."

Chantal shook her head uncertainly. "But the way that man grabbed him this morning and shoved him back into the cabin..."

"Ah, *oui,*" Pierrette said, laughing. "It was because of the dogs. Jean-Paul loves dogs, but he has the bad allergy. Maurice was afraid for him to pat them."

Denver grinned over at Chantal and murmured, "We'd have looked like idiots. Jean-Paul's just one of those thousands of ten-year-old lookalikes, after all."

"And Maurice asked me to apologize," Pierrette went on. "For the fright he gave to you on the road, with the shots."

"It *was* him shooting, then," Denver said.

"*Oui.* The road here, it is private. When he saw your van he thought you were lost in the dark, that you might drive into the fence at the road's end. He fired to signal that you should stop."

"But then he came looking in our window," Chantal said.

Pierrette nodded. "That was because he began to worry you might be robbers. But when he saw you he decided that was not so, and went back to his cabin."

"I really did leap to the wrong conclusions, then," Chantal said. "And I feel terrible about bothering you."

"That is all right. Because I came here, I got to meet your dogs. And like Jean-Paul, I adore dogs. But these two, would they rescue a person lost in the mountains? Or is that only Saint Bernards with the special training?"

"They don't need special training for that," Denver told her. "They have an uncanny sense of smell. And the Swiss have used them as rescue dogs for so many generations that the instinct is stamped in the breed."

"Well," Pierrette said, stroking McGee's head, "if we have the lost person, we will know where to come. But I should go now," she added, rising.

"I could make coffee," Chantal offered quickly. "You must still be frozen."

"Thank you, but I should get home."

Denver saw her out, then turned back to the living room. Chantal hadn't moved. She was snuggled on the couch with her legs stretched out on it, light from the fire catching pale strands of her honey-colored hair.

She smiled at him as he crossed the room, focusing his gaze on her mouth, focusing his thoughts on his feelings. The feelings he shouldn't be having.

"I guess that's it," she said. "The end of all our excitement."

He nodded, stopping a couple of feet from her and trying to decide what to say. When he'd walked in a few hours ago, he'd been primed to settle the issue of their leaving. But he'd walked straight into this final episode of all their excitement and hadn't had the chance.

And now . . . now what? The situation had changed completely. Instead of being a rifle-toting kidnapper,

Maurice Charlebois was simply Jean-Paul's grandfather. And now that Chantal knew there was no madman living down the road, she'd stay up here for sure, even if it did mean staying alone.

But now that they knew she wouldn't be in any danger, there was no real reason to worry about leaving her here. And since he wasn't going to be working with Brandy, he had no good reason to stay.

He did have a good reason to leave, though. If he spent much more time with Chantal, he'd try something they might both regret. So that decided it—he'd leave in the morning.

CHAPTER SIX

DENVER GLANCED ACROSS the living room at Chantal once more, immediately realizing he shouldn't have. Looking at her, stretched out on the couch, only made him think he'd like to kiss her.

He stuck his hands into his pockets and began silently telling himself why kissing her would be an incredibly dumb move.

"You know, I really misjudged Pierrette when we first met her," Chantal said. "Most people wouldn't have gone out of their way like she just did. And initially I thought she was...well, I thought her only concern in life was men...the way she practically drooled over you in the store."

Denver thought back, but darned if he could remember any drooling on Pierrette's part. Normally, if a woman who looked like her had come on to him, he'd have noticed. But since he'd met Chantal, he seemed to be noticing an awful lot of her and not much of anything else.

"I'm glad everything's explained," she murmured. "And that our worries about Jean-Paul were unfounded. But little René Gagnon...he's still out there someplace, Denver."

He nodded again, not really paying much attention to what she was saying, then noticed a tear trickling down her cheek.

She quickly wiped it away, but it was immediately replaced by another.

Hesitantly, he edged a little nearer. "Chantal? What's the matter?"

"Nothing... not really. It's just that I can't help thinking about what René Gagnon must be going through. He has to be so incredibly frightened. And his parents must be in agony."

Denver watched another tear make its way down her face, then tentatively lowered himself to the couch beside her, carefully staying clear of her propped-up ankle. "Chantal, with any luck it'll turn out all right for them."

"I know," she said, tears in her voice now. "But I just can't understand how anyone could be so inhuman as to kidnap a child."

He put his arm around her and drew her nearer, merely to comfort her. But somehow she ended up gazing at him, her teary eyes an impossibly inviting depth of blue, her mouth only inches from his.

Then her lower lip trembled a little, and, for the life of him, he couldn't remember why kissing her would be an incredibly dumb move. He leaned forward the fraction it took and brushed her lips with his.

She sat motionless for a moment, not responding in the slightest. And then she snuggled closer, putting her arms around his neck. Her body felt so soft against his chest, her lips so lushly moist against his, and she returned his kiss with such gentle intensity he could scarcely believe the sensations it caused.

Every fiber of his being centered on the delight of kissing her. It felt so perfectly right that, with the remnants of his thought processes, he wondered why it had taken him so long to get around to it.

Kissing Chantal Livingstone was better than anything he'd ever imagined. She smoothed her fingers up the back of his neck, drawing his lips impossibly closer to hers, and the idea of leaving tomorrow suddenly seemed the most unbelievably stupid idea he'd ever had.

He kissed her until they were both breathless, until her body began telling him things that had his own reacting like crazy. And then, in the back of his barely functioning mind, his thoughts began reaching into the past. And into the future.

The more his thoughts reached away from the present moment, the less leaving tomorrow seemed stupid. In fact, he knew it was the only sane thing to do. And the only sane thing to do right this minute was to stop kissing Chantal. Somehow, he managed to pull away.

She murmured unintelligibly and rested her head on his shoulder, gently running her hand across his chest.

He swallowed hard and captured her hand. "Chantal?"

"Mmm?"

"There's something we have to talk about." He cleared his throat, not at all certain his resolve would hold up. "Chantal, I've decided that I'm definitely going to head back first thing in the morning. I still think you should come with me but ... but obviously, it's up to you."

She eased away a few inches, gazing at him uncertainly.

He desperately wanted to draw her back, to completely forget about the past and the future, to forget everything except the here and now. That would be a mistake, though.

"I see," she finally said. "So ... what you were doing just then was kissing me goodbye."

"Chantal . . . Chantal, what I was doing . . ."

Damn. What he'd been doing was idiotic, and he really didn't want to try explaining his idiocy. "Chantal, listen to me for a minute, okay? I meant it when I said I still think you should come with me. I'd feel a whole lot better delivering you back to your town house. But now that we know old Maurice isn't the sort to wander up here during the night with an ax in his hand . . . and you said it would take at least a couple of days to do your taping. It'll likely be even longer than that with your ankle. So . . . the thing is, I can't be away from the kennel for too long at a stretch. I've just got those teenagers looking after things and . . . you understand, huh?"

"Of course. I understand perfectly," she murmured, shifting so she was sitting primly against the arm of the couch. Then she folded her hands in her lap and kind of smiled at him.

The smile didn't make it, though, and he was on the verge of simply giving up and taking her in his arms once more. Then, from the corner of the room, McGee began quietly growling.

Denver glanced over. The dog was standing facing the door, hackles raised, his low growl an unmistakable warning that something was outside. Brandy was sitting nearby, watching the display.

"What's wrong?" Chantal asked uneasily.

"I'm not sure. Don't move. Just sit there as if nothing's unusual." Denver rose and strolled across the room, glancing out the front window, seeing nothing but moonlit night. Then he wandered past the fireplace, pausing when he could see out the back of the chalet without being obvious about it.

From that vantage point, moonlit night wasn't the only thing he saw.

As casually as he could, he crossed to the couch, opened the drawer of the end table and took out Nolton's gun, slipping it quickly under his sweater before looking at Chantal.

She was staring at him, her expression saying, Oh, no, not again.

"We may have a little problem," he said quietly.

"A little problem," she repeated, trying to sound as unconcerned as Denver was trying to sound. But neither of them would make it as actors. "A little problem as in you saw someone looking in the window again, right?"

He nodded.

"Maurice?"

"No. But they're probably just more nosy neighbors."

"They?" The word barely made it out and she tried again. "They, Denver?"

"Two of them."

"Two," she repeated. "What do they look like?"

"I can't tell. They're wearing balaclavas."

"Balaclavas?" she said, starting to feel like a parrot. "You mean like bank robbers sometimes wear?"

"No, I mean like people sometimes wear when it's freezing out, the way it is tonight."

She swallowed uneasily. "Ah...Denver, you know that whoever they are, they're not just nosy neighbors. Maurice is the only neighbor we have anywhere nearby."

Denver merely shrugged, then called Brandy over.

When she bounded across to the couch, he said she was a good dog, ordered her to sit, and shoved her back end down. "Hold on to her, Chantal. I don't want her along."

"Denver, you aren't going to—"

"McGee and I are going to check on our company. We'll head out through the far end of the garage and surprise them."

"Denver, no! You can't go out there."

"Well, I'm sure as hell not staying in here while a couple of jerks play Peeping Tom."

"But you don't know who they are. Maybe they're wearing those masks because they're escaped criminals or something."

"Chantal, I have a gun. And McGee. And the element of surprise."

"Oh, Denver, call the police."

"We've been that route, remember? And I haven't miraculously learned French in the past few hours. Now, I'm going to wander out of the room as if I'm just getting something. And you sit there as if everything's fine. Try not to even look at the windows."

He turned away, McGee on his heels, then paused and glanced back. "Don't open the door, no matter what happens. And if...if anything does happen, phone Pierrette just as fast as you can and tell *her* to call the police."

Chantal felt sick. Brandy whined, and she hugged the dog's neck tightly. "It's okay, girl," she whispered. "It's okay."

But what if it wasn't okay? Denver had seen two men, but what if there were more? And what if they really were escaped criminals? What if they had guns of their own? What if Denver got hurt? Oh, Lord, what if Denver got killed?

At the thought of Denver being killed, her throat began burning and her heart racing. If something happened to him it would be entirely her fault. He'd wanted to leave, but she'd said no. And now he was going out there, into the dark, maybe getting killed, all because of her stubbornness.

Denver reached the hallway and glanced back again, giving Chantal a thumbs-up. She looked as if she were about to burst into tears, but at least her back was to the window. If those guys looked in again, they wouldn't see she was upset.

He walked rapidly down to the laundry room and out into the garage, not turning on any lights. Quietly, he felt his way along the wall, opened the door on the far side and slipped out, motioning McGee to stay right behind. After the darkness of the garage, he could see clearly in the moonlight.

He took out the gun, then eased along to the back corner of the chalet and stopped, cautiously peering around it.

They were still there. Spotlighted in the pale haze coming from the living room window. One was a little over six feet, the other maybe five-eight. It was hard to tell with them wearing ski jackets, but they both seemed fairly thin.

You never knew about thin guys, though. They could be surprising. Sometimes they turned out to have a black belt or something.

He touched McGee's head, signaling him to keep following, then started toward them, pressing against the chalet, moving slowly to minimize the crunch of his footsteps in the snow. But the two of them were whispering to each other, so he was probably safe.

"What do we do now?" one of them murmured, his words carrying through the still night air.

Three seconds, Denver said silently. Just three more seconds and you won't have any choice in the matter.

He stopped about ten feet from them, assumed a firing stance, and pointed the gun at the center of the taller man's body. "Freeze," he said. "Or I'll blow holes in the two of you."

They froze. Except for two shocked intakes of breath, they didn't move a muscle.

"Okay," he said quietly, easing away from the chalet, still aiming the gun with both hands, "we're all going inside now."

Neither of them said a word, simply stood staring at the gun, then started off the moment he gestured them to. They were just young punks, he realized. Probably out to pull a little break-and-enter at places with no one home.

He paused in the garage, located the light switch, backed the tall one against a wall and frisked him, finding nothing. "You're in charge here, McGee," he said. Then he ordered the other punk ahead of him into the chalet.

Chantal heard footsteps in the hallway and gazed anxiously across the room. A moment later she closed her eyes and offered up a tiny prayer of thanks. Denver was back inside, safe and sound, holding his gun on one of their masked intruders.

She cleared her throat to make sure her voice would actually work. Then, in her best pretending-to-be-unconcerned tone, asked if the other one had gotten away.

Denver said, "No, McGee's keeping the other one company in the garage. I thought we'd hear what they had to say one at a time. So," he added, eyeing his prisoner, "take that thing off your head and start talking. What the hell were you doing out there?"

The fellow quickly yanked off his mitts and peeled the balaclava up... only he wasn't a fellow. He was a girl, with dark curly hair, big brown eyes and an angelic face that looked more like it belonged to a high-school cheerleader than a criminal.

She didn't speak, simply stood staring at Denver's gun, looking terrified.

Chantal glanced at Denver. He was obviously every bit as surprised as she was. "Well?" he finally said to the girl, lowering his gun.

She opened and closed her mouth a couple of times, but no sound came out.

"Maybe she only speaks French," Chantal said.

"Uh-uh. I heard English outside. So, kid?" he said quietly, clearly trying not to frighten the girl even more. "What's the story?"

"Are...ahh...I guess you're using this as a hideout or something, sir?"

Denver said, "What?"

"I mean...if you are, that's ace. I mean...you aren't hurting the place. So we wouldn't tell anyone. We'll just leave and not say a word...I mean if that would be all right with you, sir."

Chantal glanced at Denver, wondering what he was making of this.

"Look, kid," he said, "I'm not going to hurt you. I just want to know what you and your friend were doing out there."

"Well...sir...we were planning on staying here for a few days. But we don't have to. Like I said, we can just leave. And not say a word about your being here."

"You were planning on staying here," Denver repeated uncertainly.

"Yes, sir. But when we saw lights on...well, we figured we'd better find out what was what. So we left the car down the drive and were trying to see who was in here. We thought it would be somebody Kip knew, thought his dad must have lent someone the place."

"Kip?" Chantal said. "Kip Bristow?"

The girl looked over and nodded anxiously.

"Oh, Lord, Denver," Chantal murmured. "Put down the gun and let Nolton's son out of the garage."

"SO WE JUST DECIDED to come here on the spur of the moment," Kip said. "It never even occurred to me somebody might be using the place. I guess," he continued, focusing on Denver, "that if I'd noticed the dogs when we looked in, I might have realized who you were. But all Cathy and I could figure was that you were a crook, holed up in a place you'd found vacant."

"Which would have made me a gun moll?" Chantal said.

"Something like that," Kip told her, grinning. "Sorry I didn't recognize you, but we only saw the back of your head."

"And I have a very ordinary-looking back of the head," she said, smiling at him. She didn't know him well, had only chatted with him at a few of Nolton's deadly cocktail parties. But he was far more likable than his father.

Kip glanced at Cathy, and Chantal couldn't help smiling again. They'd said they'd only met at the start of September, at a freshman orientation day, but they were obviously head-over-heels in love with each other. Absently, she wondered what old-fashioned Nolton would think about the two of them being here. He might be a lecher himself, but she knew he expected his son to walk the straight and narrow.

Kip brushed back some of the long dark hair that was half covering his eyes, making her suspect he'd come up here because Nolton had chased him out of the penthouse with a pair of scissors.

But that wouldn't explain Cathy's being with him. Curious, she caught his eye and asked, "Did you drive all the way from Manhattan today?"

"Ah . . . well, we actually didn't come up from Manhattan. Cathy's parents live just across the border in Maine. And I drove there after Christmas. We were going to spend the rest of the break there."

"Changed your minds, though," she said when he paused.

"Yeah. It didn't exactly work out, so . . . well, here we are. You wouldn't mind if we stayed, would you, Chantal? We wouldn't get in your way. We'd spend most of our time skiing."

"No, I wouldn't mind in the least. It's your chalet."

"Dad's chalet," he corrected her.

"Well, it's all in the family."

Kip looked at Cathy again, this time giving her a rueful smile. "It's only all in the family," he said, turning back to Chantal, "if I don't get disinherited."

She waited, unsure whether he wanted her to pick up on that. "If I had to guess what you meant," she tried when the silence grew, "I'd guess your father's upset about how long your hair's gotten."

"Yeah, well, that too. But that's not the main event. See, Cathy and I got married last week."

Chantal swallowed her surprise. "Congratulations."

"Thanks," Kip said, "but the news hasn't exactly met with parental approval."

"Your father blew up?" Chantal asked quietly.

"Wrong tense. He's *going* to blow up. He doesn't know yet. But when he finds out, he'll make St. Helena look like a kid's Roman candle."

"What the hell," Denver offered. "I guess you're both kind of young, but getting married's hardly the end of the world."

"I'm also," Cathy said hesitantly, "kind of pregnant. And that does seem to be the end of the world, at least as far as parents are concerned. Mine think I've ruined my life. They want me to have an abortion, but I just can't do that."

"*We* just can't do that," Kip said, squeezing her hand.

The four of them sat looking at each other for a minute.

Finally, Kip said, "See, the plan was that I'd go home and tell Mom and Dad. Then I'd go up to Maine and help Cathy tell her folks. I told Mom ... and, well you know Mom, Chantal. She thinks we're too young, but she'll make the best of it. When I tried to tell Dad, though ... well, I knew he'd start screaming about me being irresponsible and about disowning me. He's big on threatening to disown me. And somehow the words wouldn't come out.

"Then Mom rescued me and ... I'm a chicken, I guess, but she's going to tell him. So ... well, at any rate, then I took off for Cathy's. But things got awfully uncomfortable there, so here we are."

"And you're definitely welcome to stay," Chantal said. "In fact, I'll be glad of your company, because Denver's going home tomorrow."

Denver cleared his throat and she glanced over at him, but he was looking at the kids. "You mentioned skiing," he said.

"My doctor said it would be perfectly all right," Cathy told him. "I'll probably just get tired faster than usual."

"Well, you got me thinking," Denver said. "After driving all the way up here, I haven't even taken my skis off the van. So maybe I could get in a few runs with you in the morning and still leave around noon. If you wouldn't mind having me along, that is."

"Of course not," Kip said. "That'd be terrific. Let's head out first thing. Come on," he added to Cathy. "I'll put the car in the garage and we can unload our gear."

"That was thoughtful of you," Chantal said as Kip closed the front door.

Denver said, "What was?"

"You know. Saying you wanted to go skiing with them. After all the disapproval they've been facing...well, it was nice of you."

"'Fraid I can't take credit for being thoughtful, Chantal. I really would like a few hours of skiing, and it's better with company."

She nodded slowly, watching him, not entirely convinced he hadn't been partly trying to make them feel more at ease.

"So," he said, "Kip's in for a rough time once Nolton hears the news, huh?"

"I sure wouldn't want to be there when Marlene tells him. Nolton can be...unpleasant."

"You know, Chantal, the more I hear about that guy, the more I wonder why you put up with him."

"I've told you. He's an important account. *My* important account."

"Yeah, right, you *have* told me that. Well, I think I'll just take the dogs out, then call it a night."

"Denver?" she said as he turned away.

In the split second it took him to look back, she lost her nerve. Earlier, in those few moments between his explaining why he'd be heading off in the morning and their realizing someone was outside, she'd been certain he'd changed his mind about leaving...and certain he was going to start kissing her again...and certain she wanted him to.

But those few moments were gone forever. And she didn't have the courage to mention them.

"You were going to ask me something?" he said quietly.

The way he was gazing at her made her wonder if he wasn't thinking about those few moments too. She almost asked, but said instead, "I...I just wondered if you'd mind leaving some dog food behind tomorrow. For Brandy."

He gazed at her for another long second, then simply said, "Sure."

"I CAN'T BELIEVE YOU'RE tearing yourself away," Kip said, helping Denver lock his skis back onto the van's roof. "You sure you don't want to join us for lunch and make a few runs this afternoon? We couldn't get a better day."

Denver glanced longingly at the slopes. Sunlight was glittering on the snow, and the temperature had climbed almost to the freezing point. The skiing was perfect. He thought again about staying awhile longer, then considered how late that would mean he'd get home and shook his head.

"Tempting as it is, us old guys have to work for a living. I've got to collect McGee and get going. You two enjoy the rest of the day."

Kip said they would. "And tell Chantal not to worry about us. If we aren't dead by the end of the afternoon, we might stay for a few night runs. And we'll catch something to eat before we head back."

Denver swung into the van, gave them a final wave, then drove out of the parking lot and down to the highway. The chalet wasn't far, and he'd already packed what little he'd brought. So all he had to do was get McGee and say goodbye to Chantal and...

And why was the thought of saying goodbye to Chantal bothering him so much? He'd been awake half the night, thinking about her. And thinking how absolutely fantastic he'd felt when he'd kissed her. And wishing Kip and Cathy hadn't appeared at such an inopportune moment.

If they hadn't, he'd have gone right back to kissing Chantal. And if he'd done that, he doubted he'd be leaving today.

But he hadn't and he was. And it was for the best. Definitely for the best. His brain understood that. It was only the rest of him that was having a problem with it.

He turned off the highway onto the chalet's road, reminding himself that, with Kip and Cathy here, Chantal wouldn't be alone. So there wasn't even the slightest excuse for him to consider staying.

When he reached the chalet, McGee scrambled across the living room, tail wagging a greeting. But only McGee. No Brandy. And no Chantal. He called her name. She didn't answer, and a tiny knot formed in his stomach.

"Chantal?" he called more loudly. "Brandy?"

He hurried across the room, looked out back, and his concern vanished.

There she was, wearing a dark green ski jacket that made her hair seem a paler shade of gold. Her face was flushed and she was laughing at Brandy.

She had the dog on a leash, and they were playing the monster game, Brandy backing away on her stomach as Chantal advanced. He watched for a minute, almost laughing himself. Brandy, by far the bigger of the two, was pretending to be terrified.

Chantal was favoring her ankle, but only a little. Apparently, she was as fast a healer as she'd claimed.

McGee whined impatiently, his chin resting on the window ledge.

"Figure you're missing the fun?" Denver said, crossing to the back door. "Let's go, then."

McGee bounded over the snow to join Brandy, and Chantal turned, a delighted smile on her face. "Did you see her, Denver? I don't think anyone's ever played with her much, but she caught on right away."

He nodded. "You weren't worried about her running off again when you brought her outside?"

"Well, a little. But I'll have to take her out when you're gone, won't I? Besides, I think we've come to an understanding." She looked at the dog. "Brandy, sit!"

Brandy sat.

He said he was very impressed and Chantal laughed. "Denver, I know *you're* the one who taught her that. But she's listening to me. She sits... well, most of the time when I tell her to. And she seems to be heeling pretty well—hardly tugging on the leash at all."

"Good. And how's your ankle?"

"Not bad. I thought it was a smart idea to try it out right by the house here. But I think I could walk a fair bit, so I might take the camera and wander off later."

Dammit, but he didn't like the idea of her wandering off. Not on her own. What if she got lost? Or something else happened? Around here, weird things seemed to happen with frightening regularity.

"Why don't we have lunch?" she suggested. "You should eat before you leave, and I could make something fast."

He meant to say, No, he really had to get going, but surprised himself by saying, "Good idea."

Great. Now his subconscious was putting words into his mouth.

"So, how was the skiing?" she asked as they headed back inside.

"Wonderful. The hills are in perfect condition. I hated to leave."

She quietly cleared her throat, then said, "Too bad you have to get back to Jersey."

"Ah...yeah. Too bad. You know..."

"What?" She stopped halfway through taking her jacket off and simply stood looking up at him, waiting for him to complete his sentence.

He tried to decide what to say, but the way she was watching him was making it impossible to think straight.

Her gaze was positively mesmerizing. She had the biggest, bluest eyes in the world. And she looked so darned desirable he'd be out of his mind to stay.

No, that didn't make sense. It must be that he'd be out of his mind to leave.

Hell, he must *already* be out of his mind. He didn't even know which option made sense.

"You started to say something," Chantal murmured, shrugging the rest of the way out of her jacket without taking her eyes off him.

"Ah...yeah...I guess I did," was all he could manage. He wished she'd stop looking at him but she didn't. And to make matters worse, she smiled.

It was just a tiny, tentative smile, but he was certain it meant she really wanted him to stay. Then she began speaking again, and he simply couldn't drag his eyes from her lips.

"I said it was too bad you have to get back to Jersey. And you started to say..."

"Uh-huh. I started to say..." What he'd started to say had been entirely against his better judgment, and if he had half a brain he'd get himself out to the van this very second.

"You started to say..." Chantal repeated.

"Ah...what I started to say was...Tara's pregnant."

"Tara?" Chantal said blankly.

"One of the dogs. But she's not due for a week or so...so, well, maybe I could call home and check that everything's fine...and stay another day or two."

He thought she edged a little closer, but, if she did, it was so little he couldn't be sure.

"So you'd have the chance to do some more skiing," she said quietly.

"Yeah, that too."

"Too?" she said, almost inaudibly, maybe edging another half inch closer.

Or maybe not. He must need his vision checked.

While he mumbled something idiotic about skiing, she *definitely* moved nearer. Now he could smell her perfume. The scent made him think about how she'd felt in his arms and about how soft her lips had been against his.

"So there's the skiing and . . . what?" she prompted.

"Oh . . . uh-huh . . . there's the skiing and then there's Brandy. I mean," he rushed on before he could change his mind, "maybe you were right. The way she was sitting out there . . . well, maybe I *was* too quick about writing her off. I could have another go with her."

Chantal was smiling, telling him he was saying all the right things, and he just couldn't seem to shut up. "Then there's checking for your sites. I mean, I'll be involved in the actual shoot when we come back up. Your director will need me to work with the dog. So maybe it would make sense for me to get involved now. If you think I could be of some use to you. With evaluating potential sites, that is."

"I think you could be of great use to me," she murmured. "With evaluating potential sites, that is. And it would be awfully nice of you. I'd really appreciate it."

"Yeah . . . well . . . I guess I should go and phone then . . . just to be sure Tara hasn't started tearing up newspapers to make herself a bed or anything."

Chantal nodded, still smiling at him, but his feet wouldn't move. And his eyes wouldn't leave her face.

His arms seemed to be in working order, though, so he wrapped them around her, drew her the rest of the way to him and kissed her.

Her lips were still cool from being outside—the most delicious cool he'd ever tasted. And her body was so warm and yielding against him that he wondered if he could simply hold her and kiss her forever.

Then, from some recess of his mind, thoughts of the past came drifting forward ... and thoughts about the future ... and about Madison Avenue being light years away from a kennel in Jersey.

And the thoughts were all telling him he knew better, were all warning him he was going to deeply regret this.

But he'd never found it easier to ignore a warning. Who on earth would want to listen to a bunch of know-nothing thoughts when he could be devoting every fragment of his attention to kissing Chantal?

CHAPTER SEVEN

"STAY," DENVER SAID firmly, brushing Brandy's nose with his fingers.

Chantal bit her lower lip as he turned his back and started walking away. He must have tried this a hundred times, but maybe this time, Brandy would get it right.

The dog waited until Denver had taken half a dozen steps, then scooted over to Chantal and nuzzled her affectionately.

"Oh, Brandy," she said wearily. "You're such a sweetie, but you just don't listen, do you?"

Denver headed across the snow to them, a dark look on his face.

"Maybe if I went inside?" she suggested. "I'm distracting her."

"Chantal, if one person distracts her, how do you think she'd be with an entire film crew around?"

"She...she isn't very trainable, is she?"

"No. She's a nice-enough dog, but she's no canine Einstein."

"So...I guess you were right. I guess Nolton's straight out of luck." But, Lord, she didn't want to be the one who had to tell him that.

She stood, eyeing Denver uneasily, wondering if he was back to thinking about going home, but she was afraid to ask. She wasn't quite sure what was happening between them, and she certainly wasn't sure it was wise to be letting *anything* happen between them. But, regardless of that, she *was* sure she didn't want him to leave.

"Come on," he said. "Let's put her inside with McGee and go look for some of those darned sites you need."

She breathed a tiny sigh of relief. He wasn't thinking about leaving. In fact, from the way he was looking at her, she'd say all he was thinking about was her.

She glanced down so he wouldn't notice her smiling, but she wasn't fast enough.

"What's that about?" he said, catching her under the chin with his finger.

"Oh . . . just thinking."

"Thinking what?"

She could feel her face growing warm, and he grinned at her, saying, "I was just thinking, too. You know what about?"

"What?"

He bent forward and kissed her, his mouth deliciously cold against hers, and she happily decided he wasn't thinking about leaving even one little bit.

They left the dogs inside, and spent the next hour wandering through the hills near the chalet. Finally, Chantal admitted her ankle was bothering her and they started back.

"Oh, just let me get this one on tape," she said when they reached a clearing at the foot of a small ridge.

Denver stood, watching her pan the video camera across the setting of frosted rocks and bushes peeking out through a snowy blanket.

A snowflake landed wetly on his cheek and he glanced up. In the few hours since he'd left the slopes, the bright day had begun to cloud over and occasional flakes were drifting down. There was still enough sun that they glittered like diamonds in the crisp air, but the distant sky was steadily turning a darker gray. He suspected they were in for a snowstorm.

"That's it," Chantal called, starting toward him, smiling.

She had a smile that made him want to hug her every time he saw it. "Good," he said. "McGee and Brandy will be thinking we've deserted them." He took the camera from her and wrapped his arm around her shoulders.

She snuggled against him, and it felt so right he stopped and kissed her.

"I thought you wanted to hurry back to the dogs," she teased when they finally began walking again, his arm still tightly around her.

"Oh, I guess they'll survive without us for a few minutes longer. They have each other for company."

"And so do we," she murmured. "Denver...I'm awfully glad you decided to stay."

"Me, too," he said, pausing to kiss her once more, then taking her hand.

He just couldn't seem to stop touching her. Not that he wanted to. Not in the slightest. But he also couldn't help feeling uneasy about what was going on inside his head.

He'd never met anyone quite like Chantal...had never felt quite the same way about anyone else...had never before found himself wondering what his future would be like with one particular woman.

Yes, it was the way he kept catching himself thinking about the future that was worrisome. Because there wasn't a chance in a million of there being any bridge between their worlds. So if his feelings for her kept escalating, he was riding for a very hard fall.

But hell, maybe the time to worry about the future was when it got here.

He glanced down at Chantal. Her hair was windblown, the tip of her nose red, he'd kissed off every trace of lipstick, and a couple of silly snowflakes were clinging to her eyelashes. She looked absolutely gorgeous.

Backing away a couple of feet, he focused the camera on her and shot a bit of tape.

"And what," she asked when he clicked the power off, "am I supposed to tell my director about that little segment being in among the prospective shoot sites?"

"Just tell him your assistant cameraman couldn't resist you." He took her hand once more. The chalet was in sight now, through the trees ahead of them, and suddenly all he could think about was being alone with her in it.

"Oh?" she was saying, not quite managing a serious expression. "And exactly what is it my assistant cameraman finds irresistible about me? The way I can't walk without limping? Or the way Marlene's clothes are just enough too large that they hang on me a little. Or is it—"

"I think it's that you like me."

"Pardon?"

"I think what's irresistible about you is that you like me. I'm a sucker for that in a woman."

That made her laugh and he grinned. He liked making her laugh.

"I see," she said. "So all I had to do was tell you I'm glad you stayed—"

"Awfully glad. You said awfully glad."

She laughed again. "Okay, then. All I had to do was tell you I'm awfully glad you stayed and kiss you about four thousand times and that made you figure I like you? You sure do leap to conclusions, don't you?"

He was about to tell her it hadn't seemed like much of a leap when he heard a faint sound in the sky.

"Plane?" Chantal asked.

"Uh-uh. Helicopter."

The staccato roar grew rapidly louder, and a second later the copter appeared over a nearby hill—a yellow Sikorsky headed in the direction of the chalet. It circled the open space past the far end of the garage, then hovered for a moment and slowly began to set down.

"It's landing," Denver said, starting forward. "What the hell's going on now?"

By the time they reached the chalet, the chopper was on the ground and a man was clambering from the passenger side, the hood of his parka tugged halfway over his face, shielding it against the frosty air that the main propeller was whipping into a gale-force wind.

He scooted backward from under the prop, gave a quick wave, and the pilot lifted off.

For a moment, the man watched the chopper head away. Then he turned, shoving back his hood.

Chantal said, "Oh, I don't believe this," and jerked her hand free from Denver's. "It's Nolton. Denver, don't let him catch on that you and I haven't been strictly business."

"Chantal!" the man called over the still-loud tattoo of the engine.

"Oh, Lord, Denver," she said, waving a greeting, "do you think Marlene's told him about Kip and Cathy, or not?"

"Your guess is as good as mine."

"Oh, I'll bet she has! I'll bet she told him before she left for that spa she was going to. And now he's come up here to yell and scream at them. Oh, Denver, I'll bet he's fit to be tied."

Denver thought for a second, then told her that didn't add up. "Kip said their coming here was a spur-of-the moment decision, remember? They were planning to spend the rest of the vacation in Maine. So whether Marlene's said anything yet or not, she couldn't have told Nolton that Kip's here."

"But he is! Denver, what are we going to do?"

"Play it by ear. If Nolton doesn't know, we'll just say as little as we can until the kids get back. It's sure not our place to drop the bombshell. But we've certainly got to tell him they're here."

"You're sure we *have* to?"

"Chantal, what are we going to do? Wait until they walk in, then say, Oh, by the way, we forgot to mention that your son and Cathy arrived last night?"

"Well . . . well, maybe Nolton's only going to stay for a few minutes. If that's the case . . ."

Denver gave her a dim look. "Don't you think, if that were the case, the helicopter would still be here, waiting for him?"

"Oh, Denver. I don't like this one little bit."

He started to put his arm around her, then remembered they were supposed to be strictly business and caught himself. Nolton was walking rapidly toward them. In his mid-forties, tall and fit, he had the confident stride of a man accustomed to getting whatever he wanted.

His parka hood was heavily trimmed with silver fox— the exact shade of his prematurely silver hair. He was carrying a hand-tooled leather case, his designer jeans were cut to look good, not to work in, and the burnished riding boots he wore must have cost a thousand plus. A perfect example of taking the man out of Manhattan but not taking Manhattan out of the man.

"You must be Denver Brooke," he said, reaching them. "Nolton Bristow. Nice to meet you in person."

Denver nodded, shaking Nolton's extended hand, and Chantal said it was certainly a surprise to see him, managing to get the greeting out with her voice only a touch off its normal pitch. Nolton said, "Well, Marlene's off at her spa and—"

"Oh, Marlene!" Chantal exclaimed. "I've been so worried about what Marlene would think," she continued, launching into an apologetic explanation about wearing Marlene's clothes.

"It's okay," Nolton finally snapped, cutting her off. He stood, looking at Chantal for another moment, as if he thought the cold must have affected her brain, then went back to his own explanation. "At any rate, Marlene's away, and it turns out Kip's finally got himself a girlfriend—took off to Maine to be with her."

Denver caught Chantal's eye for an instant. At least they had the answer to that question.

"So," Nolton went on, "I was kind of at loose ends for a few days and decided to charter a copter and come up for a little skiing. And see how my dog's doing, of course. You turned her into a star performer yet, Denver?"

"Ah..." What would happen if he admitted he'd given up on Brandy?

From everything Chantal had said, Nolton would be thoroughly ticked off. And he'd probably send one Mr. Denver Brooke packing immediately. Which would leave Chantal without him, in the midst of a situation that could turn into who knew what when Kip and Cathy got back.

Eventually, Nolton would have to come around to the idea of using McGee. But under the circumstances, it might be best to just start the thought percolating.

"Well, your dog and I have been making progress," he finally said, hoping Chantal wouldn't blow it. "Brandy's sitting really well on command."

Chantal didn't say a word and Nolton laughed. "Considering what you're costing us, I assume you've got her doing a lot more than sitting. Where is she, anyway?"

Denver resisted the temptation to tell Nolton he shouldn't assume too much, and said that Brandy was inside.

"I don't think I mentioned when we spoke on the phone," he added as they started for the door, "that I'd be bringing along one of my own dogs."

"No, you didn't," Nolton said, a sidelong glance adding that he didn't like surprises.

"Well, it's easier to train a dog if you work it with one that's already trained, gives the novice something to imitate. And my McGee's a real pro. You know, you might even want to think about using him in your commercials, rather than Brandy."

"No. Absolutely not. We'll be using Brandy. That's the very heart of my great idea. Right, Chantal?"

She smiled a sick-looking smile and said it certainly was.

Denver shrugged. "Well, it's your money. I just figured you could give some thought to McGee. The shooting would go a lot quicker with him, and the film crew wouldn't be working near as many hours."

When they opened the door, Brandy and McGee came charging from the kitchen, McGee skidding to a polite sit in front of them, while Brandy raced exuberantly into Chantal, knocking her against the wall in greeting.

"Well," Nolton boomed, stepping forward and patting McGee, "Denver certainly wasn't exaggerating about how well you've learned to sit, Brandy."

Denver said, "That's McGee. It's easy to confuse the two of them."

"Oh." Nolton jerked his hand from McGee's head as if it were red hot and looked at Brandy.

Denver shoved her into a sit but Nolton clearly wasn't impressed.

"Would you like something, Nolton?" Chantal said quickly. "Coffee? Tea?"

Nolton leered at her. "Isn't the line supposed to be coffee, tea or me?"

"I'd like coffee," Denver said evenly. "And I'll make it. You sit down, Chantal, rest your ankle. Nolton? Why don't you give me a hand in the kitchen and I'll give you my ideas on how we should proceed with Brandy." *Or maybe,* he added silently, *I'll just give you a quick shot in the mouth.*

CHANTAL FORCED DOWN another sip of brandy. When Nolton had produced the bottle after dinner, insisting they try Bristow Fine Spirits' newest product, she'd hoped for the best. But she wouldn't rate Bristow VSOP brandy any higher than she rated Bristow Fine Champagne. If the brandy bombed in the stores, she just hoped Nolton wouldn't blame that on the commercials, conveniently forgetting the ad campaign had been built around one of *his* dumb ideas.

He began pacing toward the front window again, and she glanced at Denver. She'd never before believed a person's pulse could actually skip beats, but she merely had to look at him to feel hers become totally erratic.

He liked her... *really* liked her. There was no mistaking that. And the way she felt about him... well, it certainly wasn't easy sitting here beside him on the couch without reaching for his hand and snuggling closer.

She was dying to have him put his arms around her and kiss her, but since Nolton's arrival they'd been circumspectly keeping their distance.

Nolton Bristow had become angry enough, when they'd told him Kip and Cathy were here, without adding fuel to the flames. He wouldn't like the idea of his account executive and his dog trainer actually enjoying themselves on time *he* was paying for.

And he certainly wouldn't approve of his account exec playing house. Unless she wanted to play it with him, of course. And whenever he'd suggested that possibility, she'd always made it clear she wasn't interested.

Denver caught her eye, swirled the brandy in his snifter and made a face at it.

She almost laughed, then looked over at the way Nolton was staring out into the snowy night and remembered there was nothing to laugh about. Any minute now, Kip and Cathy would arrive, and what would happen then?

Nolton glanced back across the living room, muttering, "I still can't believe it. Kip sneaking around behind my back like this. It has to be that damned girl's influence. What kind of tramp would come up here with a boy she barely knows?"

"Actually," Denver said, "she seems very nice."

"Ha!" Nolton snorted. "I checked the bedrooms. I know they're only using one. Didn't you say anything to them about that last night, Chantal?"

"Well...no. I didn't really think it was any of my business."

Nolton gave her a black look, then went back to muttering. "Thought they could sneak up here for a week of hot sex and I wouldn't find out. What the hell kind of parents can she have? Don't they keep track of her? I tell you, Chantal, when I get through with Kip, he'll be one sorry boy."

"He's a good kid," she offered quietly. "Give him a chance to explain."

"Good kid," Nolton snapped. "He's started looking like a bum and acting like a sneak. I hope you don't think I approve of the way he's wearing his hair these days."

Nolton turned back to the window at the sound of an approaching car, saying, "There he is now. And about time."

McGee and Brandy clambered up from the floor and headed across to check on the arrival. Nolton simply remained standing where he was, over on the far side of the window from the door. Chantal sat wishing she could pull a vanishing act.

Kip and Cathy were laughing when they walked in, their faces brightly flushed from the day on the slopes. They paused to pat the dogs for a second, then looked across the living room.

"Denver!" Kip said, brushing snow from his shoulders. "Hey, man, you decided to stay. Terrific. You can come out with us again tomorrow, unless it keeps snowing like this and we can't make it to the slopes. I need someone with stamina. This woman here," he said, giving Cathy a quick kiss on the cheek, "called it quits halfway through the after—"

Kip's face went white as he spotted Nolton. He glanced quickly at Chantal.

She gave him a tiny shake of her head, telling him his father didn't know yet.

"Dad," he managed, his face regaining one shade of color, "what a surprise."

"I'll bet," Nolton said dryly. "What the hell are you doing up here?"

"Ahh...skiing."

"Very funny. But you know what I mean."

"Well...ahh, Dad, this is Cathy," Kip said, circling her waist with his arm.

"Pleased to meet you, sir," she said.

Chantal felt a twinge of sympathy. *Terrified to meet you, sir,* would clearly have been more honest.

Nolton merely glared at Cathy, then focused an eagle eye on his son once more. "I'm waiting for an explanation, Kip."

The boy shifted his weight from one foot to the other, took a deep breath, then said, "Dad...Cathy and I got married last week."

It was suddenly so quiet in the chalet that Chantal could hear the snow falling outside.

The muscles in Nolton's face tensed, then relaxed a little, and he said, "Should I assume that's your idea of a humorous remark, Kip?"

"No, sir, you should assume it's the truth."

"I see," Nolton said slowly. "And should I also assume your little wife here knew how much money your father had before she married you?"

"That's hitting below the belt," Kip said quietly. "Cathy and I love each other."

"Love? What the hell do you think you know about love? Dammit, Kip, you scarcely date in high school, then you just up and marry the first girl who...you just up and get married without a word about it to me? When you're nineteen years old and a college freshman. That certainly shows a great deal of intelligence, doesn't it?"

"Dad...look, nineteen or not, we really do love each other."

Nolton simply shook his head. "I have plans for your future, Kip. Big plans. And they don't include any little gold digger from Maine. I'll call my lawyer in the morning, but do you have the slightest idea how much an annulment is going to cost me?"

Cathy looked at Kip, obviously near tears as he cleared his throat. "Dad...Dad, there's not going to be any annulment. Cathy's pregnant."

For what seemed like minutes, Nolton stood eyeing Kip and Cathy with murder in his eyes.

When he finally spoke, his voice was ice. "We'll talk about this in the morning. You may go upstairs now," he added. Then, pointedly turning his back on the two of them and glancing over at Denver, he said, "When Kip walked in, he said something about not expecting you still to be here."

Chantal mentally shook her head as Kip and Cathy scurried for the stairs. She'd never met anyone who could compartmentalize things the way Nolton did. He'd just locked his anger with Kip into one tiny section of his mind, to be brought out again at his convenience.

"Well," Denver was saying, "I told the kids I was thinking about heading home. Like I mentioned this afternoon, I'd started figuring you'd be further ahead using McGee in your commercials. And if that's what you were going to end up doing, I didn't want to waste your money by working with Brandy any longer. But after Chantal explained how important it is to you to use Brandy... well, I'm still here."

"I see," Nolton said, looking over to where the dogs had curled up on the floor again, then turning to Chantal. "You know, Denver has a point about our using McGee."

She simply nodded, too stunned to even ask what the point was. She'd seen Nolton switch subject and mood like this before, but in business situations, not when one of the subjects was his own son.

How could he just dismiss Kip and Cathy while they were so incredibly upset and blithely start discussing his damned commercials?

"Denver was talking," Nolton went on, "about how the shooting would go faster with McGee. That could only save money. And when I saw the two dogs are identical... I hadn't realized they would be. But since they are, maybe I was a little hasty about insisting on Brandy. I mean, why not use McGee and claim it's her?"

"Well..." Chantal said slowly, thinking rapidly. If Nolton decided not to use Brandy, there'd be no reason for Denver to stay. And she sure as hell didn't want to be here, finishing up her site shooting, without him. She'd end up in the middle of Nolton's battle with Kip and Cathy. Or they'd leave and she'd be here alone with Nolton, a fate worse than death.

"Use McGee and claim he was Brandy?" she said. "I don't know, Nolton. I'd hate to have us nailed with a misleading advertising fine."

"Not a chance of that, because we wouldn't be misrepresenting anything about the product."

"Oh...of course...I guess that's true. But there are still the truth-in-advertising codes. They're certainly a major consideration." Although, they certainly weren't *her* major consideration at this precise moment. Right now, her primary concern was that the next thing Nolton was liable to say was—

"I wouldn't call truth a *major* consideration. So I guess you're right, Denver. We'll forget about the idea of using my dog. In which case, there's no need for you to stay past tonight."

Oh, Lord, she'd just known that was the next thing he was liable to say. She turned to Denver in panic, but he looked too cool to be true.

"I'll just need a day or two more," he said. "Since I've been concentrating on Brandy, I haven't done any work with McGee in the snow. But if I prime him before we come up for the actual shoot, it'll save time and money in the long run."

Nolton didn't seem entirely convinced of that.

"You don't," Denver pressed, "want to be paying an entire film crew to stand around while I work with McGee."

"No, no, that's a good point. You stay another day or two, then. Just as well we've got six bedrooms."

Denver nodded. "Speaking of which, I think I'll take the dogs out for their final walk and...or did you want to walk Brandy yourself, Nolton?"

"Hell, no. It's turned into a serious snowstorm out there. All I want is another glass of this great brandy. How about you, Chantal?"

"No!" she said far too quickly. "I mean, no thanks. It *is* great stuff, but the first one almost put me to sleep. In fact, I'm going to head up to bed right now."

Nolton glanced over to where Denver was putting on his battered flight jacket. "Looks like we're the only takers for a nightcap then. I'll pour refills for when you're done that walk. I want a chance to talk to you alone, anyway."

CHANTAL LAY IN the darkness, watching the snow dancing and swirling outside the glass balcony door, until she heard Denver's footsteps coming up the stairs.

She switched on the bedside light, then threw her robe on over her nightshirt and stood quietly, listening to hear if Nolton was on his way up as well. But there were only the sounds of Denver's cowboy boots and the two dogs padding heavily along after him.

When they reached the hall, she opened her bedroom door and silently motioned to him. McGee took it as a hand signal and hurried into the room first, Brandy on his tail.

"Hey," Denver whispered, wrapping his arms around her waist and shoving the door closed with his heel, "I thought you'd be asleep. This is the nicest thing that's happened to me since that damned chopper set down and spoiled our fun."

He drew her close and kissed her—a brandy-flavored kiss that made her think Bristow VSOP tasted far better secondhand. She tried to ignore the fire his closeness ignited. Then he smoothed his hands down her back, resting them on her hips, drawing her lower body against his, and the fire began to sizzle.

She forced herself to push him away gently, before she forgot about everything in the world but him.

"What's up?" he said.

"Denver, what did that rat Nolton want to talk to you about?"

"That's why I'm in your bedroom?" he teased. "Geez, you certainly know how to deflate a guy's ego. Here you are, wearing that . . . wearing not a whole lot, and I thought you wanted—"

She slid her hands up around his neck, drawing his face to hers once more, slipping her tongue between his lips and giving him another extremely serious kiss.

"If *that's* part of what you thought I wanted," she finally murmured, "you thought right. And I also wanted to thank you for insisting on staying, for not abandoning me."

"I could hardly do that. Not given the situation here."

"Well, I'm awfully glad you didn't run out on me."

He grinned down at her. "You going to demonstrate *how* glad again?"

"Definitely. Just as soon as you tell me what Nolton wanted."

His grin faded and he said, "You aren't going to like it."

"That's hardly a surprise. I absolutely hated this entire night. I've just been lying here, thinking how upset Cathy and Kip must be."

"Yeah, your Nolton's a real charmer," Denver muttered, slumping onto the edge of the bed and drawing her down beside him.

Brandy immediately hustled over and flopped into a sit, resting her giant head in Chantal's lap.

"She's what he wanted to discuss," Denver said.

"Oh?" Chantal began stroking the dog's head without taking her eyes off Denver. "Discuss in what respect?"

"In the respect that he's definitely realized he made a mistake. Before, I think he had at least some illusions about keeping her. But now he's decided a Park Avenue penthouse is no place for a dog this size."

Chantal felt her throat tightening. "And?"

"And he wants me to board her for the next few weeks. Or a month or so. Until the commercials have been shot."

"And then?"

"And then he wants me to look after selling her."

"I see . . . no, actually I don't. Not exactly."

Denver took her hand and squeezed it, telling her he knew she was upset.

She swallowed hard, suspecting she was being absurdly emotional but unable to help it. "Denver, you warned me right at the start that you didn't think he'd keep her, so I'm not exactly reeling with surprise. But what's the point of leaving her in limbo for weeks, or months, or however long he's talking about? Why not find her a good home right away? You *could* find her a good home, couldn't you?"

"Sure. I've even got a prime ownership candidate sitting right here beside me."

"Oh, I'd love to have her, but I couldn't."

"Why not? She adores you, and she isn't much of a guard dog right now, but I could train her. She may not be Einstein, but she isn't totally hopeless. And for a woman living alone in Manhattan, a big dog isn't a bad idea."

"Oh, Denver, it isn't that I need convincing. I adore her, too, and I'd take her in a minute if I were home enough to look after a dog. But when the agency's busy I'm gone ten or twelve hours at a stretch, six days a week. But...why couldn't *you* keep her? You could breed her and—"

He shook his head. "She's been spayed, Chantal. I can easily find someone who'll want her as a pet, though. That won't be any problem at all."

"But in a few weeks? Or a month or so? Denver, the poor dog keeps getting hustled from one person to another. She'll just have gotten used to being with you and she'll be moved on again. That isn't fair."

"Fair or not, that's the way Nolton intends having it."

"But why?"

"Because he latched on to what you said about truth in advertising—one aspect of it, at least. He doesn't seem at all concerned about passing McGee off as Brandy, but he isn't going to risk claiming he owns a Saint Bernard if he doesn't. And he figures as long as he's still Brandy's official owner when the commercials are shot...well, he figures as long as whatever they say is true at the time, he'll be in the clear."

"He's such a bastard," Chantal whispered fiercely, tangling Brandy's soft fur around her fingers.

"I couldn't agree with you more," Denver said, cuddling her to him.

A moment later he heard footsteps coming upstairs. Then the sound of the door to the master bedroom opening and reclosing. "Chantal," he said quietly, "you going to be okay?"

When she didn't reply, he shooed Brandy over to lie with McGee and shifted Chantal in his arms, so he could see her face. "Chantal, I promise I'll find Brandy the best owner you could hope for."

She whispered, "Yes, of course you will." But she didn't sound the least reassured, and he wished he could simply will the rest of the world away, wished they could be alone together, maybe sitting right here on this bed, but without problems, without worries, without all the differences between them that he knew made him an idiot for being here at all.

He eyed her for a moment, telling himself to simply let it go, trying to ignore the memories that were forcing their way into his consciousness. But something about Chantal made letting it go impossible. "Why do you do it?" he said.

She looked at him uncertainly. "Do what?"

"Put up with a bastard like Nolton. Work ten- or twelve-hour days. Sacrifice even something as simple as being able to have a dog for the benefit of Jay Clawson Advertising."

"I . . . it's not like that, Denver. Not really. All in all, I love my life. I couldn't even imagine a different one."

He nodded slowly. He'd known without asking that she felt that way, but her saying it made it far more real.

"My world isn't much like the one you live in," she went on. "You've got your own business and can do pretty well what you please. You don't know how things are on Madison Avenue."

He continued gazing at her, wondering if she really believed that, deciding she did. But she was actually so wrong it was almost laughable. "Chantal, I know *exactly* how things are on Madison Avenue. On Mad Ave and Wall Street and all the other fast-track sections of Manhattan.''

"No, you don't, Denver."

"Yes, I do." He knew only too well. And he also knew that what he should do right now was say good-night and go to his own room.

But instead of leaving he was searching for words, finally saying, "Chantal . . . I just can't see how you fit in. I mean, at first I assumed you did, had you pegged as Madison Avenue personified.''

When she started to speak he pressed his fingers to her lips. "I said *at first*. Back when all I knew about you was your fancy job title, when all I'd seen were your expensive clothes and jazzy town house. But now I know you aren't one of those plastic people who don't give a damn about anything but money, who don't give a damn about anyone who isn't helping them make it. You're not like them at all.''

She looked so delectable, sitting beside him in the pale light, that he couldn't resist trailing his fingers down the soft warmth of her throat and resting them against the collar of her robe.

That made her smile tentatively at him. "I guess I should take your thinking I'm not like those plastic people as a compliment, shouldn't I?''

"Yes. And the fact that you aren't is what makes it so hard for me to see why you spend your days rushing and hustling and jumping when people like Nolton tell you to. And having so little time for yourself, you don't even have a minute to stop and consider you might be missing something important.''

"Denver . . . Denver you just don't understand.''

"Yes, I do. I understand perfectly, because I lived like that for a while. I rushed and hustled and jumped with the best of them—right in the rotten heart of the Big Apple.''

"You did?"

"Yes, I did."

She looked at him for a minute, then said, "The time after the marines and before the kennel?"

"Uh-huh."

"I asked you about that once and you didn't answer."

"I . . . it's not something I talk much about."

"Want to talk about it now?"

He didn't. He didn't even want to think about those days, much less talk about them. But what if there *was* a chance for the two of them, even the tiniest chance?

No, he'd undoubtedly just be deluding himself if he started thinking . . .

"Don't want to talk about it?" Chantal murmured.

"No," he said, "I don't. But I will."

CHAPTER EIGHT

"I... YOU SEE..." Denver said. "The way it happened... when I first left the marines, I went to New York. Not to get a job, just to visit a buddy. He was my best friend in the service, but by then he'd been out about a year."

He paused, already having second thoughts about this.

"And?" Chantal prompted, forcing him to continue.

"And... his name was Mac. Lyle Macintosh, really, but Mac was all we ever called him. He was on Wall Street, with one of the big houses, doing great, and he convinced me to take a shot at the world of high finance. He talked me up to his boss, I got hired, and pretty soon Mac and I were working side by side, both making money hand over fist."

He paused again and Chantal finally said, "But eventually, you left."

"Yeah, eventually I left."

"Why?" she asked when he still didn't go on.

"Why, indeed? Why would a guy walk away from what the world sees as success to start a kennel in Jersey?"

She waited again, then said, "You must have had a good reason."

"Oh, I had a good reason, all right. Do you know how brokers live, Chantal?"

"I know how a few of them live."

"Well, with most of them it's every man for himself, anything for a buck. Everyone snorts coke and pops pills to keep going twelve hours a day. Then they drink the Wall Street bars dry after those twelve-hour days, trying to unwind from the pressure. The attitude-adjustment hour, we used to call it. Because, around Wall Street, there's no such thing as a happy hour."

"And it got to you," Chantal said.

"No. Much as I hate to admit it, I was just like everyone else. The lying and cheating and stealing didn't matter. As long as I could cover up and come out ahead...well, that's all that counted. No, it wasn't the life getting to me that made me walk away."

"Then what did?"

He looked across the room, his vision blurring. "What did...what did was my buddy Mac...killing himself."

Wordlessly, Chantal rested her hand on Denver's arm. He didn't seem to notice.

"Denver," she finally tried, "does it help to talk about why Mac...?"

He looked at her then, light from the bedside lamp playing on his face, revealing how troubled he felt. "I don't know if talking about him helps or not," he said. "I've never tried."

"Well...if you think it might...I'm not going anywhere." She didn't really expect him to continue, but he surprised her.

"You know how the market works?" he asked quietly.

"More or less. People buy stocks. Sell them. Hopefully make a profit."

"Right. Those are the mechanics. It actually runs more on psychology, though. Not for everyone, but a lot of the players are more gambler than investor. They view the market as the world's biggest crap game. Pick a few winners, get in and out at the right times, and you can make a fortune. That's what Mac expected to do."

"Only he didn't?" she said when Denver's pause lengthened.

"Well . . . actually he did. For a while, at least. He'd made some good investments before I started. Or maybe he'd just been lucky. At any rate, he had a whole pile of money in various stocks. But the more you invest, the more you can make. And he became obsessed with making all he possibly could, so he'd margined himself to the hilt."

Denver glanced a question at her, checking that she understood.

She nodded. "A margin account. The brokerage house was lending him money to invest."

"Exactly. But he made a few bad decisions. Then the market dropped unexpectedly, and his phone was suddenly ringing off the hook with margin calls."

"The borrowed money had to be repaid," Chantal said.

"Yes. And repaid immediately. If you don't have the cash, the stocks in your account are sold, even though they're in a loss position. Then, instead of becoming a millionaire, you can end up so far in debt you might never get out. That's what happened to Mac. And that's when he . . ."

The silence grew until Chantal said, "And it was after he did, that you walked away."

"Right," he murmured, nodding slowly. "In fact, I never set foot on the street again. Didn't even go in to clean out my desk. After the funeral, I just sat in my apartment with a bottle of Scotch, thinking."

"About Mac," she prompted.

"Uh-huh. And about how material things could get to mean more than life itself. About what I was doing with my own life when, of course, I was doing exactly what Mac had done. Sitting on a phone all day, everyday, hustling people. No better than a two-buck con artist wearing a thousand-dollar suit.

"And I realized that isn't a sane way of living, realized I didn't want money to ever become as important to me as it had to Mac. So I started thinking about things I'd rather do than kill myself trying to get rich. Or kill myself because I wasn't."

His voice broke a little and Chantal touched his arm again. This time, he took her hand. "Anyway, when I finally decided what I wanted to do most, I went looking for a place I could set up as a kennel."

He sat watching while she tried to think of something to say, but the phrases that came to mind seemed incredibly trite—I'm sorry about your friend, I understand why you dropped out of the rat race, I can see why you're critical of life in New York.

"So," he said when she didn't speak, "that's how I know about the fast track. And why I packed it in. And why, when I think about somebody like you caught up in it...no, what I mean is, when I think about you, specifically...oh, hell, I don't even know what I mean, so why am I trying to explain it?"

She sat gazing into his dark eyes, intensely aware of his hand holding hers. "You mean," she said softly, "that we live awfully different lives? And you don't think much of the way I live mine?"

"Something like that . . . only I . . . somehow it's your life-style I'm criticizing but not really you. Except for living it. If that makes any sense at all."

"I think I understand, Denver."

He looked at her for another minute, then shrugged. "You know, there are only seventy-odd miles between my kennel and West Eighty-fifth. And over the past few days, up here away from reality, I kind of stopped thinking that there's a lot more distance between the two of us than that. But right this minute, I'm wondering what on earth I'm doing here in your room."

"I . . . I kind of thought it was because you liked me."

"Chantal, I do like you," he said, reaching for her other hand and holding them both in his. "The problem is I like you a whole helluva lot."

"A whole helluva lot?" she whispered, loving his way with words. "And that's a problem?"

"Well . . . the problem is that it's not just in a casual, let's-have-fun-while-we're-here sort of way."

That sent a rush of emotion through her. And the way he was eyeing her, and lightly grazing the backs of her hands with his thumbs, was making her almost oblivious to everything except how she felt about him.

He wasn't the only one who'd stopped thinking about the distance between them, about New Jersey versus New York, scruffy jeans versus three-piece suits, dog shows versus theater nights. All she had to do was look at him, all he had to do was touch her, and she could scarcely recall a single one of all those blasted differences in their lives.

"And the problem with the way I like you," he went on, "is that we make a perfect example of 'never the twain shall meet.'"

She continued gazing at him, knowing he was right but not willing to admit it aloud. Because perfect example or not, they *had* met. And because, from a corner of her memory, she could hear her mother saying, *"When you meet the right man you'll know, dear. I can't explain exactly how, but you'll know he's the one."*

Well, she knew. At least, she had an awfully strong suspicion she knew. She felt good with Denver. So good. And in her entire life, she'd never felt anything even remotely similar to the way she felt when he kissed her. And given all that, she couldn't just let him walk away, not if there was even the slightest chance this might somehow work out.

"Denver," she said, "I . . . I like you a whole helluva lot, too. But I know what you're trying to say. This is pretty unlikely to lead anywhere, so the obvious thing to do is put on the brakes, not risk hurting each other. Have I got it right?"

He nodded slowly. "It *does* make sense, doesn't it?"

"Definitely," she murmured. "We simply write off what's happened as a lapse of judgment, on both our parts."

"Write off what's happened," he repeated. "Uh-huh. Walk away. Cut our losses. Yeah, that's just what I was getting at." He released her hands and sat looking at the floor, saying, "Well, then, I guess . . ."

"Denver?"

He glanced at her again.

"Denver, the only thing is that I don't often meet a man I really like. One I like a whole helluva lot, I mean.

In fact, the words *almost never* come to mind. So maybe…well, we'll be here together a little longer. Then we'll be coming back up for the shoot. So maybe we shouldn't be too quick to just…" She stopped, some ridiculously old-fashioned sense of propriety refusing to let her come right out and say it.

Finally, Denver cleared his throat. "You mean maybe we shouldn't be too quick to just dismiss this…this attraction between us?" he said, inching a fraction closer to her. "Is that it?"

"Exactly," she whispered. "You see, I try never to be too hasty about things."

"Never be too hasty…ahh…you know, that doesn't strike me as a bad principle." He edged nearer still, so near that his thigh was pressing against hers, that his body heat was invading her bloodstream as if branding her as his own.

She could feel her blood beginning to race faster, sense her body saying it was important to spread that heat through her just as quickly as could be.

Then Denver started speaking once more, and she could feel the warmth of his breath against her face, could faintly smell brandy again. The brandy that was so much better secondhand. "You know," he was murmuring, "it could be I was looking for problems that would never materialize."

Slowly…tentatively…he shifted farther onto the bed and began easing her down beside him. Her pulse rate leapt and breathing became strangely difficult, but it seemed important to finish this conversation.

"Problems that would never materialize," she said, managing a tiny, anxious laugh. "That's exactly it. Who knows? By the time we're finished the shoot, we might have decided we don't even really like each other."

He nodded slightly, as if he actually thought that could happen. But his mouth was no more than a quarter inch from hers, so just in case he really did believe it was a possibility, she leaned toward him that quarter inch and brushed her lips against his.

He breathed her name, then pressed her down onto the bed with his body, his hardness starting an aching response low inside her, making her incredibly aware she was wearing almost nothing.

"Oh, Chantal," he whispered, caressing her hip, sliding his hand up to her breast, "Chantal, please tell me we don't have to worry about being too hasty right now, because I'm absolutely crazy about you."

Covering her mouth with his, he kissed her—a long, slow, wet, deep kiss that started her heart beating a million times a minute.

She kissed him back every bit as passionately, her arms wrapped tightly around his waist, wanting him incredibly, knowing it wasn't too hasty between them. With any other man in the world it would be, but it wasn't with Denver Brooke. Not when she was absolutely crazy about him, too.

Leaning across, he turned off the bedside lamp, then drew her down on the bed with him, slipping his hands beneath her robe and caressing her body through the thin silk of her nightshirt, murmuring how beautiful she was, how he wanted to make love to her more than he'd ever wanted any woman.

She reached for the buttons of his shirt, fumbling them undone, and he slid his hands down her body to her bare thighs . . . then began slowly caressing his way back up, making her desperate to be touching his nakedness the way he was touching hers.

Finding the snap on his jeans, he popped it and eased his zipper down, the thudding of her heart filling her ears. He groaned at her touch.

The next second he was leaping to his feet, swearing. She froze, confused for an instant, then heard the dogs hurrying across to the door and realized the sound in her ears hadn't been only the thudding of her heart.

"Chantal?" Nolton said quietly, continuing to tap on her door. "May I come in? I have to talk to you."

"Oh, Lord," she whispered. She flicked the light on and scrambled off the bed, pulling her robe around her.

"Just a minute, Nolton," she called, looking frantically at Denver. "You have to hide! The closet!"

He paused half-zipped and gave her an incredulous look. "What do you think this is? A French farce? I'm not hiding in any damned closet."

"But he can't find you in here!"

"Why not?"

"Because it's the middle of the night...because it wouldn't look...dammit, Denver, just *because!*"

"Well, don't let him in, then. Get rid of him. What the hell's he up to, anyway?"

"Chantal?" Nolton said again.

"Coming," she yelled, glaring at Denver on her way past. She had a quick shot at fluffing her hair, then opened the door a crack. One of the dogs immediately nosed it open farther.

"You've got a dog in there?" Nolton said.

"Yes...a dog...yes, what I have in here is a dog. Good company, dogs are."

From the corner of her eye she could see Denver behind the door, grabbing hold of the dog's hindquarter.

"Bad dog! Go lie down!" she ordered as Denver yanked it backward.

She glanced at Nolton once more, standing in the dark hall, this time seeing he was holding his bottle of Bristow VSOP in one hand and two glasses in the other.

Oh, no, she thought. *Please not this.* "Nolton," she said. "It's way after midnight. What's so urgent that we have to talk about it now?"

"Well, actually, there's nothing special. I just thought you might like a drink."

"No. No, thank you, no drink." She eased the door closed to a mere crack again and braced her knee against it.

He gave her one of his patented lady-killer smiles. "Well, how about a little company, then?"

"No, no company. I already have company. The dog. Good company, dogs are."

"Chantal, I can be far better company than a dog. All you have to do is give me a chance."

Beside her, out of Nolton's vision, Denver menacingly clenched his fist.

"Nolton, I'm really tired. I was just about to turn out the light. So I'll see you in the morning, okay?"

He hesitated for a moment, then shrugged. "Whatever you say, Chantal. Just thought you might be up for it. I certainly am."

She forced a smile, said good-night and firmly closed the door.

"I don't believe that guy!" Denver said. "He comes knocking on your door like a horny teenager? Saying he's *up* for it? Good gawd, Chantal!"

"Shh. He'll hear you."

"So who cares? Does he do that sort of thing often?"

"Well . . . no, not often. Not to me, at least."

"But you mean sometimes he does? And to other women besides? What about his wife?"

She shrugged uneasily. She'd often wondered if Marlene could possibly not know.

"Chantal, the guy's a total jerk. Browbeating the kids, and arranging to get rid of his dog, and now this? All in one night? I'm going to go out there and pop him one. That'll make him have second thoughts if he gets any more bright ideas."

"Denver, relax, okay? He's my client. It's just a hazard of business."

Denver stared at her with undisguised disbelief. "Not of any decent business, it isn't. Because he's your client, you're willing to put up with garbage like that? Geez, Chantal..."

He stopped speaking mid-sentence and just stood looking at her, maybe counting to ten, then shrugged. "Sorry. I shouldn't be yelling at you because I'm steamed at Nolton. But the guy *is* a total jerk. I mean...well, aside from anything else, he certainly did a great job of ruining the mood. I...I guess a lot of my steam is because of that."

She nodded. "You don't suppose he was sent as divine intervention, do you? To let us know we *were* being too hasty?"

"Not a chance."

"You're sure? It...it *has* only been a few days."

"Chantal, what I meant was there's no chance any divine power would use someone like Nolton Bristow as its messenger. But...well...I guess maybe you'd rather I headed to my own room, huh?"

"I think that might be wise," she said, her brain meaning it, her heart telling her to wrap her arms around him and never let him go.

"Well . . ."

She waited, not breathing, certain that if he pressed, her heart would win out.

But he didn't. He merely murmured a reluctant, "Night, Chantal," and briefly kissed her. "Do you want me to leave McGee here? In case your *client* comes back?"

"No, I'm sure he won't. But maybe you could leave Brandy. For the company."

He kind of smiled and said, "Yeah, they're good company, dogs are. But, Chantal, I won't close my door. So if there's any problem . . ."

"Thanks, Denver."

He gave her one more light kiss, then, without another word, turned and walked out.

She almost chased after him, but her brain was screaming that both the time and place were the worst imaginable. And she didn't actually believe in divine intervention, but what if . . . after all, Denver couldn't know for sure that no divine power would use Nolton as a messenger.

"Just go to bed," she whispered to herself. "Things always seem clearer in the morning."

When she crawled between the sheets, Brandy ambled over and rested her chin on the quilt.

"You know what I'm afraid of, girl?" Chantal murmured, stroking the dog's head. "I'm afraid both you and I are heading into very troubled waters."

THE PALE MIST OF LIGHT in front of her closed eyelids was telling Chantal it was morning. Gray mist. A cloudy morning then, she decided hazily, not opening her eyes to check, not wanting to relinquish the memories of last night that were floating in the fog between sleep and wakening.

Memories of the taste of Denver's passionate kisses . . . the way he'd held and caressed her . . . of them almost . . .

She hugged herself beneath the quilt, recalling his words. He'd said he was absolutely crazy about her. And she was definitely crazy about him. That just had to be the most wonderful thing that had happened in her entire life. So wonderful she knew nothing would ever go wrong in her world again. Somehow, some way, everything would be perfect from this moment on.

Then other, unpleasant memories began to intrude on her happy thoughts. Lecherous Nolton with his bottle of brandy . . . and earlier, his scene with Kip and Cathy. Oh, Lord, he'd told them they'd talk about the situation in the morning. She certainly didn't want to walk into the middle of that.

She opened her eyes and glanced out through the balcony's glass door. Snow was coming down heavily, swirling in the wind. And given the six-inch frosting on the railing, it must have been snowing all night.

"Brandy?" she said, looking around for the dog, seeing instead that a note was propped on the bedside table.

Chantal,
    I'm giving the dogs some exercise, but we're right outside the chalet. So if Nolton even glances at you sideways, just shout.

                                        Love, Denver.

Love, Denver. She sat staring at those two words, grinning like an idiot, then climbed out of bed and

checked outside. Sure enough, he was down there playing with McGee and Brandy. So much fresh snow had
fallen that the dogs were sinking the entire length of
their legs when they tried to run.

Denver was beside the driveway, and she noticed
there were tire tracks on it—visible but fast being obliterated. Obviously not Denver's. And Nolton had made
his grand entrance by helicopter. So those tracks had to
mean that Kip and Cathy were gone.

And that undoubtedly meant Nolton hadn't done an
about-face. Hopefully, though, he'd thought things
over and hadn't been too hard on them. They *were* awfully young, but sometimes relationships worked out
when it seemed unlikely they would. And she'd gotten
such good vibes from those two kids that she had a
feeling they just might make a go of it.

She wondered if it was possible she and Denver could
ever make a go of it, too. She glanced down at him and
smiled.

There was almost never a chance to play in the snow
in Manhattan, and certainly never snow like this. And,
of course, the man she was crazy about was outside.

She got ready quickly, raced downstairs and began
tugging on Marlene's boots—then realized Nolton was
in the living room. He was sitting motionless on one of
the couches, staring toward the door, but she had a
feeling he wasn't seeing a thing. His shoulders were
slumped, and his hands were wrapped around a coffee
mug as if he were trying to strangle it.

"Nolton?" she said.

When he didn't even glance over, she tried again,
more loudly, and his gaze flickered to her.

"Nolton, what's wrong?" Of course, she had a
darned good idea what was wrong, but she could hardly

pretend not to notice that he looked like death would be a welcome relief.

He shook his head, but it wasn't a nothing's-wrong kind of shake. It said something more like, "I can't even bear to talk about it."

She hesitated, then pulled on the second boot, walked over, and sat down on the other couch.

He eyed her for a moment, then finally said, "Kip wouldn't listen to reason, Chantal. I'm going to be a blasted grandfather at forty-five."

She almost smiled. Trust Nolton to think of Cathy's having a baby in terms of himself. "I take it they've left?" she said.

"Yeah. They've gone back to college early, rather than stay here with a 'self-centered, controlling bastard.' That's what Kip called me, Chantal. And, dammit, I was only thinking about what's best for him."

"Nolton... it might turn out fine. They really are in love, you know."

"That's what they kept telling me. And they're so damned naive, they think being in love takes care of everything. But even if they were older, they'd have nothing in common, Chantal."

She bit her lip, managing not to point out that they had a baby in common.

"And even on the off chance that Cathy isn't a gold digger, she's just a little nobody from a backwater town in Maine, and Kip...oh, hell, I'll be damned if I'm going to worry about it anymore. Kip's just going to have to take his lumps. See how he likes the responsibility of a wife and kid. See how he likes a screaming baby keeping him awake all night. It won't take long before he realizes I was right."

Chantal sat silently for a moment, deciding it would be pointless to say anything more on the subject. "Nolton," she finally tried, "can I get you anything? More coffee?"

"No, this was the last of it, maybe for quite a while. The power's gone off."

"Again? It was off when Denver and I first got here."

"Happens all the time."

"Oh. Well . . . Nolton, I'm just going out for a little air. You'll be okay? Denver and I will be right outside."

Nolton didn't answer, didn't even look at her, so she simply escaped into the freshness of the icy morning, wondering how she could possibly have woken up feeling that nothing would ever go wrong in her world again.

She was going to have to take her intuition in for a major overhaul. Being stuck here with Denver and no power was one thing. But adding an unhappy Nolton to the equation made it something else again.

She started across to where Denver was standing, wanting to run but barely able to walk, sinking into the snow with each step.

He spotted her and began plowing toward her, smiling broadly, snow-covered from head to foot, his face red and his breath tiny clouds of fog. When he reached her and wrapped his arms around her, he felt every bit as cold as he looked.

"Morning," he whispered against her hair.

"Morning," she said. "I'd kiss you but our lips would probably freeze together."

"Mmm . . . what a delightful prospect." He bent and took the risk.

"So," he finally murmured, releasing her from their chilly embrace and letting the dogs greet her, "I assume you've realized it's only you, me and the father from hell still here."

"The father from hell? Should I take it you overheard the talk this morning?"

"The loudest parts of it. I left my bedroom door open last night, remember? Talk is hardly the word, though. Mostly it was Nolton yelling about abortions and annulments and about disowning Kip. Nolton's not exactly what you'd call an understanding man, is he?"

"Far from it. You don't think he'd really disown Kip, though, do you?"

Denver shrugged and said, "If he were my father, I'd look on being disowned as a lucky break. But whatever happens, I felt good about the way Kip stood up to Nolton. He and Cathy are staying married and having the baby, and that was that."

Chantal glanced along the driveway, noting that Kip's tire marks had completely disappeared now. "You think they'll be okay, driving in this snow?"

"Actually, I tried to convince them not to leave. But there was no way they were staying and listening to any more. They just wanted to get out of here."

"Denver...maybe *we* should get out of here, too. Maybe I should tell Nolton I don't really need to do anymore filming and we should leave right away."

He hesitated for a moment. "I don't know if we'd be smart to chance it. Kip had four-wheel drive, the van doesn't. We might end up in a ditch before we even made it to the highway. On the other hand, I'm sure this snow's going to keep up. So if we stay, we'll end up having to sit around all day with Nolton."

"Oh, Denver, maybe we could just stay out here—play with the dogs until bedtime."

"Sure," he said, grinning at her. "What's a little frostbite? Or hypothermia? Oh, hell, Chantal, I guess we can survive a few hours with the man. And at least it's warm in the chalet."

She shook her head. "It may not be for long. The electricity's off again."

"Tell me that's a joke, huh?"

When she told him it wasn't, he swore quietly.

"What?" she asked, hearing something in his voice that sounded more like worry than mere annoyance.

He said, "Well, it could be all the snow that's caused the problem this time. Too much weight on power lines will bring them down. And I don't know about here, but back in Colorado it sometimes took one heck of a long time for the crews to get them up again."

"One heck of a long time? Just exactly how long is one heck of a long time?"

"Sometimes days."

"Days," she repeated. "Denver, do you think we could find out for sure what's wrong? I mean, how long the power's likely to be off?"

"Does Nolton speak French?"

She nodded.

"Then let's go in and get him to phone the electric company. They might have some answers."

Inside, Nolton was sitting staring into space, looking dazed, as if he just couldn't accept the fact that Kip hadn't said, "Yes sir, yes sir."

"Nolton," Denver said, "how about calling the power company. Seeing what they have to say."

Nolton shook his head. "I've already tried, but the phone's dead. That damned snow's probably brought down half the lines in the area."

"That's just what I was thinking," Denver told him. "How fast are they about fixing things like that around here?"

"How does slow as molasses strike you?" Nolton muttered. "And if our problem's right near the chalet, we could be out of luck for days. Quebec Hydro won't set foot on the private road until it's been cleared. And the guy I pay to plow it comes around when he's good and ready."

Denver shot Chantal a look that said he wanted to talk to her, and started for the stairs.

She mumbled something about changing her clothes and headed after him.

He was waiting for her in the upstairs hall, and she had a horrible suspicion she knew what he was thinking.

"Denver, before you say anything, I want to apologize for being so stubborn the other day. I'm sorry I wouldn't leave when you wanted to, before either Kip or Nolton even got here. I'm sorry—"

"Hey, enough sorries," he said, leaning closer and giving her a quick kiss, making her feel immensely better. "But the idea of being stuck here with Nolton for days on end...Chantal, I think we should risk the road."

She nodded. "I do, too. But you realize he'll want to come with us, don't you."

"To hell with that. I'll say no."

"Denver, we can't just leave him here."

"Chantal, you were the one who first suggested we get out of here. And outside, you didn't breathe a word about us having to take Nolton along. Let him get his damned helicopter to come back for him.''

"How's he going to do that without a phone?''

"Ah..."

"Denver, when I suggested leaving, it hadn't occurred to me that there might be no electricity or working phone for *days*. Given that possibility, we can't leave him here alone.''

Denver shook his head, looking extremely unhappy, but finally said, "I guess you're right. But if we're stuck with him either way, maybe risking the road isn't such a hot idea, after all. If we ended up stuck in a ditch with Nolton for very long, I'd probably kill him.''

CHAPTER NINE

"YOU KNOW, THERE'S ONLY a shot or two left in that bottle out there," Nolton said, draining the final few drops of Bristow VSOP from his snifter. "Sure wish I'd brought along more," he added, grabbing the flashlight and heading for the kitchen.

"What I wish," Denver muttered to Chantal, "is that he'd brought along enough to drink himself into oblivion for however long we end up stuck here."

The snow showed no sign of stopping, so they'd decided they'd better ration the food, firewood and candles. And being hungry—plus having practically no light or heat—was bad enough, without having to listen to Nolton's nonstop monologues.

Chantal murmured something about escaping by calling it an early night and Denver glanced at her again.

Light from the low fire was playing on her face, making him think about *last* night. Last night, the pale light had been coming from her bedside lamp, and he'd been holding her in his arms, kissing her.

Damn. There wasn't much doubt that last night had sealed his fate. Oh, his rational side was still arguing that he was crazy to be getting even more involved with Chantal, that he was riding for a hard fall. But his irrational side was winning the argument hands down.

And every time he looked at her it gave his irrational side more ammunition.

The flashlight's beam bounced across the living room and Nolton strolled back in, an ounce or two of fresh brandy in his glass.

Chantal said, "Nolton, when the power was off before, Denver and I brought blankets downstairs and slept on the couches, by the fire."

"Good idea," he said. "'Course, with only two couches, one of us will have to make do with the floor this time." He looked at Denver, with clearly no doubt in his mind which one of them it would be. "But there are sleeping bags upstairs," he added. "You're welcome to use one of those, Denver."

"Thanks," he said. "That's darned considerate of you."

Chantal poked him in the ribs, telling him his sarcasm was showing, but Nolton seemed oblivious to it.

"In fact," he went on, "we should all use sleeping bags rather than blankets. We'll be warmer. But it's barely nine-thirty. We don't want to turn in yet."

Denver shoved himself off the couch, his movement sending McGee and Brandy clambering to their feet in anticipation. "Nolton, I don't know about you, but I'm bushed."

"Well . . . this *is* the last of the brandy. And I guess a little extra sleep wouldn't hurt us."

"Then why don't you get those sleeping bags while I take the dogs out? Want a bit of exercise, Chantal?"

"Sure," she said, following him over to the door and tugging on Marlene's boots.

"You're crazy, Chantal," Nolton called after her. "It's still snowing like the devil out there. And damned cold," he shouted as they closed the door. The dogs lumbered off ahead into the black, moonless night.

"You trust Brandy without a leash, now?" Chantal asked.

"Uh-huh. She's been listening pretty well about coming." He stopped walking, put his arms around Chantal and kissed her.

"You know," he said, finally releasing her lips, keeping her body pressed close to his, "I've been dying to do that for hours. This place was one heck of a lot more fun when there were just the two of us. Maybe we should bring our sleeping bags outside and spend the night under the stars."

She smiled up at him. "Haven't you noticed there aren't any stars, Denver? This is one of those famous dark and stormy nights. And don't I recall your mentioning the risk of frostbite? And hypothermia? Besides which, the snow's already getting my hair wet."

"Those are all minor annoyances compared to Nolton."

"Try not to let him bother you so much."

"Bother me? Chantal, a mosquito would bother me. Nolton is driving me nuts. Listen, remember the other night? When Kip and Cathy showed up and I went outside after them with Nolton's gun?"

"Yes?"

"Well, the gun ended up in the drawer of my bedside table. So if you see me looking at Nolton like a homicidal maniac, go hide it from me, okay?"

"Will do," she said, laughing.

By the time they headed back inside, Nolton had unrolled all three sleeping bags and spread one on either couch. The third lay on the floor, halfway between.

He'd obviously claimed the far couch as his own. He had moved their one lit candle to the end table by it and was busily fussing with a pillow at the top of the bag.

Denver picked up the sleeping bag from the floor and moved it over beside Chantal's couch.

"The dogs," he said when Nolton eyed him curiously. "They're less likely to step on me during the night if I'm not lying in the middle of the room." He started over to the stack of wood beside the fireplace but Nolton's voice stopped him.

"What are you doing?"

"I'm adding some logs to the fire. It wouldn't last the night, otherwise."

Nolton shook his head. "It takes forever to die down. We'll be fine till morning."

"I don't think so, Nolton. I—"

"Denver, we're rationing, remember? And this is *my* chalet. I know a lot more about this fireplace than you do. We'll be fine."

Denver merely shrugged, knowing if he tried saying anything more to the man it would come out a snarl. Instead, he told Brandy and McGee to go lie down, then turned to Chantal.

"You going to sleep in your clothes? You'll be a lot warmer if you leave your sweat suit on, rather than..." He caught himself before saying anything about the fantastic silky thing she'd been wearing last night.

"Or if I leave *Marlene's* sweat suit on, as the case might be," she said, glancing at Nolton. "You're absolutely sure she won't mind me using her things?"

He shook his head. "Now, I have the flashlight beside me here, if anyone needs it during the night. And as soon as you're both settled, I'll blow out the candle."

"Denver?" Chantal said quietly.

When he turned to her she whispered, "Just let it go."

He grinned at her for reading his thoughts, then said, "Get in and I'll zip up your bag. It's easier to do from outside."

He tucked her in, barely resisting the urge to kiss her good-night, then crawled into his own bag. Its zipper caught halfway up and he worked at it for a minute, finally freeing it and closing it completely to the top.

"All set now?" Nolton called, sounding like a primary school teacher with an extremely dumb class.

"All set," Chantal said.

He blew out the candle, leaving only dim firelight to relieve the black of night. The glow flickered onto the bearskin rug and reached a few inches to either side of the fireplace. Beyond that, the chalet was in complete darkness.

Denver lay on his back, listening to Chantal's soft breathing beside him, imagining what it would be like to spend the night in a double bag...with her...with her wearing the fantastic silky thing.

"Denver?" Nolton called across the room, interrupting just as Denver began imagining unbuttoning the fantastic silky thing.

"What?" he said.

"Denver, this isn't going to work. You'll have to get those dogs out of the living room."

"Why? What are they doing?"

"They smell."

"Nolton, that's only because the snow got their fur wet. They'll be dry in a few minutes."

"Well, they're breathing, too."

"Ah...yeah, they tend to do that. It's related to staying alive."

"You know what I mean," Nolton said. "They're breathing so loud I'll never be able to sleep. And they keep snorting. Can't you hear it?"

"Oh, geez," Denver muttered. But if Nolton couldn't sleep, he'd probably spend the entire night talking.

"Denver?" Nolton said again, this time flicking on the flashlight and shining it at Denver's head.

"All right, all right. I'll take them down and close them in the laundry room."

"Denver?" Chantal murmured. "Make sure they have something soft to lie on in there."

He yanked the zipper of his bag down, succeeded in catching it once more, and swore, certain Nolton had intentionally given him this particular bag.

DENVER JOLTED FROM SLEEP, a light shining in his eyes. He tried to scramble to his feet but couldn't move, was trapped in a giant cocoon.

Sleeping bag, he realized. Sleeping bag...living room...chalet.

"Just going up to the bathroom," Nolton announced from above, shifting the flashlight's beam away from Denver's face and shining it across the room.

"Mmm?" Chantal mumbled from the couch.

"Nothing," Denver told her as the light headed up the stairs. "Just Nolton being his usual considerate self. Go back to sleep."

"Denver, if I go back to sleep I'll freeze to death. What happened to the fire?"

"It went out," he said, pressing the light function on his watch. "And it's not even midnight. I'd better get it started again." He got the sleeping bag's zipper halfway down and it jammed.

He'd just started swearing silently to himself when Chantal said something.

"Huh?" he asked into the darkness.

"There's someone at the door!"

"Oh, come on, Chantal. There can't—" Oh, geez, he heard it. A man's voice outside, deep and muffled. Unless he was talking to himself, he wasn't alone.

Chantal said, "Could it be Kip and Cathy come back?"

"No. The voice is too deep."

Then he heard the sound of a key scraping in the lock . . . the lock turning.

"Denver?" Chantal whispered.

He grabbed the two edges of the zipper and ripped it apart. "Run down to the laundry room," he ordered, leaping to his feet. "Let the dogs out."

She murmured, "Oh, Denver," sounding terrified, but he heard her feet hit the floor as he started across the room. He was halfway to the door when it swung open—quickly, banging against the stopper.

He couldn't see a damned thing. Then the intruder clicked on a flashlight and began training the beam along the wall.

Denver dived toward the light, connecting solidly with the man, sending the flashlight flying through the air and driving the man into the wall.

He gasped as he thudded against the plaster, but the next second he was flailing his arms and shouting something. And suddenly Chantal yelled from behind them, starting Denver's head ringing with confusion.

She was supposed to be getting the dogs. So why was she standing back there? Then the words registered in his brain.

"Call the police!" was what the man had shouted.

"Jay?" was what Chantal had yelled.

When the man called, "Chantal?" Denver knew for sure this wasn't what he'd thought. He backed off, fists still raised, just in case.

The man's flashlight shone toward the front door. Chantal had picked it up, was capturing him in its light. The man . . . then the woman who was standing in the doorway.

Denver dropped his arms to his sides and stepped back. A couple in their forties. Definitely not the criminal element. Distinguished-looking man with sharp features and longish graying hair. Kind of artsy-looking. And an extremely attractive woman. Small, like Chantal, but with dark shaggy hair covered, at the moment, with snow.

"Marlene?" Chantal said, her voice like a frog croaking.

"Oh, God, Jay," the woman murmured. "I can't believe this is happening."

Chantal made a funny little noise in her throat and slowly lowered the man's flashlight until it was pointing at the floor.

For a moment, no one said another word. A long-enough moment for Denver to figure out what was going on.

Chantal's boss, Jay—not on vacation in Mexico. Nolton's wife, Marlene—not at a spa. Both here. Together. In the middle of the night. In this chalet they'd thought was vacant because neither of them had been told about Nolton's stupid advertising idea.

And son of a bitch, if Marlene couldn't believe what had happened thus far, just wait till she learned who was upstairs.

Jay Clawson stepped back and took Marlene's arm, drawing her inside. Then he shoved the door closed and asked Chantal what she was doing here.

"No..." she sputtered.

"Oh, God, Jay," Marlene said once more.

He wrapped his arm around her waist, saying, "It's okay, Marlene. We can trust Chantal."

"No..." she sputtered again.

Denver was trying to decide whether he should help her out when light appeared at the top of the stairs and there was no longer any point bothering.

"What's all the racket down there?" Nolton hollered.

Even with Chantal still pointing the flashlight at the floor, Denver could see Marlene Bristow's face turn white. He thought she was going to faint, but she merely shrank closer to Jay and closed her eyes.

"It'll be okay," he said quietly. "We knew this was coming sooner or later. I'll handle it."

Nolton thudded down the stairs, stopping dead a couple of steps from the bottom when his flashlight's beam illuminated Jay and Marlene.

The chalet was absolutely silent. No one even seemed to be breathing. Then Nolton said, "What in blazes is going on here?"

Jay cleared his throat. "Nolt...I'm just going to lay it straight on the line. Marlene and I are in love. She's leaving you. She's going to marry me."

Nolton simply stared at Jay. Finally his gaze flickered to Marlene. "Is that true?" he said, his voice frigid.

She took a deep breath, whispered, "Yes," and all hell broke loose.

Nolton charged down the last two stairs, roaring an obscenity, and bashed his flashlight into Jay's face, starting blood pouring from his nose.

Marlene began screaming. Denver threw himself at Nolton, grabbing his arm as he was going for a second blow and twisting it behind his back, sending the flashlight skittering across the floor into the darkness.

"I'll kill you, Clawson," Nolton shouted. "Then you, Marlene. Let go of me!" he yelled, kicking backward, catching Denver's shin hard and almost knocking him off his feet. "Let go of me! I'm going to kill those two."

Denver twisted Nolton's arm harder and shoved down, bringing the man to his knees, pressing his own knee into the small of Nolton's back to keep him pinned, saying, "Calm down. Just calm down."

From the laundry room, McGee and Brandy were barking ferociously.

"Should I let them out?" Chantal said, her voice still sounding as if it belonged to someone else.

Denver shook his head, breathing hard. "They're the last thing we need. But go and reassure them, okay? And can you leave Jay's flashlight here?"

She looked from Denver, both his hands securing Nolton, to Jay. Denver's eyes followed hers, and he decided Jay's nose was probably broken. The man was slumped against the wall, hands over his nose and mouth, blood all over his hands and jacket. Marlene was hanging on to his arm, murmuring to him.

"Marlene?" Chantal finally said, passing her the flashlight when she looked over, then disappearing down the black hall.

One hand still clinging to Jay, Marlene glanced at Nolton and swallowed hard. Then she focused her gaze on Denver.

He didn't know what to say. It hardly seemed the time for introductions or explanations. So he simply looked down at Nolton, wondering if it was safe to let go of him yet. Of course, his flashlight was gone. And he probably wasn't much with his fists.

"You okay, now, Nolton?" he tried. "Finished with the idea of killing people?"

"Let me up," he snapped. "Just let me up."

Denver relaxed his grip and backed off a step, ready to grab Nolton again if necessary. But the man merely got to his feet and straightened his sweater.

"Nolt?" Marlene whispered.

"Shut up. Just shut up. I need a brandy. Give me that flashlight."

Denver stepped quickly between them. "Let's hold off on that one, Nolton. Last time you had a flashlight in your hand you got a little carried away with it."

"Dammit, Denver! Who the hell do you think you are? I make the rules here."

"Not this time, you don't. You want a brandy, you go get it in the dark."

Nolton looked ready to argue, but turned on his heel and stomped off in the direction of the kitchen.

Denver waited until he was out of earshot, then told Marlene he thought she'd better get Jay to the nearest hospital, immediately.

"I can't," she said, her voice shaky. "Our car's in the ditch, halfway between here and the highway. We walked the last half mile, but—"

"There's no brandy *left*," Denver said aloud as the realization struck him. "Did he forget that or—?" He

snatched the flashlight from Marlene's hand and raced
after Nolton, shining the light directly across the kitchen
when he hit the doorway.

Sure enough, the man was frantically rummaging
through the drawer that normally held his gun. His head
jerked up when the light caught him.

"It isn't there," Denver said.

"Then where is it?"

Denver shook his head. "Nolton, I know what just
happened is tough to take, but you've got to get rational here."

"Rational? My *trusted* friend steals my *loving* wife
out from under my nose and you expect rational?
Dammit, Denver, for years Bristow Fine Spirits has paid
Clawson Advertising big, big bucks. And Jay repays me
by diddling my wife? You want even semirational, then
get them out of my sight! Throw them out of here right
this minute or I swear I'll kill them. I never want to see
either of them alive again."

"Nolton, they can't leave right this minute. It's the
middle of the night, the middle of a snowstorm, and
their car's in a ditch. Look ... let's the two of us go get
some fresh air, okay? Before you do something that'll
land you in jail for the rest of your life."

DENVER GLANCED THROUGH the darkness at Nolton
again, wondering if he could say anything that would
help the situation. Nothing came to mind, but at least
the guy seemed to have gotten most of the anger out of
his system.

Now they were just walking in silence, freezing their
butts off. But when they'd first left the chalet, Nolton
had gone on for a good twenty minutes about what he
was going to do to Marlene and Jay and everyone who

had anything to do with either of them, including him and Chantal. It hadn't been great listening, but it had been understandable. And as far as he was concerned, he didn't give a damn that Nolton no longer wanted him working on the commercials.

They reached Jay's car, sitting sideways in the ditch. Then, as if that had been their destination, turned around and started back toward the chalet.

"If it's true about things coming in threes," Nolton muttered, "I can hardly wait to see what the third thing will be."

Denver cleared his throat, hoping that would pass for a response.

"First Kip. Then Marlene. Hell, one day I've got a family and the next day I've got no one."

"It happens sometimes, I guess. But with Kip...well, I'm sure you'll work things out with him."

"Yeah?" Nolton said.

"He...they both seem like nice kids. Maybe you just need to go easier on them. Why not call them when you get back to New York?"

Nolton didn't answer, simply kept trudging along through the snow.

"That Jay," he said after a few minutes. "What a son of a bitch, eh? My best friend. Hell, there's the third thing right there. My son, my wife and my best friend. All gone."

"It's tough," Denver said, wishing he were at least a little the Alan Alda type. If there were right words for a situation like this, he sure didn't know what they were.

"Hell," Nolton muttered. "You know, I gave Marlene everything a woman could possibly want—Park Avenue penthouse, furs, jewellery. But she was always going on about dumb stuff, like saying I never talked to

her and never listened to her and never told her anything and I was never home. Hell, I'm probably just as
well out of it. And wait until I ruin Jay. She'll be sorry
then, wish she hadn't been such a fool. Because I've
been a damned good husband, you know. I mean, I fool
around, but big deal. All guys do that, eh?''

Denver just cleared his throat again. He doubted
Nolton would really appreciate hearing his opinion.
Besides, they were almost at the chalet.

They walked the last hundred yards without speaking and paused at the front door to stomp the snow off
their boots.

Chantal hadn't heard a sound, but she knew Denver
and Nolton were back when McGee and Brandy hurried to the front door.

Her gaze followed them across the living room. She
and Marlene had managed to get a new fire started and
had lit half a dozen candles. But the atmosphere in the
chalet was as far from warm and cheery as it could
possibly be.

''Here they are,'' Marlene whispered as the door
opened. ''Oh, Chantal, all Jay and I wanted was a few
days on our own, away from his phone and Manhattan
and the hurry-scurry world. But instead of turning out
to be our perfect hideaway, this place has turned out to
be . . .''

Chantal covered the other woman's hand with her
own. ''You really don't have to talk to him, Marlene.
Not now. Not if you don't feel up to it.''

''Yes, I do. I have to explain about Jay and me.
That's the only right thing. And I have to talk to him
about Kip and Cathy. I have to make him see reason.''

Chantal nodded, praying Denver had calmed Nolton
down. She doubted any of them could handle much

more tonight, and Marlene was so upset she looked physically ill.

Across the room, Nolton had taken off his jacket and was standing beside Denver, his hands jammed into his pockets, his face gray despite having been out in the cold for almost an hour.

"I'd like to talk to you, Nolt," Marlene murmured.

He didn't move, just stood staring at her.

Denver glanced at Chantal. "Where's Jay?"

"Upstairs. We cleaned him up and put him to bed under a ton of quilts."

"I'd better go have a look at him," Denver said, his expression suggesting she come with him. "You got the flashlight there?"

She nodded and picked it up, noticing as she rose that Denver was giving McGee an almost imperceptible hand signal.

The dog ambled over and flopped down directly in front of Marlene, Brandy trailing along after him.

Chantal followed Denver up the stairs, the air growing colder with each step. By the time they reached the top she could see her breath, so she aimed the flashlight at the floor. Some things were better left unseen.

She glanced back down and watched Nolton for a moment. He was still standing where he'd been, looking over at his wife.

"Marlene will be perfectly safe," Denver said quietly, drawing Chantal a few feet along the hall and circling his arms around her. "Nolton's blown off most of his steam. And McGee isn't going to let him do a thing but talk."

"Oh, Denver," she murmured against his chest. It felt so incredibly good to have him hold her. "Oh, this is just awful. Marlene was in tears most of the time you were gone. And I think Jay's nose is broken."

"I figured it was. I'll have a look in a minute. I just wanted to make sure you were okay first."

"I'd feel better if you kissed me," she whispered.

He bent down and gave her a long, tender kiss, then simply stood hugging her. "You'd feel better with something more on, too," he finally said, releasing her and heading into his bedroom, coming back a minute later with a big heavy sweater for her.

When she took it she noticed he was holding the gun, and glanced from it to his face.

"I'm going to keep it with me until this is all over," he said, tucking it away. "Just in case Nolton has any more crazy impulses."

"Do you think he will?"

"I hope not. But he's still incredibly upset. And angry. And feeling vindictive as hell."

"They didn't mean him to find out this way," she said, rolling up the sleeves of the sweater. It was about twelve sizes too large for her. "Marlene was going to tell him soon. She was just waiting until the time was right."

"Chantal, the time can never be right for something like that, can it? But it's too bad it happened the way it did—with them sending Nolton off the deep end, I mean. Because it's going to make things harder on everyone."

"Oh?"

"Yeah, his pride's hurting, and he wants to make people pay for that. Says he's going to charge Marlene with adultery, try to minimize her divorce settlement. But you know what I thought was really strange?"

"What?"

"The whole time we were outside, he didn't say a word about loving her. What seemed to concern him most, when he was ranting and raving, was what people would think when they learned she'd left him."

"It's not all that strange, Denver. It's pure Nolton Bristow."

Denver shook his head. "Talk about self-centered, huh? And Jay—most of what he said about Jay I won't even repeat. But he says he's taking his account to Carruthers and Headly the minute he gets back to Manhattan."

"That's pure Nolton Bristow, too. Frank Carruthers and Jay have had kind of a feud going for years. I guess Nolton's trying to get back at Jay any way he can."

"He sure is. In fact, he says he's going to ruin Jay. Think that's a possibility?"

"I . . . I wouldn't think so. But a major ex-client bad-mouthing an agency . . . well, it certainly won't help. Lord, Denver, if Jay loses a lot of business, I could lose my job."

Denver kissed the tip of her nose. "You'd be joining the club. McGee and I have already lost ours. No one who's had anything to do with Jay Clawson Advertising is ever going to work for Nolton Bristow again. Including me. He's back to using Brandy for his commercials. Says he'll take both his terrific idea and his dog to Carruthers."

"But what about after the commercials are shot? He's still going to let you find her a good home, isn't he?"

"Chantal, once we're out of here, I doubt I'll ever hear from Nolton again. As far as he's concerned, I'm part of this big unhappy mess."

"But what about Brandy? Somebody has to look out for her. Isn't there something you could do?"

"I . . . maybe there will be. We'll have to wait and see what happens. But right now, we'd better go check on Jay. Let him know things have cooled off."

Chantal nodded slowly, not liking the way Denver sounded so uncertain. And it wasn't only what would happen to Brandy that was worrying her. Now that she and Denver wouldn't be back here working on those commercials together . . .

She tapped on the bedroom door, then opened it. They'd left candles burning in the room, so she switched off the flashlight.

Jay looked even worse than he had when they'd put him to bed. His entire face was swollen and his eyes were mere slits, with huge purple bruises forming around them.

"How you doing, Jay?" she murmured.

"I think I'll live. Is Marlene all right?"

"She's fine."

"She's talking to Nolt now?"

"Yes. And he's calmed down. But...well, I guess it's no surprise to you that we've lost our major client."

"No, no surprise at all. It doesn't matter, though. We'll replace his business. We'll just have to put in some overtime for the next little while, drum up a few new accounts."

Denver cleared his throat and Chantal glanced at him, then back at Jay, saying, "You haven't officially met Denver."

He moved to the side of the bed, looking dreadfully uncomfortable, and apologized for slamming Jay into the wall earlier.

Jay tried to smile, but the swelling made it come off crooked. "Don't worry about that. If you hadn't hauled Nolton off me, I'd be in worse shape than I am. My nose is broken, though, isn't it?"

"Sure looks that way. We can make an ice pack out of snow, but there isn't much else even a doctor could do for it right now."

The crooked smile appeared once more. "It's so damned cold in here an ice pack would be overkill."

"Well," Denver said, grinning at Jay's remark, "at least it's almost stopped snowing. So maybe the guy who plows Nolton's road will show up once it's light out. Then we can all get the hell out of here."

Jay nodded, saying that was sure something to look forward to. But all Chantal could think of was that getting the hell out of here would mean no longer being with Denver.

She stood gazing at him. He was the most ruggedly handsome, the most amazingly wonderful man in the world, and scarcely twenty-four hours ago he'd said he was absolutely crazy about her. And there wasn't a shred of doubt she felt the same way about him. That had lulled her into believing there might somehow be a future for them, that all they needed was more time together to work out the details.

But the past twenty-four hours had changed their situation entirely. Now they wouldn't be having the next few days together, wouldn't be coming up again to shoot Nolton's commercials. All they'd be doing was getting the hell out of here.

Then she'd be back on Madison Avenue and Denver would be back in Jersey. And when they were back in the real world, weren't all those darned differences they'd been sweeping under the carpet bound to come crawling out once more?

There was a soft tap on the door and Marlene came in, followed by the dogs. She shot a wan smile at Chantal and Denver, then sat down on the bed beside Jay and took his hand.

"How bad was it?" he asked.

"I survived," she murmured.

"Ah...we should get going, huh, Chantal?" Denver said, motioning the dogs out of the room as he spoke.

Marlene looked over, saying, "I'm awfully sorry you two got dragged into this. I don't know what you want to do about sleeping arrangements for the rest of the night. I'm just going to sit here with Jay. But the beds will be so icy cold you'd be better off back downstairs...except that Nolton's still there."

"We'll figure out something," Denver said, taking Chantal's hand and hustling her into the dark hall.

"So?" he said, closing the door. "Which would you hate least for the rest of the night? An icy-cold bed or Nolton's company?"

"Oh, Denver, can't I pick neither of the above?"

"Only if you choose another alternative," he said quietly, moving closer and hugging her, warming her with his nearness.

She gazed up at him, barely able to make out his features but knowing she could never mistake him for any other man. He was special. So special. And she was more than just absolutely crazy about him. Denver Brooke was the man she loved.

"Did you have any other alternatives in mind?" she whispered.

"Only one ... body heat."

CHAPTER TEN

DENVER SHOOED BRANDY and McGee back into the hall and closed his bedroom door. The air stirred. The flame of their lone candle began to dance in the dark.

"They won't like being locked out there," Chantal said, trying to sound nonchalant, certain she sounded nervous as the devil.

Denver said dogs couldn't always have things the way they liked. "Besides, leaving them out there's a good idea, in case Nolton starts prowling around. The thought of Marlene being up here with Jay must be eating away at him."

"Maybe...Denver, maybe we shouldn't be leaving him alone. Maybe we should go back downstairs."

"Is that what you want?" he said quietly, moving forward and resting his hands on her shoulders, drawing her to him.

She leaned against him, her heart pounding. "No."

"It's not what I want, either. Chantal...I love you."

"Really?" she whispered, not meaning to, the word just slipping out.

"Really," he said, hugging her more closely. "Really, really, really. Forget about me liking you a whole helluva lot, okay? Forget about me being absolutely crazy about you. I love you. And what I want is to get into bed and spend the rest of the night holding you, keeping you warm."

Making love to you, she silently added. Just as she wanted to make love to him. And that had to be right, didn't it? When she loved him? When he loved her? When fate had thrown them together?

In fact, there must have been an entire chorus of fates orchestrating their falling in love, because even their having met was incredibly improbable. And now the two of them had been orchestrated into this room. Alone together in the middle of the night.

"Chantal?" he whispered.

"Denver...Denver, I love you, too. And the bed has to be a lot warmer than this. It's absolutely freezing out here."

He grinned down at her for a moment, then reached over, one arm still around her, and pulled back the quilts. "I'd say we should take off our shoes but nothing else, huh? Ah...I mean, not unless we get really warm."

She nodded, kicking off her shoes and scrambling into bed. "Oh, Lord!" she gasped when her hands hit the sheets. "It's freezing in here, too."

Denver blew out the candle and crawled in beside her, pulling the quilts up all the way over their heads and snuggling her to his chest, hugging her entire body to him.

He kissed her nose, pronounced it on the verge of frostbite, and then cuddled her face into his sweater— so closely that she could barely breathe.

The sweater smelled of him, and while his scent enveloped her, the warmth of his body gradually penetrated the layers of clothing between them.

She closed her eyes, imagining his body heat as a living organism, escaping from his chest and working its way through the two sweaters he was wearing, then through the one he'd given her, finally through her sweatshirt . . . warming her skin.

And lower, that body heat was slowly making its way through his jeans and her sweatpants, warming her legs and hips.

Gradually, she started feeling less like an icicle, more like a woman.

Then Denver began caressing her back, his touch smoothing the fleecy sweatshirt against her skin, making her feel even warmer . . . even more like a woman.

She was aware of her own body heat now, radiating toward Denver, was aware a liquid fire had started low inside her, simmering against the hardness of his arousal. She moved her head a little and nuzzled his throat.

"Mmm," he murmured. "Warm yet?"

"Very warm."

"Hot, even?" he teased.

"Very hot, even."

He eased the quilts down, only far enough so her nose was exposed, but it felt as if she'd suddenly stuck her head into a dark refrigerator.

"Oh, geez! Mistake," he said, covering their heads completely again and pressing her nose against his cheek until it was warm once more.

Then he slowly brushed his lips across her face and gently kissed her mouth.

She traced his jawline, rough with stubble, and his kiss grew more inviting, more demanding.

He smoothed his hands down her back, drawing her even closer, fitting her fully to him, making her wish they weren't wearing all these clothes. And then he slipped his hands beneath her sweaters and began caressing her skin, breathing her name as he reached her breasts.

She shifted in his arms, hungry for his touch, but icy air rushed into the tiny space her motion created and she gasped a shocked little gasp.

"What's wrong?" he whispered.

"Cold!" she said, hugging him so tightly that not another wisp of air could possibly sneak between them.

"Chantal, I just can't believe this."

There was something in his tone that made her smile. "Can't believe what?" she murmured.

"That I'm in bed with the most gorgeous woman in the world but—"

"Say that again," she whispered.

"You mean, the most gorgeous woman in the world?"

"Right. I like that."

"The woman I love," he went on.

"Oh, Denver, I like that even more."

"The woman I love," he repeated. "But instead of that sexy silky thing I've been fantasizing about, you're wearing so many clothes I can hardly find you in them."

"Denver, you're not exactly Mr. Nude World yourself."

"That's because you aren't the only one who doesn't want to freeze to death. But you feel so beautiful and I want to look at you, but I can't see a damned thing. And I want to touch you and kiss you all over, but I don't want you dying of exposure. How the hell do Eskimos make love?"

"Or Icelanders," she murmured, kissing his jaw.

"Or Alaskans," he said, his hands slipping to her breasts again, his arms inching her sweater up, baring the skin near her waist.

Ignoring the freezing air wasn't impossible this time. In fact, Denver's caress made it difficult to think about anything except how intensely he was arousing her.

She slid her hands under his sweaters, tangling her fingers in his thick chest hair, murmuring, "Or Greenlanders."

"Oh, Chantal," he whispered, "Antarctica... Siberia... all kinds of frigid places... maybe you stop noticing it's cold somewhere along the way."

"That could be it," she managed as he ran his hands down her sides and slid them under the band of her sweatpants.

He began easing them down, and she pressed her hand to the zipper of his jeans, feeling how very large and hard he was, making him groan. "Oh, Chantal, I think it must be right about here that you stop noticing the cold."

He covered her mouth with his, kissing her with a deep, possessing kiss that said he couldn't wait to possess her completely, then moved lower, kissing her body while he undressed her, while he helped her undress him.

It took forever—so many clothes, so much bedding entangling them. And each passing second, the aching throb of desire grew stronger inside her.

By the time they were naked she was almost frantic with wanting him. They were touching so intimately, he was so wonderfully close, but she desperately needed him even closer. Her body was moving against his hand, seeking release, telling him what he was doing to her.

"Chantal," he whispered, "in my fantasy, this was going to be slow and gentle."

"Oh, Denver, I don't need slow and gentle. Not when you're driving me crazy. Oh, Denver," she murmured again, hardly able to catch her breath, sighing at the delight of his touch, then suddenly out of control, clinging to him while her body shook with delicious little spasms.

Gradually they subsided, leaving her exhilarated and exhausted, but Denver began stroking her again, slowly banishing the exhaustion, heightening the exhilaration, until it was such deliriously painful pleasure she could scarcely bear it. She reached for him, saying, "Now, Denver. Please, now."

He entered her, murmuring how much he loved her, murmuring this was a million times beyond his fantasy, driving her to another orgasm.

This one allowed no holding back, this one sent her beyond all but the dimmest awareness of reality.

Vaguely, she was conscious of Denver's climax, of being certain she'd pleased him, of smiling with happiness that she had, of him holding her so tightly, eventually collapsing on his side, drawing her with him.

Then slowly, very slowly, full reality returned. The reality of Denver lying beside her, cradling her in his arms, their bodies so close they were still almost one. And hot. So hot when they'd been so cold.

"I love you, Chantal Livingstone," he whispered.

"I love you, Denver Brooke."

"Don't move," he murmured. "Don't even move a muscle for the rest of the night or we'll be freezing again."

"I won't," she promised, although she knew she could never feel even a little bit cold if she were wrapped in Denver's arms.

CHANTAL JOLTED AWAKE to early morning rays of the sun, thinking she'd heard an engine but not certain. The only thing she was certain of was that she was wrapped in Denver's arms, yet had never been so cold in her entire life.

"What the hell's the racket?" he said, coming to life beside her.

"I think it might be my teeth chattering. I'm shivering all the way down to my toes."

He gave her a quick grin, kissed her nose, and said he doubted her teeth chattering sounded like dogs barking. "I'd better see what's going on.

"Oh, geez!" he muttered, rolling out of bed. "It has to be forty below in this room." He scooped a pile of clothes from the floor and tossed it onto the bed. "Here. You'll be better off getting dressed under the covers."

Chantal lay watching him throw on his own clothes, until he tugged his sweaters over his head and his bare chest vanished beneath them, spoiling the show. He had the most gorgeous body she'd ever seen...and he loved her. She still could barely believe that.

He grabbed the gun from the bedside table, and she made a face at it, not wanting to be reminded of its existence.

"Chantal, don't look like I'm a reincarnation of Dillinger. From that barking I'd say the dogs heard someone outside. And the way things have been happening around here, it could be anyone."

He started for the door, then stopped. "I shouldn't rush off without saying something, should I? Last night was fantastic. And I really, really do love you. And—"

"Denver, I know. It was way more than fantastic. And I really, really do love you, too. But go see what's bothering the dogs. Then come back and say more wonderful things to me."

After he'd left she sat hugging herself under the covers, not wanting to move enough to get dressed. Even a fraction of an inch and she hit an icy patch of sheet.

But given the noise the dogs were still making, something major was going on downstairs. And if it was, Denver wouldn't be coming back.

Curiosity won out over the cold, so she clenched her teeth and grabbed at her things, deciding his estimate of the room being forty below was far too warm.

By the time she raced down the stairs, the dogs were quietly sitting at the front door, beside Denver, Nolton and Pierrette Pelletier.

She shot Chantal something that was probably meant as a smile, then continued speaking to Denver, obviously upset. "So you can drive the snowmobile, *oui?*"

"It's been awhile. But I had one years ago."

Pierrette said, "Good," then turned to Nolton. "And you have a suit Denver can use?"

Nolton nodded, saying there were half a dozen snowmobile outfits in the cupboard by the laundry room. "Everything you'll need is there, Denver. Boots, mitts, helmets, goggles."

"What's happening?" Chantal said, catching Denver's arm as he turned toward the hall.

Good question, he said silently. Pierrette's story had been the vaguest mumbo jumbo he'd ever heard, but the more he'd tried to press her for specifics, the more she'd lapsed into French and shrugged.

"What's happening," he said aloud, "is that someone's lost in the mountains near here. Half the area's snowbound, and all the phone lines are down. So Pierrette wants me to take McGee out looking for him."

"Who is it that's lost?"

"It is," Pierrette said quickly, "how do you say... a confusing story. I have already said to Denver that I will explain it to him when we go."

"What about Brandy?" Chantal said. "She could help search."

Denver shook his head. "Uh-uh. She'd be more trouble than help."

"No, she wouldn't. You told me she had good rescue instincts."

"Chantal, she isn't trained."

"You said Saint Bernards didn't need to be trained for rescue work, that it's instinctive."

"Is that true?" Nolton demanded.

"Ah... yeah," Denver admitted, wishing he'd kept his mouth shut.

"Then take her along," Nolton said.

Pierrette glanced at Denver. "There is room in the sled for two dogs. So that is a really good idea, *oui?*"

He was about to say, *No, it's a really bad idea,* when Nolton said, "It's a *great* idea. Think if Brandy found the guy. Saved someone's life. Listen, Denver, after what's been going down around here I could sure do with something to cheer me up. And just imagine how my *new* ad agency," he said, glancing pointedly at Chantal, "would be able to use a rescue story in the advertising campaign."

"Good God," Denver snapped. "Some poor guy's lost in the snow and all you can think about are your stupid commercials?" He glared at Nolton, then started down the hall.

Chantal hurried after him. "Denver? Denver, I want to help with the search. What I meant about Brandy was I could take her and you'd take McGee and—"

"Uh-uh," he said, not even breaking stride.

"What do you mean, uh-uh? Give me one good reason I shouldn't go."

He stopped walking and looked down at her. "I can give you eighteen good reasons without even thinking hard. We're talking about tromping around in snowy mountains, and your ankle can't possibly be a hundred percent yet."

"It is. It's perfectly fine."

"Don't argue, okay? I've been involved in mountain searches back in Colorado. But you're the ultimate city slicker. You admit that. You wouldn't know what you were doing, and you might run into trouble. Chantal," he added quietly, "I love you and I don't want anything happening to you."

"Denver, if somebody's lost out there in the snow, I want to help. And I'm not staying here. Not with Nolton."

"It won't be only Nolton. Jay and Marlene must have heard all the noise. They'll be down any minute."

"Oh, terrific. Just terrific. You'd leave me here with that happy trio? To get caught in their cross fire? I think I might even prefer being alone with Nolton to that."

"Dammit, Chantal, there's something funny about this whole thing, and I don't want you involved in whatever it is."

"Funny how?"

He swore to himself. The way she was looking at him told him he'd said the wrong thing. "I don't mean funny, exactly."

"Well, what *do* you mean, exactly?"

"I don't know. It's just that there's a lot Pierrette isn't saying. In fact, she's being downright evasive."

"Denver, that only makes me want to go with you more. How do you think I'd feel, sitting here worrying about whatever the something funny is? Worrying about you? Look, I love you, too. And I don't want anything happening to you, either.''

That made him pause. It was difficult to dispute his own logic. Then the clincher came to him, and he felt immensely better. ''Chantal, you can't possibly go because snowmobiles have a single bench seat. And there's only room on it for two people. So, end of discussion, huh?''

She stood gazing at him for about a heartbeat, then glanced back along the hall. ''Pierrette?''

''*Oui?*''

''Is there room in the sled for two dogs plus me?''

Pierrette didn't reply for a moment, looking as if she weren't at all certain she wanted Chantal along, and Denver willed her to say, no.

''*Oui,* there is room,'' she said.

CHANTAL STARED straight ahead, keeping her eyes on Denver's back, trying not to let them stray to the metal hitch that attached the sled to the snowmobile.

Not that she was too crazy about keeping her eyes on Denver when his arms were wrapped tightly around another woman's waist, but one look at that hitch had been one look too many.

It simply wasn't strong enough to pull over three hundred pounds of dogs, plus her, without snapping. She just knew it wasn't. Especially when Pierrette was driving like a maniac.

That snowmobile was going to go spurting ahead on its own, to the top of this hill they were climbing, and the sled would shoot back down like a runaway caboose. She and the dogs would be killed, and Denver would roar off into the rising sun, hugging Pierrette Pelletier.

Before they'd even left the chalet, she'd begun to doubt the wisdom of this. Just for starters, she looked like an enormous lemon cough drop in Marlene's yellow snowmobile suit. A stupid cough drop when, somehow, Pierrette managed to look incredibly chic in her raspberry outfit.

The suit wasn't the worst of it, though. The helmet was enough to induce an attack of claustrophobia.

But the absolute worst was the sled. The moment she'd seen it, a little voice inside her head had started telling her she was crazy to have insisted on coming along. And about three seconds into the trip, she'd decided the little voice was right.

She didn't know exactly what she'd expected, but she certainly hadn't imagined this contraption. It looked as if it belonged in a dogsled race.

Only these dogs weren't huskies. And they were back here riding with her, instead of up front, pulling. And this sled definitely wasn't moving at dogsled speed.

Pierrette had to be going four thousand miles an hour. If she didn't slow down they'd all be killed...any second now...unless the hitch snapped before that happened and sent the sled into free-fall...then only she and the dogs would be killed.

Chantal clutched their collars even more tightly, although clutching was far from easy to do with big snowmobile mitts. But she had hold of McGee with one hand and Brandy with the other and was hanging on to them for dear life.

She was also trying to cling to the front of the sled with her toes, but wasn't doing a bang-up job of that. Snowmobile boots were big, heavy things like work boots that didn't lend themselves to toe-clinging. It was a good thing Pierrette had told her to bring Marlene's boots along to wear when they started searching on foot. Assuming, of course, they lived long enough to start searching on foot.

They swerved to the right, the snowmobile almost tipped onto its side, Chantal's stomach lurched, and the skids threw up another spray of snow, about half of it scoring a direct hit on her goggles, almost blinding her.

But the snow didn't actually feel any colder than the air that had been trying to freeze every centimeter of her face. Maybe she wouldn't die in a snowmobile accident, after all. Maybe she'd die of exposure instead.

They reached the top of the hill, and she risked letting go of McGee to wipe the snow off her goggles. Ahead, a snow-covered highway stretched into the distance. Pierrette turned across a field and began driving along parallel to the road.

Not far ahead, a house stood on their left, a large, white frame affair, surrounded by snowdrifts that were acting as camouflage.

They reached its driveway and Pierrette pulled onto it. The drive had been roughly plowed, both out to the highway and back to the garage. Its double doors stood open, revealing a car inside. A new-looking pickup truck was parked nearby.

Pierrette stopped the snowmobile in front of the house. "Come," she said, hopping off. "I will explain what has happened."

She started toward the door, and Denver wordlessly helped Chantal from the sled, the dogs scrambling out with her.

He took off his helmet, so she did the same, then smiled hopefully at him. But he was clearly still angry about her coming.

"What are we doing here?" she tried. "I thought we'd go directly to where the search party is."

"Chantal," he said, shaking his head, "I don't know what we're doing here. But I have a suspicion we *are* the search party. In its entirety. So let's go find out what we've gotten ourselves into."

Pierrette had left the door ajar and they simply walked in, leaving Brandy and McGee on the porch. The house was blessedly warm. Obviously, its power was on.

Pierrette's helmet was sitting on the hall table, her heavy raspberry boots were lying on the floor, and she was standing in the living room, rapidly peeling off her snowmobile suit to reveal jeans and a sweater.

"Pierrette?" Denver said as she tossed the suit onto the couch. "I thought you were in a hurry to get started."

She turned to them, clasping her hands together, then slowly shrugging. "I must tell you how this is. But it is so awful...so terrible I do not know where to begin."

"Why don't you begin by telling us who's lost?"

"Oh, Denver...that is the hardest part of all. It is...it is René Gagnon."

It took a moment for the name to ring a bell in Chantal's mind. When it did, she decided she must have made the wrong connection.

Then Denver glanced at her, obviously not making any connection at all, so she said, "The little boy, Pierrette? You don't mean the little boy who was kidnapped, do you?"

"Oui, le petit garçon," she said, sinking onto the couch, tears starting down her cheeks. She buried her face in her hands and began to sob.

"What the hell's the story here?" Denver demanded.

Chantal motioned him to be quiet and crossed the room to sit beside Pierrette. The thought of *somebody,* some nameless adult, being lost in the snow was bad enough. But that poor little boy who'd already been through being kidnapped ...

She took a deep breath, telling herself not to get any more upset. The best thing she could do was find out exactly what had happened. "Pierrette," she said gently, "how do you know about René?"

"Oh, Chantal, I am so ashamed to say."

"It's all right. Just tell us."

"Well ... you see ... I have a brother. François."

"Yes?" Chantal prompted.

Pierrette wiped her eyes, then went on. "François is ... he is not a bad man but is sometimes doing the wrong things. He is even a few times in jail. But this time ... oh, this time he gets involved with a man who thinks to kidnap the son of Claude Gagnon. 'The ransom,' this man tells François, 'will make us rich.' But something goes wrong. I do not understand exactly, but there is a problem with the place where they take René. So François brings him here."

"I don't believe this!" Denver snapped. "Why in hell didn't you call the police?"

That started Pierrette crying again, and Chantal glared at him.

"Well, dammit, Chantal! Why didn't she?"

"She's going to tell us why. Just give her half a chance."

After a minute, Pierrette swallowed hard and started in again. "François said it would be only for two days. Then they would have the ransom and give back the boy. And he begged me...and if I told the police he would go to jail for so long...and he is my brother...and he said if I did not help he must take René to some other place.

"And I thought, at least here the little boy is safe. And I stayed with him, Chantal. He was not so frightened. But then two days was three. Then four. Then five."

Denver said, "That means you had René here when we called you about Maurice Charlebois's grandson."

"*Oui.* So I knew the child in the cabin was not René. But I did not want you to tell the police what you thought. I did not want them to maybe even suspect René was nearby. François will never, never do this again. He has sworn that to me. But the police here, they are...how do you say in English...they are trigger-happy. If they had come, they might have killed my brother."

Denver's expression said that would have been a good idea. Before he could say so out loud, Chantal quickly asked, "And where is François now?"

"He is in Montreal. He went there last night to make the contact with the father...to get the ransom."

Denver simply shook his head, looking, Chantal thought, every bit as shell-shocked as she felt.

"Pierrette," he finally said, "let's get back to why we're here. How did René get lost?"

"He ran away. This morning. Maybe he thought that with François gone...so before I woke, René dressed and left without making the noise."

"This morning," Denver said.

"*Oui.* After the snow had stopped. There were the fresh footprints."

"And you didn't follow them?" Chantal asked.

"*Certainement.* I did. On the snowmobile. But they ended at the top of a hill. There had been a . . . a snow slide. And the footprints were gone then. That is why I thought maybe the dogs . . ."

When Pierrette's words trailed off Chantal said, "You thought the dogs could track him."

Pierrette glanced at Denver, her expression saying there was more to it than that.

"The hill, it was a steep one," Pierrette said quietly. "You will see why I went no farther."

Denver nodded, looking even more uneasy.

"What?" Chantal asked him.

"A heavy wet snowfall," he said, "like the one we had, can leave the whole winter's accumulation of snow unstable."

"Unstable," Chantal said.

"It could all break loose."

"Oh, Lord," she murmured, feeling ill. "You mean there could have been enough to bury René? Like in a real avalanche? You mean that poor little boy might be dead?"

Denver stepped nearer and put his arm around her shoulders. "Let's not jump to conclusions, huh? There might not have been all that much snow."

Chantal looked over at Pierrette and she murmured, "There was . . . quite a lot."

"Well," Denver said, "could be it just slid and covered his tracks long after he'd climbed down the hill."

Chantal was still trying to decide how likely he thought that possibility was when Pierrette started speaking again.

"Denver," she said, her lower lip quivering slightly, "the footprints, they start behind the house. I am getting you some blankets to take. René will be cold. But then I have done all I can. I pray you and Chantal will find the child. I pray he will be safe."

"Chantal and I? Just a damned minute, here. Where the hell do you think you're going to be?"

"I must go to Montreal. I am right in the trouble now, and I have a friend there who is a lawyer."

"Dammit, Pierrette, don't be ridiculous. Montreal has to be over a hundred miles from here and the roads are a mess."

"I will get there. My car, it has the four-wheel drive."

Denver swore again, then said, "Look, you aren't going anywhere except off on the snowmobile with us."

Pierrette simply shook her head, and Chantal could see Denver's anger growing.

"Pierrette," he snapped, "let's get real here. Neither Chantal nor I speak French. If we went on our own and found the kid we wouldn't be able to talk to him."

"No, he speaks the good English."

Denver glared at her skeptically and she said, "*Oui*. That is true. Most Montrealers speak the English. And if I am there he will be more frightened to see me. He will think I take him back to François."

Denver looked as if he were on the verge of murdering Pierrette, so Chantal said, "Denver, that's actually a valid point. René *would* be afraid."

Pierrette shot Chantal an anxious smile, then grabbed her snowmobile suit from the couch and began digging in the pocket.

"Here, Denver," she said. "Here are keys for the house and the truck. So you can bring René back here. Or drive him to the police in Trois-Rivières. But I *must* go to Montreal. There, my friend will go to the police with me. I know I must tell them what has happened. But I am afraid to tell them unless I am with my friend."

"Never mind your friend," Denver snapped. "You've got to tell the police right now. Not in a few hours. And not a hundred-odd miles from here. We have to get a major search party organized immediately. You get on the phone to the local police this second."

"I cannot, Denver. The phone, it is not working. All the phones nearby are not working."

CHAPTER ELEVEN

CHANTAL CLUNG TIGHTLY to Denver, telling herself she was far safer than she'd been back in the sled, with Pierrette driving as if she were practicing for a snow-mobile version of the Indy 500.

Not that Denver wasn't roaring along. And not that far safer was quite the same as perfectly safe. In fact, she was feeling about as safe as she'd feel on a small motorcycle. In Manhattan traffic.

She glanced back to check that the dogs were still securely in the sled, deciding there was no point in trying to ask Denver to slow down. He'd never hear her over the snowmobile's roar. Besides, they both wanted to reach the scene of that snow slide as quickly as possible.

Snow slide, she repeated firmly to herself, wishing the word avalanche would stop creeping around in her mind. It was so much more menacing.

But avalanches were great masses of snow, weren't they? Whereas snow slide sounded minor. And Pierrette had definitely said snow slide.

Of course, Pierrette's command of English wasn't perfect. And she'd also said there'd been quite a lot of snow.

Chantal scanned the passing landscape. Snow everywhere. Under different circumstances, it would seem beautiful. Under the present circumstances, she couldn't help thinking it might be deadly.

Maybe everything would be all right, though. If René had made his way down that hill before the slide, he'd be safe. And they'd be able to pick up his trail, those little footprints with happy-face imprints from the treads of his boots.

The irony of those tiny faces, smiling in the snow, had brought a lump to her throat when she'd first seen them.

She gazed anxiously out over the dazzling whiteness once more, wishing for a miracle, wishing she'd see a ten-year-old boy. But all she saw was the smoothly covered ground and trees, their blanket marred only by René's trail and the odd set of fresh animal tracks.

And then she saw something moving in the distance. Another snowmobile. She poked Denver sharply in the back to get his attention, then pointed across the snow. He slowed to a stop, and they waited while the other machine drew nearer.

As it did, Chantal could see there was a passenger clinging to the driver. A small passenger. A child.

Her spirits soared. Maybe, just maybe, the child was René. Maybe this person had found him wandering in the hills.

Then the snowmobile pulled to a halt in front of them, the driver shoved up his goggles, and her spirits sank. It was Maurice Charlebois. So that was undoubtedly his grandson with him. Jean-Paul, she recalled Pierrette saying his name was.

"Bonjour," Maurice said, then turned to the boy and spoke rapidly in French.

Jean-Paul hopped down and tugged off his helmet, saying, "My *grandpère* wants me to ask if you're lost."

Denver said, "No, we aren't. But someone else is. A boy about your age. Do you think you and your grandfather could go for more help? Contact the police and ask them to organize a search party?"

The boy translated for his grandfather and Maurice nodded. *"Oui. Certainment,"* he told them.

"Good," Denver said, looking at Jean-Paul again. "The lost boy's name is René Gagnon. Will you remember that?"

"Oui. René Gagnon."

"Right. The police are already looking for him, but this is his trail we're following. Can your grandfather tell them exactly where it is?"

Maurice nodded again when Jean-Paul repeated the question in French.

Jean-Paul scrambled back onto the seat, waved goodbye, and Maurice roared off, spraying snow to either side.

Denver reached for Chantal's hand and squeezed it through the bulk of their mitts. "It's going to be all right. The cavalry always arrives in time to save the day."

She tried to smile, but this particular cavalry could be a long while in coming. And right now, there were only the two of them with a chance of saving the day.

They started off again, following René's footprints along a level stretch and up a hill. Denver slowed as they neared its crest, then cut the engine. "Look," he said, gesturing ahead as the noise died.

"Pierrette was right," he added when they got off the snowmobile. "I was hoping she'd somehow figured this wrong, but see how the footsteps just vanish where the slide started?"

Chantal merely nodded, doubting she could manage words, barely aware of Denver taking off his helmet and goggles, digging his cowboy boots out of the sled. She simply stood staring down the incline, no longer able to tell herself there was any chance it had been a relatively gentle snow slide.

Of course, she was only looking at the aftermath, but even a city slicker could picture what had happened. The drop-off was both steeper and stretched down much farther than she'd been imagining—fifty yards or so from top to bottom. When people talked about ski *hills,* they actually meant mountains.

To either side of where they were, the snow lay clean and blanket smooth. The center of the hill, though, looked as if a giant river of churning water had rushed down, carrying earth and rocks along in its path, wiping out trees.

But the huge, chunky, debris-filled mound of snow that had come to rest at the bottom told her it had been a mass of snow and ice that had hurtled down, not water.

Now all was quiet again, the drift sprawling out over an area maybe half as big as a football field, the upper portions of several evergreens and a few enormous, topsy-turvy root formations sticking up from the rubble.

"I'll just go have a preliminary look," Denver said. "You stay with the dogs, okay?"

"Denver?" she murmured. "Be really careful."

"Piece of cake," he said. "Everything that could go down has already gone."

She took off her own safety gear and waited beside the sled, absently patting the dogs and watching Denver slowly head down the center of the hill.

He reached the chunky sea of snow at the bottom, and she held her breath as he began cautiously picking his way over its surface.

It seemed forever before he'd crossed to the far edge and started back, longer than forever before he was safely beside her once more.

"What?" she asked, not actually needing to. His grim expression was telling her she didn't want to know what he'd seen. Or rather, what he hadn't seen.

"Bad news. There aren't any footprints leading away from the other side."

Her throat began to sting and her eyes filled with tears. "Then he's dead?" she managed.

Denver shrugged, looking as if he were in danger of crying himself. "It's possible he's not. It's possible he found a hiding place—maybe beneath a ledge or behind a boulder or someplace. If he did, he's just trapped under the snow—like being in an igloo."

"I see. So... what do we do now?"

"I'll go back down. Take McGee with me this time. We'll search the surface of the drift until he scents the boy."

"What about me? And Brandy?"

Denver looked as if he wasn't the least bit keen on the idea of her helping, but she certainly hadn't risked her life on that damned snowmobile to sit here and watch. "Denver," she said quickly, "with Brandy and me, we can cover the area twice as fast. And time's important, isn't it?"

He eyed her uneasily for another moment, then said, "Well...I guess maybe you're right. You'd better change your boots."

She grabbed them before he could have second thoughts, saying, "Tell me what I should do once we're down there."

"You don't really have to do anything except follow McGee."

"McGee?"

"Yeah, I'll go with Brandy. Just in case she does something dumb."

"She won't."

"Well, no, probably she won't. Even a puppy would instinctively sniff out a person."

Chantal was pulling on Marlene's second boot when the strangest feeling seized her. "Denver?" she said.

"Uh-huh?"

"I want to go with Brandy, not McGee."

"Chantal—"

"Woman's intuition. We'll be fine. Really. And we won't be out of your sight."

He shook his head, almost smiling. "Well...how can I argue with woman's intuition?"

Once they started down the center of the hill, she realized the walking was trickier than Denver had made it appear. And the jagged roughness below meant the going would get far worse.

When they reached the drift Denver said, "Look, the surface is fairly stable, but be very, very careful about testing each step before you take it."

"I will."

"And Chantal?"

"Yes?"

"I love you."

"Love you, too," she whispered.

They headed the dogs off in opposite directions, and Chantal slowly followed Brandy, easing her weight cautiously from one foot to the other, fearing she'd pitch off balance any second. If Denver thought this was fairly stable, she'd hate to try walking on anything he figured was *unstable*.

She glanced across at him. He and McGee were about forty feet away now, moving gradually forward. Just ahead of her, Brandy was sniffing her way along, her behind wiggling and her tail waving, closing in on the upper portion of a fir tree the drift had partially buried.

The dog reached it and stopped dead, her entire body beginning to quiver. She pressed her nose into the snow until her snout was covered all the way to her eyes, then jerked it back out and began digging like crazy.

It took Chantal a second to realize what was happening. When she did, her heart started racing. "Denver!" she shouted. "Brandy's found him!"

Denver motioned McGee ahead and the dog lumbered quickly across the drift, his tail beginning to wag as he neared the tree. He let out a single deep bark, then began digging alongside Brandy.

By the time Denver reached them, snow and tiny bits of the fir tree were flying furiously from beneath their paws, and they'd already dug a fair-sized hole.

"Oh, they've done it!" Chantal said, grinning with relief. "They're wonderful. I love them both."

"And what about me?" he said.

"Oh, Denver, I love you most of all."

He wrapped his arm around her shoulders and hugged her to him, not wanting to destroy her elation but finally saying, "Chantal...honey, don't get too excited just yet. They'd know he was down there even if he wasn't still alive."

She closed her eyes and pressed her face against the cold fabric of his snowmobile suit, murmuring, "Oh, Denver, I just assumed their digging meant..."

He hugged her more tightly, silently urging the dogs to hurry. For all he'd been worried about Chantal walking around down here, she'd been right. Every second might make a difference.

The dogs had dug out an area about five feet across and a good three feet down when he saw a flash of neon purple. "There's his arm," he said, releasing Chantal and dropping into the hole beside McGee.

He shooed the dogs back up and began scooping the remaining loose snow away with his mitts, his hopes rising when he realized the bottom branches of the tree had created an air pocket.

Then he shoved a large branch aside, fully exposing the body of a little boy, and his hopes plunged.

The child was lying on the the ground, eyes closed, tiny clumps of snow clinging to his dark hair, his face covered with scratches and a large bruise on his forehead that could mean concussion. From the looks of things, the rush of snow had caught him and slammed him against the tree trunk.

And worst of all, he was perfectly still—no visible sign he was breathing.

"That's definitely him," Chantal said, her voice shaky. "That's the jacket he was wearing in one of the pictures I saw on TV. But is he alive? Oh, please," she added in a whisper, "please let him be alive."

"I'm checking for a pulse," Denver said, ripping off his mitts and pushing up the sleeve of the child's jacket, inching his fingers across the skinny wrist but not feeling what he desperately wanted.

He glanced back at Chantal, wondering how hard she was going to take this, then realized his thoughts must be written on his face when she said, "Oh, Denver...no."

Tears began trickling down her cheeks. "We're too late, aren't we?" she murmured.

He leaned over the little body for another moment, his own eyes growing moist, then unzipped the top of René's jacket and tried under his jaw...and found a pulse. A weak one, but a definite pulse.

He scooped the child up in his arms and started clambering up the sloping side of the hole saying, "Chantal, he's still alive."

Tears kept right on streaming down her face but she began smiling through them. Then she felt the child's throat, checking his pulse for herself, and her smile faded. "Denver, it's awfully slow. And faint."

"I know. He's really cold. Probably hypothermic."

Chantal took a deep breath and said, "He could still die. Oh, Denver, we can't let him. We just can't let him."

"We won't. Come on," he said, starting across the drift with the child in his arms. "Let's get him to a hospital."

PIERRETTE'S PICKUP HAD far more guts than Denver had expected, and he drove as fast as he dared, clutching the wheel so tightly his knuckles were white. Trying to get René to a hospital, knowing he might die right there in Chantal's arms, would have been a nightmare under any conditions. Driving an unfamiliar truck on a killer highway was just adding terror to the trip.

The surface had been plowed of snow but was a sheet of ice. In the more than half an hour since they'd left

Pierrette's house, they'd passed precisely two cars. On the road, that was. They'd passed at least a dozen in ditches. Probably every one of those French radio stations they couldn't understand was telling people not to take their cars out.

He risked looking across at Chantal. She was still hugging René tightly to her, still massaging his little body through the blankets.

They'd paused at the house only long enough to close the dogs in the basement, change the little boy into dry clothes, and grab warm blankets to wrap him in. There was nothing else they could do for him—nothing except get him to Trois-Rivières alive. Chantal glanced over and he asked how René was doing.

"He still feels terribly cold," she said anxiously. "And he hasn't stirred. Not even a twitch. You don't think...you don't think he couldn't breathe enough under the snow, do you? You don't think he might have brain damage."

Denver wanted to reach across and take her hand, try to reassure her. But he was afraid to let go of the wheel, so he simply said they had to hope for the best.

Chantal nodded, cuddling René even more tightly, and Denver turned his attention back to the highway. His entire body sagged with relief when he saw a sign that said Trois-Rivières was only five kilometers farther.

Those five kilometers seemed like five million miles, but they eventually reached the first turnoff into town. He eased off the gas and told Chantal to start watching for anything that looked like either a hospital or police station.

Once off the exit, he followed a main street, and she finally said, "Up there, Denver! There's a hospital on the right."

"Hallelujah," he murmured, spotting the sprawling brick building with a giant H sign. "Now, let's just hope we recognize the French for emergency entrance."

"There!" Chantal said, pointing. "Look, it says Urgence/Emergency. Oh, Lord, half in English! With any luck, someone in there will understand us."

Denver sped up the driveway, blasting the horn, and jerked to a halt beneath the emergency sign. "Open your door, Chantal. I'll carry him in."

He threw open his own door and raced around to lift the little boy from her lap.

They'd run halfway up the walk when a man in white rushed out of the hospital, yelling a question in French.

"English?" Denver called back.

"*Oui*. Yes," the man said, reaching them.

"The boy's in bad shape," Denver told him, not slowing down.

The man wheeled back toward the entrance, saying, "What happened?"

"Buried by a snow slide," Denver said. "Hypothermia. Maybe concussion."

"Lucky to be alive," the man said, sprinting ahead to open the door.

He shouted something in French and several people came running along the hall, one pushing a gurney, another taking René from Denver's arms and putting him on it.

A second later, they were whisking the little boy away.

Denver turned to Chantal and she collapsed into his arms. He hugged her so tightly he was certain he could feel her heart beating against him, even through their snowmobile suits.

"We did it," she whispered. "We did it. Now he just has to pull through. He just has to be okay."

A nurse touched Denver's arm and said if he gave her the keys she'd have someone move his truck to the parking lot. "And you two just have seats in the waiting room. Someone will inform you about your son's condition as soon as they've examined him."

Denver said, "He's not our son. But I wonder if you'd call the police for us? Tell them you have René Gagnon here—the little boy who was kidnapped in Montreal."

DETECTIVE VEILLEUX'S helicopter had touched down on the hospital's rooftop pad almost two hours ago, and they'd finally finished their second run-through of everything that had happened, had repeated every word they could remember Pierrette saying this morning.

Chantal glanced at Denver, sitting beside her on the waiting-room couch, then looked back across at Veilleux and watched him scribble a few more notes into his book, thinking big city detectives all projected the same image.

Not that she'd had much to do with the police, but she'd as easily have believed Veilleux had arrived from New York as Montreal.

Middle aged, conservatively dressed, quiet and thorough. She had a suspicion those maverick cops in the movies were entirely figments of Hollywood's imagination.

"All right, then," he said, his English perfect despite his French name. "You're positive Pierrette Pelletier didn't mention who the other kidnapper was?"

Denver said, "No. The only thing she told us was that the kidnapping wasn't François's idea. That he'd gotten involved with a man who suggested it."

"But she said nothing at all about the man?" Veilleux pressed. "Nothing about what his part was in the actual snatch?"

"Nothing except that he told François the ransom would make them rich."

Chantal said she didn't think Pierrette even knew who the other man was. "She really didn't seem to have been involved. Her brother had just shown up with René and she didn't know what to do."

Veilleux shook his head, as if he wasn't convinced of Pierrette's innocence. "And you're positive," he went on, "that she believes her brother's in Montreal at the moment? You don't think there's any chance she was trying to throw you off track?"

"Uh-uh," Denver said. "I really think she was terrified about having gotten herself into this. And worried sick about what might happen to the boy. So I'm sure everything she told us was true."

Chantal added, "And she definitely said François had gone to Montreal last night—to make contact with René's father."

"Well, he hasn't tried to make contact so far, and when he does we'll know about it."

"You've got the phones tapped?" Denver asked.

"Ever since the child was taken," the detective said. "And both Gagnon's business and residence are under surveillance."

Veilleux glanced at the fax pages he'd requested as soon as they'd told him about François, and muttered that he'd be glad when they picked up the SOB. "You can tell he's a real bad actor just by looking at him, can't you?'' he added, flashing the faxed picture at them again.

Chantal stared at it for a minute. How could a woman as attractive as Pierrette have a brother who looked as if he made his living collecting for loan sharks? The man had a scar that ran from his ear all the way across his face to his chin.

"We got the impression from Pierrette that François wasn't all that bad, just misguided," Denver put in.

"Not that bad, eh?" Veilleux said, looking at one of the sheets. "Let me see his priors again . . . a couple of assaults to his credit, served six years in a federal pen for armed robbery, arrested on suspicion of arson but they couldn't nail a conviction, now we add kidnapping. . . ."

"Not exactly the type you want wandering around loose," Chantal murmured.

Veilleux grinned at her and said, "No, not exactly. But he won't be loose for much longer, thanks to you two telling us who we're looking for. We put his picture on the wire an hour ago. The entire force and every stoolie in Montreal will be watching for him. We'll get him. Then he'll be locked up for a long time."

"What about Pierrette?" Chantal asked.

"Depends on the details of her story," Veilleux said. "And on how cooperative she is. And on what the boy has to say, assuming he's okay. If he doesn't make it . . . well, things could be far worse for her if that happens. Look, I'm going to grab another coffee. You two want some?"

Denver said, "Yeah, regular, thanks."

Chantal said, "No, thanks," her gaze flickering across the waiting room to rest on Hélène and Claude Gagnon once more.

She didn't want to think about René not making it. Both the little boy and his parents had been through too much already. And they seemed like a decent, thoughtful couple—the way they'd taken so much time thanking her and Denver when they were obviously emotional wrecks.

The Gagnons had arrived from Montreal by police helicopter not long after Detective Veilleux's own copter had landed, but they still didn't know whether René would be all right, and the waiting had to be torture.

"He's holding his own," the doctor had said, "but it's the next hour or two that'll tell the story. And we won't know about brain damage until he regains consciousness."

Denver covered Chantal's hand with his, and she made an effort to smile at him.

"What are you thinking about?" he asked.

"Oh . . . about how strongly we react to some things. How easily we can get emotionally involved. I mean, we've never even seen René conscious, yet I'll feel awful if he's not perfectly fine. And it'll hurt so much if he dies."

Denver nodded, squeezing her hand.

"Oh, Denver," she murmured, "can you imagine how his parents must be feeling?"

Veilleux was heading back across the room with the coffee, and Denver simply nodded again.

The detective slumped into his chair and handed Denver one of the cups, saying, "I checked in with headquarters, and we don't have any news on Pelletier yet. The sister and her lawyer have come in, though, so they're getting her statement right now. I imagine . . ."

Chantal followed Veilleux's gaze as his words trailed off. The doctor who'd spoken to the Gagnons earlier was striding back into the waiting room, his expression unreadable.

She held her breath as he approached the couple and started speaking to them. And then her eyes began to tear up as Mrs. Gagnon broke into sobs.

"Denver," she murmured, her voice cracking, "he didn't make it."

Veilleux rose and started across the room. Denver wrapped his arms around Chantal and drew her to him, saying, "Honey, there was nothing more we could have done."

She sat crying into his shoulder, trying unsuccessfully to regain control, until a man's voice said, "Chantal?"

She took a deep breath and looked up.

The Gagnons were standing in front of the couch. Hélène was still sobbing, and it took Chantal a moment, through her own tears, to realize Claude was grinning. Took another moment for his words to register.

"The doctor says our son is going to be fine," he said. "He's awake and alert and talking."

"But... but I thought..." Chantal stammered, gazing at Hélène.

"Oh, thank God," Denver whispered, hugging Chantal again. "We did it, honey. We did it."

"My wife just broke down with relief," Claude explained. "We're going up to see René now. But we can never thank you two enough. I'd like to give you a reward. I—"

"No," Denver said, rising and shaking the other man's hand. "That's not at all necessary. We're only glad we could help. And I can't tell you how happy it makes us to know René's okay."

"Well, if there's anything I can ever do for either of you..."

Claude continued speaking to Denver while Hélène sat down beside Chantal and hugged her, still crying but managing to murmur her own thanks.

Finally, her husband took her hand and said their son would be waiting for them. "Try to stop crying, Hélène," he added, "we want René to know how happy we are to have him safely back."

"Claude," Chantal said, "there *is* one thing you could do for us."

"Anything."

"Well, I...would it be all right if Denver and I said hello to René? After you've seen him? Just for a minute?"

"Of course. Of course. He'll want to thank you himself. My son...my son is a polite little boy," he added, a single stray tear escaping down his cheek.

CHAPTER TWELVE

"I WISH I'D BEEN AWAKE," René said, propped up against his pillows and grinning. "I wish I could have seen the dogs."

Denver simply sat, watching him in amazement. Kids sure were resilient. No one would ever guess the boy had just been through a week or so that must have been terrifying for him.

"You know what?" Chantal said. "I've got some videotape of the dogs. Not of them rescuing you, but if you'd like to see them, I could send you a copy when I get back to New York."

"Would you?"

"Sure."

"And you know what my mom said?"

"What," Chantal asked.

"She said I can get a dog of my own. I've always wanted one but she used to say they were too much trouble. But I guess your dogs showed her different."

Chantal laughed and said she'd tell Brandy and McGee how wonderful they were.

"And you'll thank them for me, too?"

"Yes, I'll thank them for you, too."

A nurse popped her head into the room and said, "Some people need to rest for a while, now."

Chantal rose, clearly reluctant to leave, and Denver reached for her hand, saying, "Bye, René. You take care of yourself, huh?"

"Yes, you do that," Chantal told him. She hesitated a second, then leaned over and gave him a quick kiss on the cheek. "And I'll send you that tape just as soon as I get home," she told him again.

"Thanks...thanks for everything," he added as they left.

"Happy?" Denver asked on their way down the hallway. Not that the question was necessary. Chantal hadn't stopped smiling for a second in the past half hour. Now she smiled up at him and said, "You know I'm happy. René's a real sweetie, isn't he?"

"Sure is."

They stopped to wait for an elevator, and Chantal glanced at the pay phone in the corner, then asked what time it was.

"Almost four."

"And we left the chalet before eight. Think the phones back there are working yet? We should probably try to see what's happening."

"You might as well have a shot at it," he said, then stood watching while she dialed.

When she gave him a quick nod, saying she'd gotten a connection, he wandered over to the window and stood looking down at the street, thinking the last place in the world he wanted to go was back to the Bristows'.

It had been a long day, and he wasn't up to facing the romantic triangle again. Or maybe that wasn't the right term for those three. Whatever, all he wanted was to be alone with Chantal.

He heard her hanging up and turned.

"The power's been back on there for an hour or so," she said. "The road's been plowed, Marlene and Jay have left, and Nolton has a helicopter coming to pick him up any minute now. I . . . I told him we'd probably stay the night. He wasn't very pleased about that, but I said it was too late to drive back to New York today. Staying's okay with you, isn't it?"

He nodded, eyeing her uncertainly, trying to decide what the problem was. Her expression was distinctly unhappy, even though everything she'd said sounded like good news. Fantastic news, in fact. Suddenly, the chalet was topping his list of places he wanted to go.

"Staying is far better than okay," he finally said. "It's great. With everyone else gone, we'll be alone together—all night long. But you don't look as if . . . Chantal, am I missing something here?"

"It's Brandy," she said. "Nolton wants you to deliver her to his apartment as soon as we get back to the city. He said, and I quote, 'Tell Denver if I'm not there to just leave her with the doorman.' Like she was nothing more than a package," she added, her voice breaking a little.

He nodded slowly. "Chantal, she is *his* dog."

"Well, she shouldn't be. And we both know that's only until his blasted commercials are shot. It's just not right."

"Chantal, I'll talk to Nolton, okay? I won't leave Brandy there without talking to him and working something out."

She gazed at him for a long moment, then said, "You think you'll get anywhere? At least make him promise he's still going to let you find her a good home."

"Don't worry. I'll take care of it," he said, trying to sound confident.

He must have succeeded, because she smiled at him again as the elevator door opened, making him feel more than a little guilty. She apparently had far more confidence in his powers of persuasion than he did.

When they reached the main floor, Detective Veilleux was waiting.

"I'm here to reroute you," he told them. "There are about twenty reporters outside, but there's a side door that opens onto the parking lot.

"If any of them catch you," he added as they started down a corridor, "just tell them no comment. We don't want François hearing on radio or TV that we've identified him as one of the kidnappers."

They walked a few more yards, then Veilleux glanced at Chantal, saying, "You were asking earlier what would happen to Pierrette."

"Yes. Have you heard anything?"

"Just got off the phone from Montreal. The word is she probably won't stand trial. Her lawyer had her volunteer to be a Crown witness. He must have convinced her François is a lost cause. So even if she's charged as an accessory, probably the worst she'd be looking at is a suspended sentence."

"Oh, that's really good news," Chantal said.

Veilleux grinned at her. "Because it means you two won't be stuck coming up to Montreal to testify?"

"No," she said, laughing, "because I'm sure Pierrette was dragged into the whole thing against her will. And that she mostly went along with François because she was afraid of what would happen to René if she didn't."

"Well," Veilleux said, "if that's true, the Crown won't likely charge her at all. It's François they'll want to nail to the wall."

They stopped at the door, and the detective shook their hands. "Thanks again for all your help. And I expect you'll be hearing from us soon. There's bound to be some sort of civic award for rescuing the boy."

Chantal said it was the dogs who deserved the award, and Denver practically groaned, thinking back to what Nolton had said this morning, about hoping Brandy would save someone's life so he could use the story in his advertising campaign.

Hell, Nolton would probably have every one of his stupid commercials start with a shot of the certificate or plaque or whatever it was. "Come on," he said, taking Chantal's arm, "let's get going before those reporters spot us."

They said a final goodbye to Veilleux, then headed across the parking lot to the truck and made it to the street unnoticed.

The snowplows and salt trucks had obviously been out in full force, so the trip back to Pierrette's, to pick up the dogs, would probably take only half as long as getting to the hospital had. And then they'd head for the chalet...and there'd be only the two of them there.

Denver glanced across at Chantal once they'd turned onto the highway, scarcely able to believe they were together without a hundred other people around.

"Denver," she said, "you *do* think finding René had to be the end of all our excitement up here, don't you? There can't possibly be anything more that can happen, can there?"

"Oh, I don't know. I was thinking of some pretty exciting things that could happen when we get back to the chalet."

She simply smiled again, but it was a smile that started his heart racing and his blood pumping like crazy. "You know," he said, "the road's in far better shape now. There's no reason I need to keep both hands on the wheel."

"Oh? And what would you like to do with the free one?" she teased.

"Well, if you moved a little closer, I could put my arm around you."

"Or, if I moved a lot closer, I could put *both* my arms around you." She moved a lot closer, stroking the side of his neck with her fingertips, then tracing his jaw, murmuring that he hadn't shaved today.

Her breath, soft and warm against his neck, sent a rush of excitement through him.

He tried not to notice how easily she'd aroused him and said he hadn't shaved yesterday, either. "There was the small matter of no hot water. Guess I look pretty scruffy, huh?"

"A little rough trade," she admitted.

"Guess you don't like that, huh?"

"Guess again," she whispered, easing down the zipper of his snowmobile suit, then smoothing her hand across his chest, making him wish they were already at Nolton's place.

"Maybe I shouldn't be doing this while you're driving," she murmured. "It isn't really safe, is it?"

"It's okay," he said quickly. "I'll keep both hands on the wheel."

She unbuttoned a button on his shirt, slipped her fingers through the space and tangled them in his chest hair.

He put his hand on her thigh and began caressing it, thinking that if she weren't wearing that damned, thick suit ...

"I thought you were going to keep both hands on the wheel," she whispered, pressing even closer and nuzzling his neck.

He swallowed hard, keeping both hands right where they were and shoving his foot down on the accelerator.

Making love to Chantal last night, even in that freezing chalet, had been incredible. But the heat was back on now. The next time they made love, they'd be in a nice warm room...in a nice warm bed...assuming Chantal didn't get him so crazy he'd have to stop the pickup someplace along the highway.

"What are you smiling about?" she said.

"Oh...just thinking how nice and hot we're going to be when we get to the chalet."

DENVER WHEELED UP Pierrette's driveway, parked in front of the house, and they hurried in out of the cold, greeted by the sound of Brandy and McGee barking from behind the basement door.

"It's obvious they want up," Chantal said. She started down the hall, but Denver caught her hand and stopped her.

She glanced back at him and laughed. It was obvious what he wanted, too.

"They can stand it down there for a minute longer," he said. "But I doubt I can stand a minute longer without kissing you."

He drew her to him, kissing her with a hungry, yearning kiss. He tasted deliciously of fresh cold combined with hot desire. Lord, but she wished they were at Nolton's right now instead of Pierrette's.

"Good gawd, you drive me crazy," he finally murmured. "Let's get the dogs and go to the chalet."

They headed along the hall, Denver shoved the kitchen door open... and they froze in their tracks.

Chantal simply stood staring at the man, her heart pounding, her brain screaming they were about to die.

There was no mistaking who he was. Not with that angry scar slashing across his cheek. They were face-to-face with François Pelletier, and he was pointing a revolver at them.

She tried to force her gaze away from François, tried to look at Denver, but her eyes wouldn't move. They seemed mesmerized by the scar's ugliness.

François gestured with his gun, motioning them the rest of the way into the room, and she found her legs wouldn't do what she wanted them to, either.

Denver took her hand and dragged her forward a few steps.

"Qui êtes-vous?" François demanded.

"Ah...do you speak English?" Denver asked, sounding as if someone were strangling him.

"Oui. Who are you?"

Denver cleared his throat, then said they were friends of Pierrette's, shooting Chantal a quick, sidelong glance that told her he wanted to try bluffing their way out of this.

She swallowed hard, looking back at François with his gun, certain they didn't have the slightest chance of succeeding. She'd realized, days ago, that neither of them would ever make it as actors.

"And you are...?" Denver was asking François.

"I am Pierrette's brother. So those dogs in the basement, they are yours?"

"Uh-huh, I'm afraid they are. They've been barking? Bothering you?"

"Oui."

Denver said he was sorry about that and yelled at them to be quiet. "They don't like being in the basement," he explained, "but I didn't want them roaming around loose in Pierrette's house."

"I see." François continued watching them intently, clearly trying to decide what they were doing here and what they knew.

Chantal tried to meet his gaze. His eyes were as black as his leather jacket. As black as his slicked-back hair.

They were such a cold, unfeeling black that she shivered and looked away.

"So…" Denver said, stretching the word into three syllables, almost managing to sound casual, "I guess when you heard us coming in you must have figured we were burglars or something."

He stared meaningfully at the revolver until François slowly lowered it to his side, giving Chantal a shred of hope that he might not kill them, after all.

"*Oui,* that is it. I thought you were burglars. But my sister, she is not with you?"

"No," Denver said, "no, she isn't."

"Where is she?"

Chantal told herself to think. If she could come up with a plausible answer she'd try to speak. But she couldn't even come up with an implausible one.

"Where is she?" Denver repeated François's question, sounding so idiotic that Chantal winced. "Ah…well…" he stammered.

"The hospital," she managed, as an idea popped into her head. "We had to take Pierrette to the hospital…in Trois-Rivières. She…she fell and hurt her wrist."

"And went to the hospital?" François said skeptically.

"Uh, yeah...it...it looked as if her wrist might be broken," Denver said.

"She was waiting to have it X-rayed when we left," Chantal added.

François nodded slowly, finally saying, "When I put my car in the garage, Pierrette's, it was not there. If you drove her, where is her car?"

"Ah...I don't know," Denver said. "Maybe there's something wrong with it. Maybe it's somewhere being fixed."

"I think not. There was nothing wrong with it yesterday."

"Ah...well, I really don't know anything about that," Denver tried.

"I think you do," François said, raising his gun once more, aiming it at Denver's chest.

Chantal's own chest suddenly felt so tight she couldn't breathe.

"And I think," François went on, "you will tell me where Pierrette has gone. And where the boy is."

"The boy?" Denver said.

François cocked the revolver with a deadly click and simply stared at them.

This was it, then. He *was* going to kill them.

Chantal tried to swallow but her throat was every bit as tight as her chest. She couldn't take her gaze off the tiny black hole in the end of the barrel, just stood staring at it, expecting her entire life to start flashing before her eyes any second. She'd never been as terrified as she was this minute.

"Okay," Denver said quietly. "I'll tell you what happened," he went on, his voice so strangely calm she knew he was just as certain as she was that they were about to die. "The boy escaped and got himself hurt. It was him we took to the hospital."

François snarled something in French, and his cheek began to twitch, making the scar look like a long worm writhing grotesquely on his face. "They know who he is?" he demanded.

Denver nodded.

"And they know about me?"

"Yes, they do. Look, the best thing you can—"

Without warning, François slammed his gun at Denver's head, sending him reeling to the floor.

Horror swept Chantal, its intensity paralyzing her for an instant, then she started toward Denver.

One step, half a second, and François grabbed her arm and jerked her to him, twisting her so her back was against his chest, wrapping his arm around her waist and thrusting the gun into her ribs—so hard she cried out.

The dogs were barking furiously again, and François began muttering something about a hostage saving him. And, oh Lord, *she* was going to be that hostage!

She tried to look down, tried to see if Denver was even conscious, but François was shoving her ahead of him, out of the kitchen. She screamed at him to let her go, kicking back as hard as she could and connecting, but all he did was jam the gun barrel into her harder.

They reached the front door. He fumbled with the handle, muttering in French now. She squirmed so much that he couldn't get the knob turned, and he finally flung her against the wall, the impact stunning her.

She managed to regain her balance and wheeled toward the kitchen as François threw the door open. But a hand shoved her against the wall once more.

An instant of confusion, then she realized it was Denver who'd pushed her this time, that he was right there.

Suddenly, everything was a blurred collage of motion and sounds. Denver grabbed François around the throat and wrenched him away from the door, kneeing him in the back and smashing him to the floor.

Flesh thudded, metal crashed, a shot roared, leaving the air vibrating.

A second later motion ceased. All was quiet...and Denver was lying in the hallway...the side of his jacket ripped, a growing, blood-red stain slowly soaking it.

Chantal cried his name, starting to drop to her knees beside him, but François grabbed her hair and yanked her back up.

He shoved her outside, then began dragging her toward the garage.

She had to get back to Denver. Had to help him. Had to be sure he wasn't...no, he couldn't be dead. He just couldn't be.

She did her best to ignore the tears stinging her eyes, the lump choking her throat, and tried to pull away from François again, tried with all her might. But his grip was too strong. He merely jerked her forward and snarled that she could either cooperate or he'd kill her here and now.

She told herself he wouldn't do that. He wanted a hostage. But in the heat of the moment he might forget that.

They reached the garage. He pushed her inside ahead of him, pinning her against a big black car while he opened the driver's door.

"Get in," he snarled, shoving her so hard her ribs smashed against the steering wheel.

Quickly, she crawled past it. If she were fast enough, maybe she could escape out the passenger's side. Then François grabbed her hair again and pulled her back beside him, pressing his gun to her ribs once more.

"You just sit right here," he muttered. "Try anything else and you're dead."

The engine roared to life. Chantal stared out through her tears as they shot past the house. Denver was inside. Maybe dying. Maybe dead.

DENVER DRAGGED HIMSELF along the hall, reaching the door just in time to see an old black Cadillac fishtail from the driveway onto the highway.

"Oh, God," he whispered, catching a glimpse of Chantal's honey colored hair. He grabbed the doorframe and pulled himself to his feet. His side felt like it was on fire, but the pickup was parked only a few yards away. He could make it that far. He *had* to make it that far.

He stumbled across the porch and down the two steps, almost falling, but managed to lurch across to the truck and haul himself into the cab. He fumbled with the key, finally getting it into the ignition.

The engine grumbled to life, then stalled. Denver swore, trying again, praying he hadn't flooded it.

This time it caught and held. He wrenched the wheel to the left, stomping on the gas, and the searing pain that knifed through his side made him groan.

By the time he reached the highway, the Caddy was nothing more than a black speck racing in the opposite direction from Trois-Rivières and Montreal.

He wheeled onto the road, pain stabbing him again, then straightened the truck out and floored the accelerator, blessing the pickup's power as it sprang forward. God, but he hoped that old Caddy wasn't souped-up.

He kept his foot to the mat and his eyes straight ahead, until he was certain it wasn't simply his imagination saying that he was gaining on François. François and Chantal. The thought of her in that car...and François with a gun...oh, God, if anything happened to her...

He was closing on them rapidly now, the pickup quivering, the speedometer's needle so far past a hundred he didn't want to look at it. The tachometer was almost red-lining at sixty-five hundred.

If he hit a patch of ice going this fast...but he couldn't think about that. All that mattered was stopping the Caddy without getting Chantal killed.

The faint wail of a siren caught his ear, and he glanced into the mirror. In the distance, a car was trailing him, blue-and-white roof lights flashing. But he was far closer to the Caddy than the cop car was to him.

What the hell was he going to do, though, when he caught up to François? The truck had enough weight to force that Caddy off the road. But he couldn't do that. Not at this speed. Not when Chantal was in the car.

He was only a couple of car lengths back now. Decision time. He shifted into the left lane, barely breathing as the truck drew even with the car. If he could just pull in front of it, just slow it down...

Then pain shot from his side through his entire body as metal scraped metal, as the steering wheel tore at his hands and the truck swerved. That bastard François was trying to send him into the ditch!

Next time he'd have to be ready for it. Next time the cab of the truck had to be far enough ahead.

Denver barely managed to get the pickup under control before the Caddy rammed into its side again.

The impact jolted pain through him once more. The scream of grinding metal against metal drowned out the engine's roar.

He gave the steering wheel a quick twist to the right, praying the old car's structure was still solid. The pickup spun sideways in front of the car. Another searing jolt as the Caddy's grill locked under the truck's rear wheel well.

For one horrible second, he thought the pickup's momentum was going to tear it free and he'd go smashing into the frozen snowbanks that were rushing by. But the locked metal held...and now the Caddy was forced to push the truck's deadweight before it.

They began to slow. The siren wailing behind them was quickly growing louder. And then a horrendous blast shattered the passenger's window of the pickup. François was shooting at him.

Denver hit the floor in a hail of glass, crying out with pain that quickly dissolved into black nothingness.

DENVER FOLLOWED CHANTAL stiffly from the back seat of the car Detective Veilleux was using, still thinking they were lucky to be alive. If it hadn't been for that cop, hot on their tail for speeding, François would undoubtedly have done them in on the side of the road.

He took Chantal's hand and smiled at her through the evening darkness. Her hair seemed pure gold in the glow of yellow light coming from Pierrette's porch.

"I'd like to hug you," she whispered, "but I think we'd both regret it."

He nodded, trying to ignore the pain in his side. According to the doctor in Trois-Rivières who'd stitched him up, the bullet had merely grazed him. Mere graze or not, though, it hurt like hell. And Chantal was pretty bruised from being roughed up by François, then bounced around in the Caddy.

Veilleux walked around the car to them and gestured at the marked car that was going to transport Brandy and McGee back to the chalet. "Want André to go in and get the dogs for you?"

Denver said, "Thanks, but they'd probably bowl him over after being in that basement all this time." He started for the house, Chantal's hand still in his.

Veilleux fell into step beside them, saying, "I have to admit I'm starting to feel a little repetitious, thanking you two. But if you ever want a job with a police department anywhere, feel free to use me as a reference."

"We'll keep that in mind," Denver said. "I doubt I could take many days like today, though."

"Fortunately," Veilleux told them, "there aren't many days like today. But we really do appreciate everything you've done. Pelletier won't be a free man again until he's old and gray, if then. If you two hadn't come by here, though...well, once he learned René had escaped, François would have tried to drop out of sight."

"What made him come back from Montreal, anyway?" Chantal asked.

"His partner realized it was too hot for them to make contact with Claude Gagnon."

"His partner," Denver repeated. "Have you identified him yet?"

"Not yet. François wasn't talking much. But he will, once we convince him things will be harder on him if he doesn't." The dogs began barking excitedly when they heard the front door opening, and they'd only marginally calmed down by the time Denver got them scrunched into the back of the police car.

"You know the Bristow chalet, André?" Veilleux asked the officer in the driver's seat.

The man nodded, glancing unhappily back at the drooling dogs.

"We'll see you there, then," Veilleux said.

Chantal gave Brandy a final pat, murmured to her that she wasn't to howl, and closed the door.

The officer started his engine and Brandy began wailing. With a final, tortured look at Veilleux, André headed down the driveway.

CHAPTER THIRTEEN

VEILLEUX GAZED AFTER the departing police car for a moment, listening to Brandy howl, then turned, laughing, to Chantal and Denver. "That's a trained dog, is it? If André switched his siren on, she'd drown it out."

"She still needs a little work," Denver said as they climbed into the detective's car.

When they hit the highway, Veilleux glanced back at Denver. "You really going to feel up to driving home tomorrow?"

"I have to," he said. "I've got a pregnant bitch about ready to whelp, and I really don't want my kennel sitters having to deal with that."

Chantal glanced down at Denver's hand, holding hers, his words echoing uneasily in her mind. Tomorrow they'd be going back to their two separate worlds.

And then . . . then what? Denver hadn't said a single word about the future. He'd said he loved her, though. Didn't that have to mean . . . ?

She looked over at him, suddenly seized by the most dreadful feeling that falling in love up here, and having a future back home, weren't necessarily one and the same. And for the remainder of the trip home, she couldn't shake off the sinking sense that tomorrow was going to be the beginning of the end.

When they reached the chalet, she halfheartedly offered Veilleux coffee.

"Thanks, but I'll just get going," he said. "You both look as if you could use a good night's rest. Thanks again for everything," he added, shaking their hands, then giving Brandy and McGee quick pats.

Halfway to his car he paused, glancing back. "You two make a good team. Take care of each other, eh?"

"Think that's true?" Chantal asked quietly as they went inside.

"What is?"

"That we make a good team."

"I think, Ms. Livingstone, we make a fantastic team. And I'd give anything to spend the night showing you just *how* fantastic. But these stitches pull whenever I move, and every inch of me is aching."

She nodded slowly. "Me, too. Every inch. I think I'll take a hot shower and see if that helps."

Denver gave her a rueful smile. "If my chest wasn't wrapped up like a mummy, I'd join you. Guess I'll just get cleaned up as well as I can in the en suite."

Chantal headed upstairs, grabbed a clean nightshirt from her bedroom, then stripped off her clothes and stood under the pulsating water, trying to wash away the memories of François's hands on her, of her terror that he'd kill both her and Denver.

Those memories would be a long time fading, though, so she mostly tried not to think about how much she wished Denver were right here with her now, tried not to imagine how wonderful his touch would feel on her wet skin.

Finally, she shut off the water, dried herself and tugged on her nightshirt. She reached for the door handle, then stopped.

Last night, she'd slept in Denver's bed. But tonight he'd made it clear he wasn't up to making love. And even if he was, she just didn't know...Lord, tonight she just didn't seem to know anything.

She started along the hall, pausing uncertainly at his doorway. The dogs were curled together in one corner, and Denver was sitting up in bed, the top edge of the bandaging visible around his chest. He looked so incredibly desirable she felt a warm rush merely gazing at him.

"Hey," he said, "what are you doing standing out there when you should be in here?"

"I...well, I thought maybe...with your stitches and all..."

"You didn't think a little pain would keep me away from you entirely, did you?"

She managed a smile and started over to the bed, feeling a strange urge to both cry and laugh. He took her hand and she slipped into bed beside him.

"Hey," he murmured, grazing her cheek with his fingers, "that's a nasty bruise. Must hurt."

"You didn't think a little pain would keep me away from you, did you?" she whispered.

"I'd like it if nothing would keep you away from me," he murmured, turning off the light and smoothing his hands possessively down her body. His touch made her quiver, and he kissed her so tenderly that the silly urge to cry grew almost overwhelming.

Too soon, he drew away, then gingerly cuddled her to him. "I like this," he murmured, brushing her neck ever so lightly with his lips. "I'd like to hold you forever."

He'd like to, she thought, loving his warmth against her. If only he'd say he intended to.

CHANTAL GAZED AROUND the chalet a final time, half listening to Denver on the phone. He was telling one of his kennel sitters he'd be home later today.

"And Tara's okay?" he was asking. "No signs she's getting close?"

He listened for a moment, finally saying, "Then there's nothing to worry about. I'll call again when we get to Manhattan.

"Know what day it is?" he asked, hanging up and glancing across at Chantal.

She thought for a moment and guessed Wednesday.

"Actually, it's Tuesday. But that's not what I was getting at. It's December thirty-first."

"Really?" she said, thinking that meant they'd met only six days ago. How could she conceivably have fallen so deeply in love so quickly?

She didn't know how, only knew she had. Just waking up in bed with Denver this morning, remembering he might have been killed yesterday...

"I hadn't realized it was New Year's Eve, either," he was saying. "It's a good thing I called, though. The older kid has a big party on, and he was getting worried I'd want them both there, that he'd be seeing the New Year in with only his brother and the dogs for company. I...ah, I guess you must have plans for tonight, huh?"

She gazed at him, trying not to smile, finding she couldn't help it. How could he possibly think she wouldn't change any plans she might have had to be with him? And how could she possibly have been thinking he might simply walk out of her life once they got back? His question about tonight, and the way he was looking at her, were sending an entirely different message.

"I was invited to a party," she said. "But I didn't promise to be there. Wasn't sure I'd be back in the city."

He grinned at her, then crossed the room and draped his arms around her waist. "So, how would you feel about spending New Year's Eve at a kennel? I want you to see my place."

He wanted her to see his place. The words began zipping around in her head, each zip making her happier.

"We could pick up some champagne," he added, as if she needed coaxing.

"Well...I guess," she teased. "As long as you promise me something better than Bristow Fine."

"Better than Bristow Fine shouldn't be hard at all," he murmured, bending to kiss her.

Vaguely, she thought how amazing it was that even a gentle kiss like this one started her wanting him. But she could feel the bandaging through his sweater and made do with snuggling gently against him when the kiss ended.

"And you'll stay with me till tomorrow night?" he said. "There's no one in the world I'd rather start the new year with than you."

"Mmm...yes, I'll stay. But only because I'll need time to figure out the difference between Julie, Lily and Tara."

He grinned at her again, saying, "Tara will be a cinch By now, her stomach must be almost dragging on the ground."

"Oh, well, if I'm only going to find two of them confusing, maybe I won't have to stay over."

"Chantal..."

"Yes?"

"Honey, don't joke, okay? Not about spending time with me, I mean. Because whenever I start thinking you might not…hell, I don't know how to put this…don't even know if I should try. It's happened so fast it's just too soon to talk about the future, isn't it?''

She pressed her cheek against his chest, reminding herself not to hug him too tightly but feeling an incredible surge of relief. All her worrying really *had* been for nothing. He believed they had a future.

''I mean,'' he went on, ''I know it's too soon to even think about anything permanent. Isn't it?''

''I…I don't know, Denver. A week ago I'd have said this sort of thing was impossible. But now it doesn't seem that way at all.''

He exhaled slowly and smiled down at her—a smile that made her weak in the knees.

''That's good,'' he murmured. ''Because after waking up beside you the past couple of days, I really hate the thought of waking up without you. Look…what I'm trying to say is that I don't want to lose you when we go back. I want us to…Chantal, if we keep on feeling the way we're feeling, I want us to end up together.''

She closed her eyes for a moment, thinking she'd never been so happy in her life.

''Chantal?'' he said anxiously.

She smiled at him. ''Oh, Denver, I don't want to lose you, either. So we won't let it happen. We'll figure out something, some compromise. Lots of couples do. It'll just take us a little time.''

Ideas about how they might manage things began racing madly through her mind. Then she realized Denver was eyeing her uneasily and said, ''What?''

''Ah…it was just the word compromise. Not that I don't believe in compromising,'' he added quickly.

"But...well, I can't help thinking about something you said the other night."

"What was that?"

"You said you love your life, that you couldn't even imagine a different one. And there are some compromises I can't make, Chantal. I can't move the kennel to midtown Manhattan."

"No, no, of course you can't. And I guess compromise wasn't the best word. I only meant there'd be things to work out. For instance, maybe we could think about alternating weekends between Jersey and Manhattan."

Denver nodded slowly, saying, "Yeah, I could arrange weekend help for a while. But...hey, maybe now isn't the best time to get into this, huh?"

She gazed at him uncertainly. He was the one who'd started the discussion.

"I mean," he went on, "we don't have to sort everything out at once."

He stood watching her for a minute, as if trying to decide whether he really wanted to drop the subject or not, then said, "Chantal, it's just that...well, in the long run, I don't want some sort of weekends-only relationship. And the kennel's over seventy miles from Mad Ave."

"There's commuting," she said slowly, trying not to think about the two-, sometimes three-hour, traffic jams getting in and out of Manhattan during rush hour.

"Uh-huh...there's commuting."

That was all he said, but she heard what he hadn't said—loud and clear. In that "long run" he was thinking about, he figured she wouldn't be able to stand the commute. And she suspected he was right.

But she couldn't imagine there were many advertising agencies around Somerville, New Jersey. And she couldn't imagine changing her entire life. There had to be other possibilities, though.

"Denver," she finally said, "I think you were right about not having to sort everything out at once. There are probably all kinds of options we could consider."

"Uh-huh, there probably are...ah, can you think of any? Just offhand?"

"Well...I don't know...maybe we could somehow live in both places?"

"The kennel's a full-time job, Chantal. I have to be there most of the time."

"Well...what if you hired someone out there and did more work for advertising agencies? It would mean you'd be spending more time in New York and..." She stopped speaking, realizing Denver was shaking his head.

"Chantal, the only reason I do advertising work is because I can use the extra money. But I don't need *that* much extra. Honey, I've made my choice about how I want to live my life. And being a money-grubber just isn't it. And spending any more time than I do on Mad Ave *definitely* isn't it."

She stared down at the floor, thinking that the relief she'd felt, only minutes ago, had been premature. There was no guarantee at all that they'd be able to work anything out. Denver was being completely one-sided.

Maybe she should call him on it. She considered that, then decided to wait until she'd had a chance to think. But from what he was saying, any future for them would involve him continuing to live his life precisely the way he was and her doing every bit of the compromising. And she didn't know if she'd ever be prepared to do that.

"Hey," he said, tilting her chin up with his fingers, "how did we get into such a downer of a conversation? You were right. We'll work something out. The important thing is that we love each other, huh?"

She nodded slowly. There was no doubting that. But was loving each other enough?

Then Denver bent and kissed her... and made her wonder how she could possibly think it might not be.

"Come on," he said after he'd kissed her half senseless, "we'd better hit the road. Don't want all the good champagne to be sold out."

They locked the chalet and headed over to the van. Brandy and McGee were waiting inside, both peering expectantly out the windows.

When Denver slid open the passenger door, Brandy stuck her head between the seats and greeted Chantal with a loud snuffle. It made her throat tighten. By the time Denver climbed into the driver's seat, she was fighting tears.

He glanced over and asked what was wrong.

"Denver, I've been forgetting about Brandy. But I don't want to take her to Nolton's. I really, really don't."

"We don't have any choice," he said, reaching for her hand. "You wouldn't want us charged with dognapping, would you?"

She tried to smile but could feel the corners of her mouth turning down instead of up. "Well... well, we could keep her for another day, couldn't we? Take her to your place with us for the night?"

"That wouldn't make things any easier, Chantal. Not for you and not for her."

"But—"

"Tell you what," he said, "I'll call Nolton when we get to your house. If he's not home, we'll keep her with us. And if he's there, I'll take her over and talk to him about her."

"But what if he won't listen? What if he tells you to get lost?"

"Honey, everything's going to be all right. He'll have calmed down by now. And after his commercials are shot, I'll find her a terrific home. You'll see."

"Promise?" she murmured.

"Promise," he said.

DUSK WAS GATHERING when Denver pulled off the parkway onto Riverside Drive.

Chantal gazed absently out at the familiar sights. On their right, the Hudson was quiet, its water gray. Actually, everything was gray, from the sky right down to the slush-covered ground.

Manhattan seemed incredibly dirty after the pure white snow they'd left behind. But at least the city had started coming brightly alive for the evening. And reflections of lights from the far shore were beginning to sparkle faintly in the river.

That was New Jersey over there, of course. Across the Hudson, somewhere to the southwest, lay Denver's kennel.

She looked at him, trying once again to convince herself that things would somehow work out. They just *had* to. She loved him too much for them not to.

She'd have liked to have talked more about exactly *how* they'd work out, but Denver had been as quiet as on the trip up, had switched into his strong and silent mode before they'd even reached the border this morning. It was almost as if he'd been a different person up north.

A different person . . . she forced away that thought. She was being absurd. Regardless of where Denver was, or where she was, they were the same people.

He glanced at her and asked what she was thinking.

"The truth?"

"Uh-huh."

"I was thinking how much I love you."

"Then just carry on," he said, grinning at her.

"That wasn't the *only* thing I was thinking," she teased.

"What else?"

"Oh, I was remembering the night we talked about life-styles . . . about how you didn't figure mine was the greatest. And I was thinking there are going to be changes in it, because of you. And thinking that maybe one change could be...well, your suggestion that I buy Brandy from Nolton. Maybe I *could* manage a dog. So . . . you still think it would be a good idea?"

Denver reached across and took her hand, saying, "I think it would be a terrific idea. I'll talk to him about it tonight, huh?"

She nodded, looking back at the sleeping dogs and feeling far better.

But the good feeling dissipated when they pulled up in front of her town house. Then Denver said they'd just leave the dogs in the van while he phoned Nolton.

He reached for the champagne he'd bought at the duty-free. "Might as well let this chill in your fridge for a while," he said, opening his door.

She swallowed hard and reached into the back to pat Brandy goodbye, worrying about what would happen to her if Nolton didn't go for their idea.

The dog wiggled her behind and tried to push between the seats.

"Oh, Brandy," she murmured, leaning down and wrapping her arms around the furry neck. "You be a good girl."

She could barely get the words out past the lump in her throat, so she simply hugged the dog for another minute, then gave McGee a quick pat and got out of the van. She followed Denver across the sidewalk and up the steps, trying unsuccessfully to keep her tears from escaping.

"You going to be okay?" he asked, brushing them from her cheeks once they were inside.

"I guess so. I just feel so badly for her. She's going to hate it in that penthouse with Nolton, you know."

"It'll only be for a few weeks. I wouldn't be surprised if he's already got Carruthers and Headly hard at work on his damned ad campaign."

She nodded, glancing into the hall mirror, knowing she must look awful. Even so, she was taken aback by her reflection.

"You look like you're seeing a ghost," Denver said.

"I . . . I don't look like me." She tried to smooth her hair, but it insisted on staying fluffed out every which way.

"I think you look great," Denver told her, setting down the champagne and gently wrapping his arms around her from behind. "I like the casual look."

She continued staring at the woman in the mirror. Hair a mess. No makeup. An unsightly bruise on her cheek. One of Denver's far-too-large sweaters hanging shapelessly past her hips. And he liked this look?

But... but it wasn't her. The last time she'd looked anything like this was after she'd spent three days in bed with the flu.

Her gaze flickered to Denver's reflection and she thought once more about how quiet he'd been on the trip back. But it wasn't actually possible they'd been different people up north. Wasn't actually possible they'd each fallen in love with someone who didn't exist in the real world. No, of course it wasn't.

Denver kissed the top of her head and asked where the phone was, so she dragged her eyes from the mirror, telling herself not to think like a crazy lady, and led him down the hall to the living room.

He paused in the doorway and whistled quietly.

"What?" she said.

"This is nice. I mean, I realized that the first time. I just didn't realize it was quite so... you didn't decorate it yourself, did you?"

She nodded, glancing around the familiar room, trying to see it through Denver's eyes.

Undoubtedly too feminine for his taste—all pastels and raw silks. The fireplace smooth pale marble. And white Berber wasn't carpeting you'd choose if you owned dogs. Undoubtedly it wouldn't take Brandy long to turn the white into off-white.

"The phone's over there," she said, gesturing toward her desk.

Denver stared at it for a moment, then said, "That looks like it belongs in the Met. A reproduction?"

"No, it's a real antique," she told him, suddenly feeling guilty because it was.

"Beautiful," he said. "Ah... Chantal, my kennel's nothing like this."

She smiled at him. "I didn't imagine a house in the Jersey countryside would be much like a Manhattan town house."

"No...I mean it's *nothing* like this. *My* desk is a beat-up old oak thing. And its legs are covered with puppies' teeth marks."

"Distressed."

"Pardon?"

"You know, when antiques have worm holes, the wood's referred to as distressed." She'd hoped that would make him laugh, but it didn't.

He simply said, "Yeah, well you'd be hard-pressed to find a desk any more distressed than mine. But what I'm trying to say is I don't want you to be disappointed. My place needs a little work. In fact, it needs a complete renovation. I just haven't had either the time or money to get going on it."

"All right. Pre-renovation. I'm forewarned." He finally smiled at her, but his smile seemed uncertain. Or maybe her imagination was playing games.

"Guess I'd better make that call," he said. "You've got Nolton's number?"

"In the book on the desk," she said, then stood watching him dial, hoping Nolton wouldn't be home.

That was silly, of course. Denver had been right. He'd arrange for her to buy Brandy, so she'd be here permanently in no time. And keeping her with them for another day now wouldn't really make much sense.

Then Denver said, "Hello, Nolton?" and whether or not it would make sense didn't matter.

She retrieved the champagne from the hall table and made space for it on the door of the fridge. By the time she returned, Denver was hanging up.

"All set," he said. "I'll head over to Nolton's now. But you don't mind if I just check in with the kennel, do you? Leave them this number in case anything comes up before we get on our way?"

"No, of course not."

While he made the second call, she remembered that she'd promised to phone her parents as soon as she got home. She'd make it quick, though, and leave time to get herself looking human before Denver got back. That would make her feel better. Maybe she'd put on her new black silk dress. After all, this was New Year's Eve. And she'd be spending it with the man she loved.

"Everything's fine at home," he said, hanging up, "so I'll get going. Should be back in less than an hour, easy."

She walked him to the door, resisting the urge to go outside with him. Saying another goodbye to Brandy would only leave her feeling worse.

Once Denver had driven off, she went back to the living room and dialed her parents' number.

"Hi, I'm back," she said when her mother answered.

"Oh, I'm glad, dear. I was starting to think you'd miss seeing the family tomorrow."

"Ah..." Damn, she hadn't even thought about New Year's dinner. And if Denver had to drive her from the kennel to her parents' place...should she invite him?

"Is anything wrong, Chantal?"

"No. I just...well, I might bring a friend, Mom. Would that be all right?"

"Of course, dear. Someone I know?"

"No...actually, he's the fellow I went to Quebec with."

"Oh?" her mother said curiously.

"Yes, he turned out to be…well, he turned out to be very nice." She smiled to herself, thinking how much beyond very nice Denver had turned out to be.

"Your trip was enjoyable, then?" her mother said.

"Yes…enjoyable."

"That's lovely, dear. We'll look forward to meeting him. Come before six, all right? You know how your Uncle Harry can't bear to miss the news, and you'll want time to say hello to everyone before the television goes on."

"Before six. But, Mom…my friend might not come. I haven't asked him yet, and he may already be busy."

"Well, you ask him and see, Chantal. There's always room at the table for one more. And what about tonight, dear? You have plans?"

"I…yes, I'm spending the evening with him."

"Oh." This time, Chantal could hear a smile in her mother's voice.

"See you tomorrow, Mom," she said, smiling herself. "Give my love to Dad," she added before they said goodbye.

She hung up slowly, realizing she had no idea how Denver would feel about meeting her family. Especially en masse. Maybe inviting him wouldn't be wise. But if she didn't, she'd have to spend the evening without him. And she didn't want to spend a single minute without him if she didn't absolutely have to. Not another single minute of her entire life.

CHAPTER FOURTEEN

DENVER PARKED in the first space he came to past the town house, then sat gazing into the darkness, not wanting to go in and face Chantal. They were still so new together that he wasn't always sure how she'd react to things, but right now he had no doubt about how unhappy she was going to be.

He glanced at McGee, saying, "What am I going to do, fella? Get it over with right away or wait?"

He reached back to scratch behind the dog's ear, knowing there really wasn't any choice. The minute he walked in, she'd ask. And lying to her would just be stupid. Reluctantly, he got out of the van.

Chantal had obviously been watching for him because she opened her front door as he reached the steps. When he didn't even try to smile, her expectant expression faded.

She closed the door behind him and waited—the way she was looking at him making him certain she was going to cry if he said the wrong words. But there were no right words.

He shrugged, feeling like a total failure, and said, "Honey, Nolton told me to go to hell. I hardly even got to the part about your buying Brandy. He doesn't want anything more to do with either of us."

He'd been right. A tear trickled down her cheek. He stepped forward and folded her into his arms, wincing a little even though she barely leaned any weight on him.

"Look," he tried, "when Nolton *does* sell her, the Kennel Club will record the ownership transfer. If you want, we can try to buy her from her new owners."

"Oh, Denver," she murmured, gazing up at him, her eyes luminous with tears, "they wouldn't be likely to go for that."

"We can give it a shot."

Chantal nodded, drawing back and wiping her eyes. "I guess we'll just have to see what happens, then do what we can, won't we?"

She kind of smiled—and didn't remind him he'd promised her this morning that he'd work things out with Nolton, even though he knew she remembered. Damn, he loved her so much. He only wished there was something more he could do.

"I was just making coffee," she finally said. "Want some before we start for the kennel?"

"Sure, that'd be great." He followed her down the hall to the kitchen. The far wall was mostly glass. Beyond it, the miniature backyard was awash with garden lights. A stone Japanese lantern stood in one corner, behind a tiny, frozen pool.

The kitchen itself looked as if it should be featured in a glossy magazine... and was about as different from his kitchen as a kitchen could possibly be.

Dog toenails would destroy that white ceramic floor in no time flat, he thought, glancing down. And the table was gleaming glass and brass. It wouldn't last three seconds at the kennel without being covered from beneath with nose prints.

"It'll just be a minute," Chantal said, heading over to the coffeemaker.

Denver looked around, deciding she had every kitchen appliance and gadget known to man, and he couldn't help wondering how she'd feel about washing dog bowls ... by hand. The way she looked right now, he couldn't picture her even loading her dishwasher.

While he was gone, she'd changed into a low-cut black dress that was absolutely sensational. Probably silk. Definitely expensive. She was wearing makeup, too, so carefully applied he could hardly see the bruise on her cheek. And her hair was all smooth, just the way it had been the first moment he'd seen her.

It was almost as if the calendar had been turned back a week. She looked like a glamorous fashion model again. He picked a tuft of McGee's fur off his sweater ... then didn't know where to put it.

Suddenly, he started having trouble imagining Chantal at the kennel. Hell, five minutes after she walked in, that silk dress would be ruined by dog drool.

And what was she going to think of his place? Oh, she'd love the exterior. The fieldstone was what had sold him on sight. But once she got inside ... well, his place definitely had potential. Yeah, it had the old *P* word in spades, but fixing it up was going to take forever.

What had she said when he'd tried to explain the state things were in there? Pre-renovation, that had been her word. "All right," she'd said. "Pre-renovation. I'm forewarned."

But he doubted she really was. Hell, maybe he was out of his mind to even have been thinking what he'd been thinking. Chantal living with him? Bringing her brass-and-glass table and her antique desk to his place?

She carried a formal silver tray over to the table. He glanced at it and added her silver and expensive china to the list of things that would make his surroundings seem even more tacky.

And right now, after the kids had been in charge for a week, the house was bound to look worse than usual. If Chantal walked in there tonight, she'd wonder what the hell she was even thinking of getting herself into.

The last thing he wanted was to scare her off, so maybe they'd better stay here. If he kept her away from the kennel for a while, did a little work before she saw it...

Yes, as soon as he'd finished his coffee he'd call home. The younger of his sitters was a reliable kid. And a sixteen-year-old would be okay on his own for the night, with his parents just down the road.

Chantal glanced across the table, saying, "I just don't know how Nolton can be the way he is."

"You mean how he can be pond scum?"

She laughed at that, and Denver reached over and took her hand. "You know, I'm so damned glad you won't be having anything more to do with that guy. If I'd known about him before I agreed to do those commercials, I'd have told Rachel there was no way."

"Then you and I would never have met."

"Ah...that's true. I guess it was worth putting up with him once, then."

"You guess?" she said quietly.

He laughed, silently reassuring himself. They could make each other laugh, and that would take them a long way. All he had to do was kind of ease her into things...not waltz her into his place when looking at it would be enough to give her culture shock.

"Okay," he said aloud, "it was *definitely* worth putting up with Nolton once. But even if I was stone-broke, there's not enough money in the world to make me work for him again."

"Since he told you to go to hell," she teased, "there isn't much chance he'll ask you to."

"Well, that's true. But if he ever did, my integrity would certainly be more important than the money."

The phone on the counter began ringing, and Chantal rose to answer it. "Yes," she said, "he's right here."

She held out the receiver to him, saying, "It's for you, Mr. Integrity," then moved away and stood watching him, wondering if he always looked so serious on the phone. So serious, but so absolutely gorgeous, she could scarcely keep her hands off him.

She reminded herself he was recovering from a bullet wound, that she'd darned well better keep her hands off him. But a hundred-percent healthy or not, he was filling the room with raw masculinity. Even those scruffy cowboy boots she used to hate, now struck her as mere accents to his virility.

"Sounds like it, all right," he was saying.

He'd only given her number to his kennel sitters, so that had to be who'd called. And even from the one-sided conversation, she knew something was happening with Tara.

"Okay," he said, "I'll leave right now. Be there in plenty of time...yeah, just sit with her in case she starts getting more upset, huh?"

He hung up, saying, "Sounds as if Tara's pups are about ready to face the world."

She smiled across at him. "Playing midwife's going to make this the most unusual New Year's Eve I've ever spent."

"Ah...honey, when I invited you to the kennel, your playing midwife wasn't exactly what I had in mind. I think maybe you'd better just stay here. I'm going to have my hands full tonight."

"That's all right. I don't mind helping."

His expression was saying he doubted that, and when she realized why, she laughed. "I guess a silk dress isn't exactly delivery room scrubs, is it? I'll just run upstairs and change. Then we can—"

"No, Chantal, listen, your coming along really isn't a good idea. This sort of thing can get awfully messy."

"Denver, I honestly don't mind. In fact, I'm really interested."

"Well...see, the thing is that having a stranger there might make Tara nervous. And anyway, this definitely isn't the way I want to introduce you to Brooke Kennels."

She stood watching him for a moment, trying to decide what to say next. Half of her wanted to insist on going with him. The other half was saying that would be a bad idea when he so clearly didn't want her along.

Finally, she quietly said, "Denver, don't worry about me, okay? I don't faint at the sight of blood, and if I make Tara nervous I'll just stay out of the way."

He hesitated for a second, then said, "Okay, but get changed fast, huh?"

She nodded and hurried up the hall to the stairs, wondering whether the strong sense of unease she was feeling was warranted.

BEFORE THEY REACHED Somerville, Denver turned off Highway 22 onto a secondary road. In the back of the van, McGee clambered to his feet and peered expectantly out into the night.

"Almost there," Denver said. "The kennel's just down this road."

This *dark* road, Chantal thought. If the moon weren't shining, it would be as dark as the road to Nolton's chalet.

Of course, the moon *was* shining. And this road's surface was clear and dry. And there weren't huge drifts of snow lying on the roadside fields, only an inch or two. And there was no sign of a Maurice Charlebois clone, but you never knew. "Denver, you don't have any rifle-carrying neighbors who wander around at night, do you?"

He grinned across at her. "I don't have any rifle-carrying neighbors at all. This is a pretty peaceful community. That," he added, pointing to the house they were passing, set back from the road about fifty feet, "is where the kids who've been looking after the kennel live. And this," he said a minute later, slowing the van, "is home."

The headlights captured a weathered split-rail fence on the right. Just behind it stood a stretch of evergreens that concealed the property. Ahead, a driveway was marked with a large hanging sign that read Brooke Kennels Reg. Saint Bernards.

Denver pulled into the drive and she gazed down it, surprised by what she saw. The house was gorgeous. Not the dilapidated farmhouse she'd been imagining, but a fieldstone beauty at least a hundred years old.

A series of landscaped terraces, lightly dusted with snow, reached away from the house and off into the darkness. A rambling front porch, bathed in soft light, ran its entire width, and lights glowed invitingly through the windows.

"Denver, it's beautiful. After what you said, this isn't at all what I expected."

"Well, it isn't the outside that needs work. Not much, anyway. But the interior really is a little rough."

He parked in front of the house, and even before he turned off the engine she could hear barking from inside. Fierce, resounding barking.

"Sounds like the main event hasn't started yet," Denver said. "Tara's barking along with the others."

Behind them, McGee whined impatiently.

"Ready for a little turmoil?" Denver asked. "The girls can be pretty exuberant."

"Ready," she said, opening her door. The barking immediately sounded much louder. If she didn't know there were only three dogs in there, she'd have guessed a lot more. And if she didn't know how gentle Saint Bernards actually were, the idea of going into that house would be unnerving. But she'd gotten used to being around two big dogs. Four couldn't be much more difficult to deal with, could they?

Denver let McGee out, and he bounded ahead onto the porch, barking a deep gruff greeting when he reached the front door. That raised the level of noise inside to an excited frenzy. Chantal followed Denver up the steps, reminding herself once again just how gentle Saint Bernards actually were.

He stuck the key into the door and put his arm securely around her waist, saying he didn't want her getting bowled over, then opened the door, and the porch was suddenly a sea of dogs.

Denver ordered them to calm down, but she couldn't see that it did any good. She felt as if she'd been dropped into an old western, smack dab into the middle of a stampede scene. Only instead of running, bawling cattle, they were surrounded by jumping, barking dogs, with McGee joining right in with the others.

Four, she told herself. It might seem like a dozen, but there were only four of them.

"Quiet!" Denver shouted over the din, and the noise subsided.

"Good dogs," he said. "Now sit."

They sat, and a quick head count assured her there really were only four. Somehow, though, four seemed about ten times as many as two. Maybe it was because one of them—obviously Tara—was so fat she looked about ready to explode.

A teenager appeared in the doorway, a sheepish look on his face, and said, "Sorry about that, Denver. They listen to Ken better, but he's already left for his party."

Denver told him not to worry about it, motioning the dogs inside. "Right into the kitchen," he told them, and they ambled off down the hall.

"Chantal, this is Ron," he said, nodding at the boy and taking her coat.

She barely had time to say hello before Ron was talking to Denver about Tara. "I had her settled in the box," he said, "but when she heard the van there was no keeping her there."

Chantal glanced around while Ron told Denver about how anxious Tara had been for the past couple of hours.

Now that Chantal was inside, she could see what he'd meant about the house needing a complete renovation. He hadn't been exaggerating. It was a gracious center-hall design, but showed the wear and tear of a century.

To either side of the foyer lay the living and dining rooms, their French doors standing ajar...badly scarred

French doors. Each had one or two panes of glass that were cracked.

In one corner of the living room sat his desk, and he hadn't been exaggerating about it, either. She could see the teeth marks in the legs all the way from where she was standing. And the recliner behind it didn't look to be in any better shape.

Ahead, a wide staircase led to the second floor. It would have been imposing once, but now its woodwork was covered with badly chipped paint. She tried to imagine how long it would take to strip and stain all those balusters and came up with a mind-boggling number.

"I'll get her settled back down," Denver was telling Ron. "Her box is in the kitchen," he added, glancing at Chantal. "Just down the hall here."

She headed after the two of them, then paused, seized by a sudden sneeze.

Denver looked back and asked if she was coming down with a cold.

"I don't think so," she said. Then a second sneeze caught her. She blinked rapidly, realizing her eyes were starting to water.

Denver's grin faded as she wiped them. "Allergies," he said. "You told me way back when that you had some allergies, didn't you."

"Only a couple," she said uneasily. Once she got going like this, she didn't magically stop.

"Well, are you going to be okay?"

"Sure," she lied. "It's probably just a little dust. Old houses are sometimes bad for that."

The sheepish expression appeared on Ron's face again and he said, "I guess maybe we should have cleaned a bit."

"That isn't what I pay you for," Denver told him, not taking his gaze off Chantal. "You know, I can actually see your eyes getting redder."

"No, I'm all right. Really. Let's get Tara settled."

He gave her a doubtful look, but started toward the kitchen again. Chantal followed him along the hall, mentally swearing at herself for having the damned allergy. She tried to ignore the way her throat was beginning to feel scratchy. Then her nose started running, and she dug in her pocket for a tissue.

Denver shooed the other dogs out of the kitchen and coaxed Tara into a low-sided, roomy wooden box lined with shredded newspaper. "You're just about there, aren't you baby," he murmured to her, stroking her head.

Chantal tried to stifle another sneeze but couldn't. It was the loudest one yet and was immediately followed by three more.

Tara looked up at her and whined. Chantal rubbed her eyes, said she was sorry, then sneezed once more. This time, Tara growled.

"Ah . . . Chantal . . ." Denver said. "We've got a problem here."

"I'll just get out of the way," she said.

"And do what?" he said sharply. "Sit in the living room and sneeze all night while I'm in here?"

Tara gave an urgent little cry, then began to pant loudly.

Chantal sneezed again and started wishing she were dead.

Denver looked at Ron, saying, "How would you feel about driving into Manhattan and back?"

Ron said, "No problem."

"Oh, no, Denver," Chantal said. "I don't want to go home. Really."

Tara gave another cry—far sharper and louder than the previous one.

"Chantal...I don't have time to argue. Look, I'm really sorry about ruining your New Year's Eve," he said, tossing Ron his keys, "but I know best here, okay? Hell," he added, looking down at the dog, "I don't think I've even got time to walk you to the door. I'll call you first thing in the morning, huh?"

THE CLOCK RADIO CLICKED on mid-song, and Chantal reached for Denver...an instant before she realized she was in her own bed. Alone. For the second morning in a row.

She lay perfectly still, telling herself she shouldn't spend every waking moment thinking about him. She couldn't help it though, because she still hadn't decided whether something was wrong or not. She'd been darned upset about the way he'd unceremoniously sent her packing on New Year's Eve, but after they'd talked...maybe if she let herself relive yesterday's conversation one more time...

He'd phoned first thing in the morning, just as he'd promised. He'd wished her a happy New Year and apologized for being sharp with her the night before. "I just got a little edgy, worrying something might go wrong," he'd said.

She'd decided not to point out that he'd gotten a little bossy, too, and the tension had started to evaporate when he'd begun talking about the pups.

"Nine's a good-sized litter," he told her. "Not too many for Tara to cope with."

"But enough to make a canine baseball team," she said, and he laughed as if he thought she was wonderful.

"Do I get to see them today? I can take some antihistamines," she added anxiously when he didn't answer immediately.

"Ah...Chantal..." he said hesitantly, raising her anxiety level further. "Chantal, I'm dying to see you today, but I've got a million things to do around here. After being gone for a week, I mean. And I have to keep an eye on Tara. And the pups...well, newborn pups look like blind, bald rats. You don't really want to see them just yet."

She considered her options for about two seconds, then said, "Yes, I really do."

There was a long silence before Denver said, "Chantal, the thing is that I don't like leaving a litter alone in the house for the first twenty-four hours. If any problems are going to develop, that's when it happens. So I can't come and get you, then take you back. Not when it's over an hour each way."

"Oh," she said, wondering why he hadn't explained that in the first place, instead of giving her that million-things-to-do line. Maybe she could borrow her father's car...but it wouldn't make much sense to go all the way to Queens and pick it up, then drive all the way to the kennel, when she had to be back in time for the family dinner.

Well, at least she no longer had to worry about how Denver would react to the idea of meeting her relatives. There was no point in inviting him to dinner if he couldn't leave the kennel.

"Denver?" she finally said. "What about tomorrow? Maybe I could come out there after work. I really *do* want to see the pups, bald and ratlike or not." *And,* she added silently, *I really, really want to see you.*

"Tomorrow," he repeated. "Uh-huh, let's figure out something for tomorrow. I'll call you in the morning, okay? Before you leave for work?"

"Great, I'll be up about seven," she told him, breathing a little more easily, telling herself everything was fine.

"I'll call you then. Love you, Chantal."

"Love you, too, Denver."

And those had been their parting words. So why was she lying here, worrying?

The song on the radio ended, and the announcer brought her abruptly back to the moment, saying, "Good morning, Man-hat-tan!" in the same abominable imitation of Robin Williams he'd been doing for years. "It's January second, boys and girls, and that means it's either back to school or back to work, so roll out of those beds and hit those showers."

Chantal groaned. She hated that man—only tuned him in so she wouldn't be tempted to linger in bed. Not that there was anything tempting to linger for this morning. Not when she was here and Denver was in Jersey.

She closed her eyes and tried to pretend he was beside her, but the blasted announcer made it impossible.

"Don't go closing those eyes again," he ordered. "Remember your New Year's resolutions. You're going to start being on time, right?"

She reached over and pressed the snooze button, then found she was already too wide awake to conjure up an imaginary Denver. Besides, nothing she'd be able to conjure could come close to the real thing.

The real thing she hadn't seen for the past thirty-odd hours. The real thing she'd been missing so incredibly. Even at dinner last night, she'd kept wishing he was with her. He could have helped her out when all her relatives insisted on firsthand accounts of the adventure in Quebec.

The story about two locals rescuing a kidnapped child up in Canada, and their subsequent encounter with the kidnapper, had made the six o'clock news. And thanks to Uncle Harry's obsession with watching it, everyone had seen the segment, so it had been the major topic of dinner-table conversation.

She'd refused the TV reporter's interview request, and apparently Denver had, too. He'd likely figured the same thing she had, that Nolton would sue them if they breathed a word about his top-secret idea for his ad campaign.

Someone had gotten photographs of them, though, and splashed those across the screen. And every single one of her aunts had asked whether she'd fallen for that handsome man she'd been alone with in the wilderness.

If he'd been at dinner with her, they wouldn't have had to ask. They'd have seen it every time she looked at him.

The phone began ringing and she grabbed for it, willing Denver to be on the other end.

He was. And just the sound of his voice was enough to make her hug herself under the blankets.

"I didn't get you out of the shower or anything, did I?" he said. "This isn't a bad time for me to call?"

She almost said there were twenty-four hours a day when it wouldn't have been a bad time for him to call. Instead, she just said, "No, it's fine."

"Good, because I couldn't wait to tell you how much I love you."

She smiled, sighing such a giant sigh of contentment, Denver would have heard it in Jersey without the help of a phone line.

"And tell you how much I miss you," he added, making her smile even more broadly.

"Denver, I miss you, too." She sat waiting for him to suggest picking her up at the agency after work today, but there was a pause at his end. The longer it grew, the more anxious she felt.

"Chantal," he finally said, "about your coming out here today...something unexpected's come up."

"Oh?" she said uneasily.

"Yeah, I got a call yesterday about a job and—"

"You got a call about a job on New Year's Day? What kind of job?" The moment the words were out she wished she could order them back. She didn't want to sound suspicious or disbelieving. And she didn't want to feel that way, either, but it was exactly how she was feeling.

"Well...it's just a job. Nothing worth talking about. But there's a big rush on it, and the guy didn't care what day it was. He was lining everything up so we could get going today. And we'll be working long hours till it's done, even through the weekend. So, between the litter and this, I'm going to be tight for time."

"Oh, I see," she said, not really seeing but suspecting the worst. What kind of rush jobs did kennel owners do? And the idea of even some workaholic lining things up on New Year's Day was pretty hard to buy.

"But," Denver went on, "it'll only be tight for the next week or so."

"Oh, I see," she repeated. And now she really *was* starting to see. The feeling she'd had on New Year's Eve, when he'd hustled her out of his house, was back. Stronger than ever. Denver was having second thoughts. He'd taken one look at her, red-eyed and sneezing away like an idiot, being absolutely no help whatsoever, being in his way, even, and he'd decided maybe she wasn't the woman for him, after all. He'd decided there was no way she could ever fit into his world.

She swallowed hard and tried to think more rationally. A few sneezes wouldn't have caused the end of everything. It could be that there really was a job. It could be that someone actually had called him yesterday.

But even if he was telling the truth, he intended to go for the next week or so without spending any time with her. And if he could go for that long not seeing her, then what he felt for her didn't come within a country mile of what she felt for him. She swallowed once more and said, "So, you'll call me when you have some time?"

"Chantal...look, I'll call you everyday. And if I get a chance to see you...Chantal, I know this must seem awfully strange, but I can't explain it right now. Just trust me, huh? I really do love you."

"Of course," she murmured. "I'll talk to you soon, then." She hung up and sat staring at the phone, her eyes filling with tears. He really loved her? One of her father's favorite sayings was, "Actions speak louder than words." Or, in this case, lack of action.

And another of his favorite sayings was, "If something seems too good to be true, that's probably because it is."

Well, she had a terrible feeling that what she and Denver had found together up north, or what she'd thought they'd found, was too good to be true.

She sat quietly for a minute, desperately trying to reassure herself that her feelings were sometimes wrong. When it didn't work, she tried forcing her thoughts to her job.

With Nolton's sudden departure, her major account was gone. As soon as she got to the agency, she'd have to sit down with Jay so they could figure out what she should be doing and how they were going to replace the Bristow revenue.

Jay would probably want her to start trying to drum up new clients. So that's what she'd concentrate on.

Yes, she'd concentrate on that and not even think about Denver. She wiped her eyes, telling herself she'd been a damned fool to fall for him so fast. And she was being a fool right now. She'd never before let a man make her feel miserable, and she wasn't about to let Denver Brooke do it.

If he wanted to cool things down, she wasn't going to be even more foolish by throwing herself at him. In fact, if she could fall in love with him in the blink of an eye, then she could fall out of love with him every bit as quickly.

She headed for the shower, telling herself that maybe he wasn't as great a guy as she'd been thinking he was, anyway. He could be darned arrogant. Bossy, too. Right from the start he'd tried to tell her how to do her job. And what exactly had he said on New Year's Eve?

I know best. Ha. Well, maybe cooling things down with a guy who always thought he knew best wasn't a bad idea.

CHAPTER FIFTEEN

AN HOUR LATER, walking into the building that housed Jay Clawson Advertising, Chantal had herself believing Denver Brooke was securely out of her thoughts.

Exactly three minutes and thirty-six seconds after that, the time it took her to get from the lobby to Jay Clawson's office, she started thinking about Denver again. One look at Jay flooded her with memories of the week at Nolton's chalet.

"Good Lord," she murmured, staring at him, "you've seen a doctor, haven't you?" His broken nose had left him looking like a purple-and-yellow raccoon, his face still badly discolored around his eyes and nose, and bruises running down either side of his throat. "Saw one the minute we got back," he said, motioning her into a chair. "Marlene insisted on it."

"And you're all right?"

"Unless I end up with trouble breathing. Then they'll have to rebreak it. But right now it doesn't feel nearly as bad as it looks."

She nodded slowly, wondering how things stood with Jay and Marlene and Nolton, thinking there'd been a whole lot of relationship-type issues left hanging. If a psychiatrist had happened into that chalet, he'd have had a field day. "So..." she said tentatively, "is everything *else* all right?"

"Everything's fine. Marlene's seeing a divorce lawyer this morning."

"Oh, I'm glad for you, Jay. For the two of you. And Kip and Cathy?"

"They're okay. Marlene has spent hours on the phone with them, checking that they were all right and explaining about leaving Nolton and everything."

"That must have been rough," Chantal murmured.

"Yeah, well...Kip didn't seem to handle the news too badly." Jay leaned back in his chair, watching her for a moment, finally saying, "And what about you? I could hardly believe my eyes when I saw your picture on the news last night. Why didn't you call me when you got back? Tell us what happened?"

She merely shrugged, hoping he'd let the subject drop. By the time her family had finished with her, she'd grown tired of talking about it.

"I tried phoning you," he continued, "but there was no answer. They made it sound as if Pierrette's brother might have killed you."

"I guess he might have. But here I am, safe and sound."

"And Denver? They said he was shot."

"He's all right. A little sore, but otherwise fine."

"That's good. He seemed like a hell of a nice guy."

"Uh-huh," she murmured, trying to ignore the way that darned lump was forming in her throat again. Surely just talking about Denver wasn't enough to upset her. And the way Jay was eyeing her, he clearly expected more than an "uh-huh."

"One of his dogs had puppies," she said to fill the silence. "Nine of them. On New Year's Eve. We just made it home in time."

Jay smiled. "I'll bet they're cute."

"I... I haven't seen them." Damn, she *was* getting upset. In fact, tears were stinging her eyes. She looked at the floor so Jay wouldn't see them.

"Chantal?" he said, his tone telling her she hadn't looked down fast enough.

If she tried to say anything more, those damned tears were going to spill over, so she simply sat, willing them away.

After a moment, Jay rose and shut the office door. Then he sat down beside her, saying, "Anything I can do?"

She shook her head, not looking up, not trusting her self-control.

"Hey," he finally said, "I realize you just went through a lot. Practically getting killed would upset anyone. So why don't you take today and tomorrow off? By Monday you'll feel better."

"Thanks, but I'll be all right," she managed. The last thing she wanted was four straight days to sit around wondering what was going on in Denver's mind. What she needed to do was keep busy and not think about him. "It's just... it's nothing, Jay."

"A nothing by the name of Denver Brooke?" he said quietly.

She gave up the pretense, wiped her eyes, and asked if it had really been that obvious.

"Actually, it was Marlene who picked up on it."

Chantal tried to smile, knowing she wasn't managing much of an imitation. "I'm surprised Marlene noticed anything at all, considering the situation."

"She's pretty observant about things like that. Even at the worst of times. And to hear her talk, I'm at risk of losing you. She says you two have fallen so hard that you might chuck your career to take up kennel-keeping.''

"Oh, Jay, could you really imagine me at a kennel in Jersey?''

"Well . . . actually, no.''

Chantal merely nodded. That was precisely the reason she'd known, right from the moment she'd realized she was falling for Denver, that there was very little chance of them turning out to be a permanent item. The way she felt for him, though, she'd wanted to at least give it a chance. But from the looks of things, Denver had decided it wasn't worth giving any chance at all.

"Chantal," Jay went on, "you know I don't meddle in my staff's personal lives, but I figure I owe both you and Denver. Hell, Nolton might have killed me if you two hadn't been there. So if I can do anything . . . even act as a sounding board. . . .''

She thought about that for a minute, not knowing if a sounding board would help, but deciding it couldn't hurt. She certainly hadn't managed a bang-up job of convincing herself that Denver wasn't really a great guy. And Jay was long on common sense.

"I . . . I don't know," she said. "We seemed . . . well, we seemed to really click. That one-in-a-million sort of thing, you know?''

"I know.''

"But . . . I think he's dumping me, Jay.''

He gazed at her for a moment, then slowly shook his head. "He didn't strike me as the love 'em and leave 'em type.''

"He didn't strike me that way, either," she said unhappily. "But when we got back home . . . well, he'd invited me to his place to celebrate New Year's Eve. Then he got a call, while we were still at the town house, telling him his dog was ready to whelp, and he did an abrupt about-face. Suddenly he didn't want me to go along. I went anyway, but it turned out to be a big mistake and . . . well, I ended up back at home long before midnight."

"You've heard from him since, though," Jay said. "About the litter, at least."

"Well . . . yes. He called yesterday. And again this morning."

Jay sat looking at her with the faintest hint of a smile.

"What?" she said.

"Chantal, let me get this straight. The two of you drove back down on New Year's Eve."

"Right."

"And today is January second. So it's been one whole day since you've seen him. And he's called you twice."

"Ah . . . I guess you could look at it that way."

"Well, it doesn't sound to me like you're being dumped."

"Oh, Jay, there's more to it. This morning he said he's suddenly gotten some job that'll take all his time, so he won't be seeing me for a while."

"Chantal, the man has to earn his living."

"He . . . oh, Jay, I guess that was part of it. But there was something else."

"What?"

"I don't know. But something. Just the way he was talking this morning, saying he won't have any time at all to see me. I somehow knew he didn't really want to."

"Women's intuition?"

"I guess that must have been it. I . . . I have a feeling he decided he can't imagine me at a kennel in Jersey any more than you can. I mean, I think he's decided we're too different."

Jay nodded thoughtfully, making her even more sure she'd hit the nail on the head.

"I just don't know what's going on for certain," she continued unhappily. "One minute he was saying he can't see me and the next he was saying he'll call me everyday. It's as if he doesn't know what he wants. And that has to mean he doesn't really want *me*. Doesn't it?"

"Not necessarily," Jay said slowly.

She gazed at him, his words igniting a tiny spark of hope. "What do you mean?"

"Well, you two hadn't even met before you went up to Nolton's place, had you?"

"No."

"So you've only known him . . . ?"

"A week," she said, feeling ridiculous just admitting it.

"A week. And you're two single, attractive people who got thrown into a nutty situation together—alone together. The outcome's hardly surprising. But maybe it happened so damned fast that it scared him when he started thinking about it."

"Second thoughts," she murmured. Exactly what she'd figured, and that's what Jay figured, too.

"Not necessarily second thoughts," he said. "But maybe he decided it made sense to pause and catch his breath. And that wouldn't be a bad idea, would it? For either of you?"

She didn't answer, just sat wondering if Jay might be right. Denver pausing to catch his breath certainly wasn't as scary as the idea of serious second thoughts. But she was just so afraid of what conclusions he might reach while he was catching his breath.

"Chantal, if it's really love, it isn't going to evaporate overnight. Hell, I've been in love with Marlene ever since I met her. It just took her twenty-odd years to realize she married the wrong man."

"No one can accuse you two of rushing things, then, can they?" she said, managing a smile.

Jay laughed quietly. "But we *are* ending up together. Sometimes it just takes time, Chantal. So, as far as Denver's concerned, why not play it cool? When he calls, don't ask about seeing him. Just let him take things at his own pace."

"You don't think his own pace would be twenty-odd years, do you?"

He smiled at her. "No, I doubt it'll even be twenty-odd days. Men sometimes get skittish, that's all. I'm completely certain things will work out."

She nodded slowly, wishing *she* was at least a little bit certain. Even if Denver got over whatever was bothering him, there'd still be all those differences in their lives, still be no guarantee they could come up with any workable compromise.

But maybe... well, maybe she should take Jay's advice and be patient. Maybe her idea about trying to fall out of love with Denver in the blink of an eye wasn't the best idea she'd ever had.

As if you actually could have, whispered a sardonic little voice inside her head.

CHANTAL SAT STARING at the engagement calendar on her desk, unable to force her eyes from the date and unable to force her thoughts from Denver.

Monday, January 6, the calendar proclaimed. And she'd never before had a blue Monday that held a candle to this one. It had been six entire days since she'd seen Denver. And every one of them had been a hundred hours long.

She missed him so incredibly much that she was dreaming about him every night, dreaming about being in his arms, about making love to him.

But he couldn't be missing her the same way at all. No matter how busy he was, if he'd really wanted to see her he'd have made the time. And she was devastated he hadn't.

"Why not play it cool?" Jay had said. "When he calls, don't ask about seeing him. Just let him take things at his own pace."

And that's what she'd been doing, because the advice had made sense. Besides, she still had at least some of her pride. If Denver didn't want to see her, she wasn't going to beg.

So each day, when he called, she simply told herself his phoning was a good sign, then bit her lip to keep from pressing him. But she'd reached her limit. She couldn't play this waiting game any longer. She felt as if her life was on hold, that she just had to start getting on with it again. And if Denver wasn't going to be a part of it, then she had to start getting on with forgetting him.

Tomorrow it would be an entire week since she'd seen him. And tomorrow she was going to ask him exactly where things stood. Of course, deep down she already knew—was certain that what he'd tell her would break her heart. If only a fairy godmother would appear and grant her a wish.

"Hi, Chantal," someone said from the doorway.

She looked up and managed a smile, even though Marlene Bristow was hardly a fairy godmother. "Hi. What are you doing here?"

"Meeting Jay for lunch," she said, sinking into a chair. "Well, actually, I'm meeting Jay and Kip and Cathy, but I'm early."

"Kip and Cathy are in town?"

"Uh-huh. They flew in Friday night, courtesy of Nolton."

"Oh, Marlene, he's had a change of heart, then."

"I hope so. He called Kip at school and invited them to spend the weekend with him. *Warmly* invited them, according to Kip. Said he wanted a chance to get to know his new daughter-in-law."

"That's really good news. I was worried he wouldn't come around."

Marlene nodded slowly. "I've just been a little concerned because . . . well, you never know with Nolton. So I asked them to stay over long enough for lunch— wanted to see them before they went back to make sure Nolt hasn't done anything outrageous."

"Kip . . ." Chantal paused, realizing the question on the tip of her tongue wasn't any of her business, but Marlene was eyeing her expectantly and she couldn't think of anything else to say. "Kip feels all right about coming to the agency? About Jay . . . about you and Jay, I mean?"

"He's going to be okay with it. He was upset when I told him what was happening, of course, but I think he's been wondering for years why his father and I were still together. And the saving grace is that he adores Jay, grew up thinking of him as kind of a favorite uncle. Jay's always been around our place . . . even before he and I . . .

"At any rate, I think we're all going to be fine," Marlene continued. "Even Nolt. We had a meeting with our lawyers on Friday morning, and he's accepting the divorce now. In fact, knowing Nolt," she added with a rueful smile, "he'll probably be running around with some glamorous twenty-year-old model in no time."

Chantal didn't have any idea what an appropriate response might be, so she simply smiled uneasily.

"You see," Marlene went on, "it's been years since Nolt and I...well, there was nothing left between us but old habits. So any hurt he feels isn't really from losing me. It's just hurt pride. And he'll rationalize that away in no time. I guess—"

"Knock, knock," Kip interrupted from the hall.

"If that's a lead-in to a terrible knock, knock joke," Chantal teased, "you aren't welcome in my office."

"Nope, no terrible joke," Kip assured her, ushering Cathy in. "It's just hard to knock on an open door."

They were both all smiles and easy hellos, a sign Chantal took to indicate the weekend had gone well. Marlene's relieved expression said that's how she was reading things, too.

"We just ran into Jay," Kip said. "He's going to be a couple of minutes yet."

Marlene made polite chitchat with Cathy for the next few moments, but was clearly dying of curiosity. "So, Cathy..." she finally asked, "how was the weekend, dear?"

"Very nice, thanks."

Kip grinned at his mother. "What she means is that Dad didn't do a repeat performance of Attila the Hun."

"Well, I'm certainly glad to hear that. He really did only want to apologize and make up, then?"

"Well, he didn't exactly apologize," Kip said. "It was more like he pretended everything had always been just ace, like the scene at the chalet never happened. And making up wasn't exactly the *only* thing he wanted."

"Oh?" Marlene said.

"Yeah." Kip shook his head. "Dad's never going to change, is he?"

"I doubt he will, Kip. What's he up to now?"

"Oh, he's had his new ad agency really putting a push on shooting the dog commercials. I think..." Kip paused, suddenly looking uncomfortable. "I think he's been trying to keep real busy...you know what I mean, Mom?"

"I know, Kip," Marlene said softly. "It's a difficult time for all of us, huh?"

"Yeah...well, anyway, he was even working on the weekend. There were cameramen following him and Brandy around, getting supposedly unstaged footage. And right now, they're shooting just outside the Carruthers and Headly offices, filming Dad walking Brandy to the ad agency as if he actually does walk her places. I think the whole series of ads is almost a wrap. The filming part, at least."

"And I think he's really been enjoying himself," Cathy offered. "I mean," she added, glancing uncertainly at Marlene, "as much as he could under the circumstances."

"It's all right, Cathy," Marlene said. "Nolton's a great one for shutting things up into tiny little boxes in his mind and not thinking about them. I'm sure he'll manage to enjoy himself just fine most of the time."

"He *has* been having fun, Mom," Kip said. "In fact, he's gotten such a blast out of being the star that he wants to personalize the follow-up campaign, too. He's planning it already, even though they won't shoot it for six months or so. And guess what his idea is for that one."

"I couldn't even begin to guess."

"Well, get this," Kip told her, patting Cathy's stomach. "He wants them to feature him with his newborn grandchild."

Marlene eyed her son skeptically. "You're kidding...aren't you?"

"Nope. Dad told me..." Kip paused, thrusting his jaw forward in an imitation of Nolton, then saying, "Son, there's nothing like animals or babies to sell products. And if I'm going to pay somebody's grandchild residuals, it's going to be my own."

"And what did you say?" Marlene asked, almost laughing.

"I said, 'Well, Dad, Cathy and I will just have to give some thought to whether or not we want our baby in show business.'" Kip grinned a grin that said he intended to make the most of having a little power over his father.

"And then," Cathy added, "Kip said, 'Give give us a couple of months, Dad, and we'll get back to you on this.'"

Marlene laughed out loud at that. "And then your father turned purple, right, Kip?"

"Yeah, he definitely made purple."

A second later, Jay stuck his head into the office and asked if they were ready for lunch.

"Would you like to join us, Chantal?" Marlene said.

"No, thanks, the four of you enjoy yourselves. But Kip, just before you go...?"

"Yes?"

"With the shooting almost finished, did your father happen to mention what he's going to do with Brandy?"

"Not exactly. I know he isn't planning on keeping her, though. Says she's too much trouble."

Chantal nodded slowly, barely paying attention as the others said their goodbyes and headed off. If Nolton was coming to terms with everything else, maybe he'd removed her name from his blacklist. Maybe he'd reconsider selling Brandy to her. It certainly wouldn't hurt to ask. She'd phone him tonight.

No, she decided after a moment's thought. It would be better to ask him in person and better yet if other people were around. Then he'd be far more likely to play Mr. Nice Guy. And if they were shooting outside Carruthers and Headly right now...well, that was only a short walk down Madison Avenue.

WHEN SHE REACHED the corner of Fifty-second and Madison, Chantal could see an enormous equipment truck parked part way down Fifty-second, blocking one lane of traffic. And she could count at least eleven camera crew up ahead, outside Carruthers and Headly.

Some were busy arranging light standards, others peered intently at notes, a couple were just standing around looking half frozen.

They had a long stretch of the avenue blocked off and were rerouting pedestrians, to their obvious annoyance. In any other city, people would stop to watch a crew filming. Not in Manhattan, though.

She stood shivering, waiting for the red light to change. It was a typically cold, gray January day. No longer snowing, but threatening to start again any minute. And the sharp wind at her back kept blowing her hair around. She pushed it off her face once more, then shoved her hands into her pockets.

Her thin leather gloves were fashionable, not warm. Just like her boots, she thought, struck by a sudden sense of déjà vu. She could almost see Denver standing before her, saying, *"You've got to wear warmer clothes. And you can't wear those ridiculous high-heeled boots."*

"They're not ridiculous," she'd protested. *"They're fashionable."*

"On the sidewalks of New York, they might be fashionable. In the ski hills of Quebec, they're ridiculous."

Chantal sighed. She wished . . . she wished she were back in the ski hills of Quebec, with Denver, instead of on the sidewalks of New York, without him.

No, she told herself firmly, she didn't wish that at all. She didn't want any man who didn't want her, and she didn't need any man with a penchant for bossing her around. And Denver or no Denver, she was going to start getting on with her life, right here in the real world.

She took a deep breath and forced her attention back to the slushy street ahead. Frank Carruthers was obviously sparing no expense on Nolton's commercials. Of course, it was Nolton's money. And both he and Frank would want to produce a campaign that would make everyone at Jay Clawson Advertising ill.

There was no sign of Nolton and Brandy, so they were probably waiting someplace warm while the crew set up for the next shot.

The light changed and she started across Fifty-second, thinking that if anyone from Carruthers recognized her, they'd assume she'd come on a spying mission.

Just as she got to the curb, Nolton walked out of a building at the far end of the blocked-off stretch. Nolton—with Brandy on a leash.

Chantal felt a tug at her heartstrings when she saw the dog. She simply had to convince Nolton. But barging in when they were probably about ready to shoot wouldn't

get negotiations off to a good start, so when she reached
the barricades she stopped and simply stood watching
Brandy, wishing New Yorkers weren't so darned blasé.
If a crowd was viewing the proceedings, she wouldn't be
so obvious.

No one would likely notice her, though. Not from
half a block away.

Nolton stood talking with a fellow holding a clip-
board, and Brandy was sitting beside him, as good as
gold. Absently, Chantal wondered who'd taken over her
training. She wasn't moving a muscle...well, actually,
she *was* starting to look around a little.

Another gust of wind whipped at Chantal's hair. She
brushed it back out of her eyes and moved over against
the sheltering wall of a building.

When she focused on Brandy again, the dog was
staring straight at her. Of course, it couldn't see well
enough to know it was her. Not from this far away.
Denver had told her dogs didn't have the distance vision people had.

And then...oh, no, Brandy's big black nose hadn't
really begun to twitch, had it?

Suddenly, that sense of déjà vu was back again. Now
she was recalling Denver saying, *"Saint Bernards have
an uncanny sense of smell."* And this certainly wasn't
the first time she'd seen Brandy's nose twitch. There'd
been that cat...and that rabbit...and each time, right
after the twitching...

At the exact instant Chantal realized what was about
to happen, Brandy became a moving, howling blur. She
leapt into the air, then hit the sidewalk, charging toward Chantal, sounding like an entire pack of wolves.

And, oh Lord, Nolton hadn't let go of the leash. He
was flying through the air after the dog, his body par-

allel to the ground, his arms stretched straight out in front of him, his hands still clinging to the lead. All he needed was a blue cape and he'd be a perfect Superman.

Only Superman didn't yell while he was flying, and Nolton certainly was. She could hear him hollering even over Brandy's howling. Then she saw that one of the cameramen was racing along after them, filming the action. Oh, Lord, she thought fleetingly, what a commercial this could make!

And then, as suddenly as Nolton had taken flight, he crash-landed, twisting onto his backside just as he hit the pavement, then bouncing along on his behind a couple of times, still yelling, finally letting go of the leash and skidding to a halt.

For a second, Chantal's gaze was frozen on him, sitting there in a pool of pained surprise, his usually perfect silver hair sticking out every which way and his cashmere coat covered in slush.

Vaguely, she realized they'd collected a crowd. Even for Manhattan, this had been quite a spectacle. Then a huge ball of brown-and-white fur barreled through the barricade and leapt at her, knocking her against the building, and she forgot about the onlookers.

Shakily, she knelt to hug Brandy and was rewarded with a face full of wet doggy kisses. She could hear Nolton uttering a nonstop string of obscenities. Some of them were directed at the cameraman who'd been shooting the excitement, but both her name and Brandy's were coming up frequently.

By the time Brandy had stopped quivering with excitement, the cameraman had vanished and Nolton was glowering down at them.

"She...I guess she was glad to see me again," Chantal murmured inanely.

"What the hell are you doing here?" Nolton shouted.

"I...I..."

"What?" he yelled again.

This had to be the worst time possible to ask, but she wouldn't likely get another chance, so she said, "Nolton, I want to buy Brandy from you."

"No." He grabbed the end of the leash and muttered, "Stupid, damn dog."

"Nolton, wait," Chantal said, scrambling to her feet. "I know you're angry with me, but you have to sell her to someone and I really—"

"You're too late," he said. "I've already arranged to dispose of her."

"Dispose of her? Dispose? Dammit, Nolton, she isn't some bag of garbage! I'll give her a good home. Don't you care about that?"

"She's going to a good home. Now just...oh, there you are," he snapped, glancing past Chantal. "Hell, it's about time. You're late. Take this damned dog off my hands, will you? I've had it with her. I'm not shooting another frigging foot of tape. You just go do what I'm paying you to do and keep her away from me."

Chantal turned to see who Nolton was snarling at now, and her heart stopped. "Denver?" she said.

CHAPTER SIXTEEN

"DENVER?" CHANTAL SAID a second time, still unable to believe her eyes. It couldn't be anyone else standing before her, though, not with those rugged good looks. And not dressed in that battered flight jacket, worn jeans and scuffed cowboy boots.

But the way Nolton had been snapping orders it had sounded as if... She glanced from Denver to Brandy, to Nolton, then back to Denver, finally saying, "What are you doing here?"

"I...I...well, I..."

"What the hell do you think he's doing here?" Nolton snarled. "He's making himself a major fortune at my expense, while I'm standing here freezing. Here," he said, handing Denver the leash, "I'm going inside to warm up."

Chantal's brain seemed to be on pause. Tiny disjointed facts were swirling around inside it but refusing to come together. One thing was clear, though. *This* was the job Denver had told her would be keeping him so busy. "You're working for Nolton," she said.

"Ah...it isn't exactly the way it seems, Chantal."

"You're working for Nolton," she repeated.

"Ah...well, yeah. Kind of."

She stood there feeling more sick and more angry by the second. He'd been working right here in Manhattan and hadn't seen her in a week. Hadn't seen her because he'd been too busy chasing the almighty dollar, chasing after money he *claimed* wasn't important to him.

Well, apparently it was more important to him than she was. Which told her precisely where he rated her.

So much for his loving her. And so much for his talk about having principles, about never working for Nolton again, about hating to work on Mad Ave.

Denver Brooke could obviously be damned quick to forget his principles if there was enough money at stake. This...this snake she'd thought she was in love with was the biggest hypocrite she'd ever known.

She fixed him with her highest-voltage glare, saying, "You're working for Nolton because he offered you a whole pile of money."

"Ah...Chantal...I can—"

"Mr. Integrity!" she yelled at him. "Mr. Holier than Thou, Phony Baloney Integrity! Criticizing me! Criticizing my life when all the time—"

"Chantal," he snapped, grabbing her arm, "people are listening."

"Let them listen!" she yelled even more loudly, smacking his hand away. "Maybe they've never heard of anyone as phony as a three-dollar bill before."

Brandy whined and pressed her bulk against Chantal's hips. She knelt and hugged the dog again, burying her face in its fur, trying to keep from crying. She couldn't have Brandy. That hurt. But what hurt more was that the man she'd fallen in love with wasn't the man she'd thought he was.

"Chantal, look—"

"Don't *Chantal look* me," she said, getting back up to her feet. "Because I've got a great memory for things people say. And I recall your saying so many dillies I don't know where to start. Maybe with, 'How can you work for a bastard like Nolton, Chantal?' And saying it in such a superior tone, as if *you* would never stoop that low.

"Or how about that if you'd known what Nolton was like, before you'd agreed to work with Brandy, you'd have told Rachel there was no way?"

"Dammit, Chantal, will you at least—"

"No. No, the best one was definitely, 'Even if I was stone-broke, there's not enough money in the world to make me work for Nolton again.' But that was back when you were sure he wouldn't ask you to, wasn't it? Back when it was easy to say your integrity was more important than money. Ha! You've got about as much integrity as a toad."

Suddenly, tears were streaming down her face and she knew she'd couldn't manage another word. She wheeled away from Denver and ran toward Fifty-second Street.

Through her tears she spotted a cab, hailed it and gave the driver her address. She had to repeat it twice before he could understand what she was saying, but by the time he turned onto West Eighty-fifth she'd regained a modicum of control, enough to think of calling the office to tell them she was ill. Enough to drag herself upstairs and change from her dress into jeans and...and it had to be positively pathological, some warped bit of masochism, but something made her put on the sweater of Denver's she'd worn on their trip home from Quebec.

She wandered miserably back downstairs, made a pot of coffee, then sat at the kitchen table for hours, trying not to think, trying not to cry, staring out into her tiny garden until it grew too dark to see...then simply staring into the darkness for hours more.

By that point, she'd cried so many angry tears there were none left to cry. All that was left was emptiness, both inside and out.

She felt hollow. And the town house had never been as lonely as it was right now. She wanted a dog she couldn't have and a man who didn't exist.

The man she'd fallen in love with was an illusion... or maybe delusion was a better word. She'd deluded herself into believing he was something he wasn't. Not that he hadn't helped her along. He'd put on a damned fine performance as Mr. Integrity. And she'd bought his act completely.

Ms. Gullibility. That was her. What a terrific combination they'd been. Ms. Gullibility and Mr. Phony Baloney.

What had she been thinking of, letting herself get so involved with a man she barely knew? Believing he loved her when undoubtedly all she'd been to him was a warm body in a cold chalet?

She'd been such a fool. And the most foolish part of all was that she'd actually been ready to make major changes in her life for him, when he hadn't even considered changing a damned thing.

"I've made my choice about how I want to live my life," he'd said. *"And being a money-grubber just isn't it. And spending any more time than I do on Mad Ave. definitely isn't it."*

No, Denver hadn't considered compromising one bit. Not for her, at least. But Nolton's offer of a major fortune had obviously started him falling all over himself to compromise those phony principles of his.

She glanced at the clock. Was 3:00 a.m. late enough that she'd actually fall asleep if she went to bed? She doubted it. And she didn't really want to go to bed.

That would only make her feel more lonely, so she simply rested her head on the table, using her arms as a pillow, burying her face in the soft wool of Denver's sweater.

The scent of him surrounded her...making her more miserable than ever....

The next thing she was aware of was a loud knocking. She opened her eyes to find the first pale fingers of a January morning poking into her kitchen and all the terrible memories of yesterday flooding back into her mind.

Her neck was so stiff she could barely raise her head from the table, but the front door knocker thudded a few more times, and she forced herself to her feet, running her fingers through her hair, then heading along the hall.

She peered through the peephole. Standing outside was a man wearing some sort of dark uniform. "Yes?" she said through the door.

"Ms. Livingstone?" he asked.

"Yes?"

"Ms. Livingstone, I'm with Elite Limousine Service. And I'm supposed to give you this before we leave," he added, holding up a white envelope.

Before we leave? she silently repeated, looking out to the curb. Sure enough, there was a big navy limousine parked in front of her town house. Curious, she opened the door, leaving the chain on—you could never be too careful in Manhattan—and took the envelope.

Inside it was a birthday card with a cute picture of a dog on the front. But whatever this was all about, it was crazy. Her birthday was in June. She opened the card and her breath caught in her throat. She'd only seen

Denver's writing once before, but she recognized it instantly.

> Chantal,
>   I don't know when your birthday is, so I guess what I've got for you at the kennel is actually an un-birthday present. Please come and pick her up. I couldn't have her delivered because she'd have howled all the way there.
>
> Love, Denver.

She stood staring at the "Love, Denver," feeling tiny hot-and-cold prickles over her entire body.

"Ms. Livingstone?" the driver said. "Will you be ready to leave shortly?"

She barely heard his words over the pounding of her heart. Somehow, Denver had gotten Brandy for her. But he hadn't even bothered to see her once in an entire week. So if he figured giving her Brandy was going to make her think he was wonderful once more, he was mistaken. She didn't even want to see him again. Not ever.

She glanced at the card again. "Please come and pick her up." Outside, that limo was waiting. What would happen if she didn't go? Would Denver change his mind? Not let her have Brandy, after all? She couldn't risk that happening. But if she went, she'd have to face him.

"Ms. Livingstone?" the driver said.

"Yes, yes," she murmured, deciding. She wasn't a child. She could handle this. It wouldn't be easy... in fact, it just might be the hardest thing she'd ever done, but she couldn't take the chance of not going. "I'll only be a few minutes," she told the man. "Would you like to wait inside?"

"No, ma'am. Thank you, but I'll wait in the car."

She closed the door, raced upstairs and got ready in record time, just throwing her jeans on again after her shower and not even bothering with makeup. She didn't want Denver to think she'd fixed herself up for him. She threw some antihistamines into her purse and hurried back downstairs.

"I'll be polite, of course," she murmured absently, opening the front door. Maybe she should even consider apologizing for screaming at him yesterday.

Not that he hadn't deserved it. He'd hurt her more than anyone had ever hurt her before. But screaming hadn't exactly been the most adult way of dealing with her emotions.

And Denver might be a world-class phony, but she *did* appreciate his getting Brandy for her.

He wasn't the man she'd thought he was, though. And he *certainly* wasn't the man for her. So she'd be polite but distant. Yes, she could manage that.

CHANTAL'S STOMACH HAD begun feeling queasy the minute she got into the limo, developed butterflies when they hit the Lincoln Tunnel, and began positively churning as they were passing through Hoboken. By the time she saw the sign that said they were nearing Somerville, she was decidedly ill.

She *definitely* didn't want to see Denver. And the farther they'd driven, the more she hadn't wanted to see him. She knew it was going to hurt—a whole helluva lot, as he would put it. Because even though he was a phony, the instant she looked at him she was going to start thinking about how things might have ended if he'd been for real.

The limo slowed and turned onto the secondary road, and soon the kennel sign appeared ahead. Her heart had somehow climbed all the way up into her throat and was racing at a million miles an hour by the time they turned down the driveway. This was the last place on earth she wanted to be.

The house looked even prettier in the daylight, and sitting on the front porch was Brandy, a huge red bow around her neck.

Seeing her almost started Chantal crying.

The driver stopped in front of the house and opened her door. She got out and simply stood looking at the porch for a moment—until that big black nose twitched and the dog bounded down the steps in a barking frenzy of excitement.

"Brandy," Chantal murmured, stroking the huge head with both hands. "I thought I'd never see you again."

Behind her, the limo's door clicked closed. Then she heard the hush of its wheels on the drive and whirled around.

But the car was already heading back to the road. Oh, Lord, she was trapped here.

"It's all right," Denver said.

Her entire body froze at the sound of his voice.

"I only hired it for a one-way trip," he continued. "I'll drive you home in the van."

She reminded herself she wasn't a child, that she could handle this. Polite but distant, she said silently, then slowly turned.

Denver was standing just outside his front door, and seeing him hurt even more than she'd expected it to.

Despite what her head had been telling her heart, falling out of love with him was going to take a long, long time.

He looked utterly gorgeous—freshly shaven, hair still damp from the shower, a sweater the same warm brown as his eyes, and those stupid, scruffy cowboy boots she'd grown so used to seeing.

She swallowed hard. "Thank you for Brandy. It was very kind of you."

He merely nodded, watching her, his gaze making her hot despite the cold morning air.

"I . . . I'm surprised Nolton let you have her," she finally said.

"We made a deal. She was part of it."

It was her turn to merely nod. She really didn't want to hear the details about his dealings with Nolton.

"I thought," Denver said, "you might still like to see the pups."

She managed a smile and began forcing one foot in front of the other. Inside, McGee greeted her almost as enthusiastically as Brandy had.

Julie and Lily bulled their way forward, and Chantal patted each of them, then glanced around, looking everywhere but at Denver, trying to think about anything except him.

"You four," he said, gesturing to the dogs, "just stay out here."

Even Brandy obediently flopped onto the floor.

"Coming, Chantal?" he said, starting for the kitchen.

She followed him along the hall, still trying to keep her eyes off him, but unable to . . . and unable to stop wishing he actually was what he'd once seemed . . . to stop wishing he really loved her as much as he'd claimed . . . to stop wishing the two of them could have at least tried to—

"There they are," he said, moving aside so she could see.

She knelt down beside the low-sided box and spoke softly to Tara. Little sleeping bundles of brown-and-white fuzz were curled up along her stomach, half hidden in the shredded newspaper.

"By this time next week, their eyes will be open," Denver said.

"They're darling," Chantal murmured. "Could I hold one?" she asked, glancing up at him, instantly wishing she hadn't. Just looking at him was almost enough to break her heart.

"Chantal," he said quietly, the way he spoke her name making her pulse leap, "first let's talk about this past week, okay?" He eased himself down onto the floor beside her without taking his gaze off her.

She shook her head, not wanting to hear. All she wanted was to take Brandy and get out of here, get as far away as possible from this man she didn't want to love. "You don't have to explain," she whispered over the lump in her throat. "I understand."

"I don't think you do."

She risked glancing at him again, and again it was a mistake. His warm brown eyes were saying he loved her, but she knew they were lying.

"Look, Chantal, I'm sure you realize that I only took Nolton's job because I needed money—a whole helluva lot of money, in fact. I'd been racking my brain trying to figure out how I was going to come up with it, and suddenly he was on the phone, so desperate for me to help him out that I could name my own price. It was like he was handing me that money I needed on a silver platter."

"And all you had to do to get it," she said, knowing she sounded terribly sarcastic but not caring, "was compromise the hell out of those high-and-mighty principles you were spouting to me, right?"

"That's right," Denver said quietly. "But there's just one person in the world I'd have done that for...just one person in the world I love enough to have done it for...and she's sitting right here on my kitchen floor."

Chantal stared down at that old wooden floor, fighting tears. If only he meant what he was saying. "You love me so much," she whispered, "that you haven't even seen me once since we got back." He reached for her hands but she pulled them away.

"Chantal, listen to me, huh? I wanted to be with you every damned minute we've been apart."

"Then why weren't you? I wanted to come out here again. You knew I did. And you were working in New York all week and didn't even—"

"No, you've got this all wrong. With nine pups, I've barely been out of the house."

"Denver, don't lie to me! I was there. You were training Brandy for Nolton again and—"

"Oh, geez, Chantal, I wouldn't have put up with Nolton again. They hired some other guy to work with Brandy. The only time I saw Nolton was yesterday. And that was the only time I was in New York. And running into him then was accidental. Hell, I made them put that into the agreement, that I wouldn't even have to see Nolton."

She shook her head in frustration, not understanding any of this and not knowing why she was even trying to. Then she looked at Denver again and her heart told her why she was trying.

"What agreement?" she asked. "And if you weren't working with Brandy, then what was the job you told me about, the one that was going to keep you too busy to see me?"

"Chantal, I had to give you *some* reason for not seeing you. It was the best one I could come up with."

"You lied to me," she whispered, telling herself to stop thinking with her heart, brushing away a tear she couldn't manage to contain. "All you've ever done is lie to me."

"Oh, dammit, Chantal, that's just not true. It was one little white lie. And I wanted to see you so badly it hurt. But I knew that if I saw you, I wouldn't have been able to stop myself from telling you what was happening. And I just couldn't tell you what I was doing...not until it was over...not until I was certain it would work out."

His words started a tiny hope flickering inside her. She couldn't possibly have figured this out wrong...could she? He couldn't possibly have a wonderful explanation for everything...could he?

She was almost afraid to hear the rest of what he had to say, afraid there was no wonderful explanation at all, but yearning for there to be one.

"What was happening," she said hesitantly, "that you couldn't tell me about?"

"I agreed to be in one of the commercials Carruthers and Headly were going to shoot for Nolton."

"What?" she cried, her hopes plunging all the way to her toes.

"Chantal, listen to me for a minute. Remember when we went out on the snowmobile to search for René?

Remember what Nolton said just before we left that morning?"

She shook her head, knowing she was going to dissolve into a terminal state of tears in a matter of seconds.

"He said," Denver continued, "'Think if Brandy saved someone's life. Imagine how I could use a rescue story in my advertising campaign.'"

"But—"

"Chantal, Frank Carruthers thought that was a great idea. He wanted to do a commercial that featured an eye-witness account of Brandy's locating René. But you and I were the only eye-witnesses. And the last person in the world Nolton would use was someone who works for Jay Clawson. So that left me.

"That's what I meant about him being so desperate for my help that I could name my own price. Aside from you, I was the only person in the world who could do that commercial for them."

"So you demanded a small fortune," Chantal murmured.

"And I demanded Brandy. But Chantal, don't you want to know why I was so desperate to have that money?"

She nodded uncertainly, her thoughts a tangled confusion.

"To renovate this place. I used all my savings to buy it, and I'd planned on fixing it up a little at a time. But you're allergic to dust."

She gazed at him blankly. His mind seemed to be jumping all over the place and she wasn't following at all.

"Chantal, even without the kind of dust a renovation would mean, this old place had you sneezing like crazy. And you've had enough of a look around to see how much work has to be done here. If I renovated a little at a time, it would be a dust-bowl for years. God, I can't live without you for years, Chantal. And even aside from your allergy, how could I possibly have asked you to come and live here with me in this . . . this pre-renovation?''

He kept on talking but she stopped hearing. The words *"live here with me"* were repeating themselves inside her head, blocking out everything else.

She'd been wrong. All wrong. What he'd done, he'd done for her. He *did* love her.

"Chantal?" she heard him say uncertainly. And that was when she started crying.

"Chantal?" he said again, even more uncertainly. "Chantal, I thought you wanted us to be together. I thought you—"

"Oh, Denver," she sobbed, throwing her arms around his neck, "do you have any idea how miserable I've been this past week? Why didn't you trust me enough to tell me what was going on?"

He didn't answer, merely wrapped his arms around her and kissed her as if he was never going to stop.

"Your side," she whispered when he finally did.

"What?"

"Your side. The bullet wound. You shouldn't be holding me so tightly. It must hurt."

"Chantal, even if it hurt like hell, it would feel good to hold you."

He snuggled her closely against him, saying, "To answer your question, it wasn't that I didn't trust you. It was that I didn't trust Nolton. That's why I couldn't tell you what was going on. The agreement his lawyer drew up was twelve pages long, and I just kept thinking he might have snuck in a clause that my lawyer missed, one that would have let Nolton sucker me.

"Chantal, what if I'd told you we were getting Brandy, that I'd be able to renovate the house right away, and then it had all blown up in my face? I just couldn't say anything until I was completely certain. But now I am. We've got Brandy right out there in the hall, and I've got a certified check in my desk. And best of all, I've got you in my arms. So," he murmured, nuzzling her neck, "can you see living happily ever after with me?"

"Oh, Denver, if there was anything beyond ever after, I could see living happily with you for that long, too."

That earned her a smile, and Denver said, "I'll bet I can have this place in fantastic shape in a couple of months. I'll even get a central vac put in."

She rested her head against the warmth of his chest, wondering if anyone in the world had ever felt this ecstatic while sitting on an old kitchen floor. And then, from a corner of her mind, a dark thought crept into her consciousness. "Denver?" she said uneasily.

"Uh-huh?"

"Denver . . . I'm absolutely positive I could live happily ever after with you . . ."

"But?" he said, his tone uneasy.

"But . . . but there's still a problem with the logistics. We never did get around to figuring out exactly how . . . I mean, if I was living here and trying to get back and forth to Manhattan every-day without the traffic driving me insane . . ."

"Uh-huh," Denver said. Then he gave her the biggest Cheshire cat smile she'd ever seen. "Well, I've had a lot of time to think lately, and I had an idea. Hey," he added, kissing her quickly, "don't look so anxious. I think you might like it."

She waited for him to go on, praying she *would* like it.

"What if you could work out of the house here? What if you only had to go into Manhattan now and then, and not during rush hours?"

"I..." she paused, trying to smile so her disappointment wouldn't show. That just wasn't a realistic option. And what if there turned out to be *no* realistic options? Could she really bring herself to give up her entire life? Could she really live happily ever after if she did? Not just for a few years but for ever and ever?

"Denver," she said slowly, "Jay wouldn't go for one of his account execs working at home. I have to meet with clients all the time and—"

"Who said anything about Jay? Chantal, remember I once told you I've got a knack with most animals?"

She nodded.

"Well, some of my thinking the past few days has been about how damned selfish I was being, expecting you to do all the compromising. And dammit, if you're willing to change your life, then so am I. In addition to the kennel, what would you think about us starting a booking agency? One that specializes in animal actors?"

"I...I don't know," she murmured, her mind racing. She'd never thought about having her own business.

"It makes perfect sense," Denver pressed. "You know the ins and outs and the people in ad-land. And I could do the training. And we'd both be here, but you wouldn't feel cut off from civilization. You could go into the city whenever you had business to take care of, and I could go in when there was a shooting and— Hey, does that smile mean you like the idea?''

"No, this smile means I *love* the idea. And I love you, Denver Brooke. I love you a whole helluva lot," she added, kissing him, trying to show him just exactly how much.

When she thought she'd probably succeeded, she said, "And have you come up with a good name for this agency of ours?''

"Well . . . I was considering Brooke and Livingstone.''

"Or Livingstone and Brooke,'' she teased.

"Uh-huh, that's a possibility, too. But the one I'd really like us to go with is Brooke and Brooke.''

Chantal smiled a smile that she knew out-Cheshired Denver's. "Brooke and Brooke, huh? I definitely like that one the best.''

"I was hoping you would," Denver told her. "That's why," he added, pulling a blue velvet ring box from his pocket, "I picked up a second un-birthday present for you.''

"Oh, Denver," she murmured, opening the box, "it's beautiful. It's the most beautiful diamond I've—''

Her words were cut off by a dog beginning to howl out in the hall.

"That could only be Brandy," she said, laughing. "Guess she still needs a little training, huh?''

A moment later, a second dog took up the chorus . . . then a third . . . finally, a slightly deeper wail that had to be McGee.

And then Tara began howling from her box, practically into Chantal's ear, and the other four dogs came thundering into the kitchen, skidding across the wooden floor to where Chantal and Denver were sitting, pushing one another aside in their eagerness to be patted.

Brandy, her huge red bow askew, was doing her best to fit her hundred-and-fifty-odd pounds into Chantal's lap.

"I think they're welcoming you to the family," Denver shouted above the din.

"And what about you?" she asked, leaning closer so he could hear her. "Aren't you going to give me a proper welcome, too?"

He gazed at her for a moment, and this time she believed the message of love in his warm brown eyes. Then he wrapped his arms around her and kissed her... and she believed they really would live happily ever after... and if possible, longer.

HARLEQUIN SUPERROMANCE®

COMING NEXT MONTH

#522 JUST BETWEEN US • Debbi Bedford
When Monica Albright volunteered to be a Big Sister to
troubled teen Ann Small, she never expected to fall in
love with the child's father. But now that the inevitable
had happened, she and Richard were running the risk
of alienating Ann forever.

#523 MAKE-BELIEVE • Emma Merritt
Marcy Galvan's roots were in San Antonio. She had
her business, her family and her Little Sister,
Amy Calderon. Brant Holland's life was in New
York—his business needed him there. Though love had
brought them together, would their obligations keep
them apart?

#524 STRING OF MIRACLES • Sally Garrett
A lot of slick young legal eagles had made a play for
lawyer Nancy Prentice, but she was saving herself for a
real man: Mark Bradford. The only problem was that
Mark had always treated her like a sister. Well, no
more. Now *she* was going to take the initiative . . . !

#525 RENEGADE • Peg Sutherland
Former country-and-western star Dell McColl lived up
to his reputation as a renegade. He never backed down
from anything or anyone. Then he met never-say-die
Daylene Honeycutt. Daylene wanted two things from
Dell. She wanted *him,* and she wanted to sing in his
bar. Dell refused to give in on either count. Never again
would he be responsible for a woman's destruction on
the road to stardom.

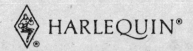 **HARLEQUIN**®

THE TAGGARTS OF TEXAS!

Harlequin's Ruth Jean Dale brings you
THE TAGGARTS OF TEXAS!

Those Taggart men—strong, sexy and hard to resist...

You've met Jesse James Taggart in FIREWORKS!
Harlequin Romance #3205 (July 1992)

Now meet Trey Smith—he's THE RED-BLOODED YANKEE!
Harlequin Temptation #413 (October 1992)

Then there's Daniel Boone Taggart in SHOWDOWN!
Harlequin Romance #3242 (January 1993)

And finally the Taggarts who started it all—in LEGEND!
Harlequin Historical #168 (April 1993)

Read all the Taggart romances!
Meet all the Taggart men!

Available wherever Harlequin books are sold.

HARLEQUIN HISTORICAL

CHRISTMAS

• STORIES • 1992 •

Capture the magic and romance of Christmas in the 1800s with HARLEQUIN HISTORICAL CHRISTMAS STORIES 1992—a collection of three stories by celebrated historical authors. The perfect Christmas gift!

Don't miss these heartwarming stories, available in November wherever Harlequin books are sold:

MISS MONTRACHET REQUESTS by Maura Seger
CHRISTMAS BOUNTY by Erin Yorke
A PROMISE KEPT by Bronwyn Williams

Plus, this Christmas you can also receive a FREE keepsake Christmas ornament. Watch for details in all November and December Harlequin books.

DISCOVER THE ROMANCE AND MAGIC OF THE HOLIDAY SEASON WITH HARLEQUIN HISTORICAL CHRISTMAS STORIES!

HARLEQUIN®

Temptation®

Rebels & Rogues

Alex: He was hot on the trail of a career-making story . . . until he was KO'd by a knockout—Gabriella.

THE MAVERICK
by Janice Kaiser
Temptation #417, November

All men are not created equal. Some are rough around the edges. Tough-minded but tenderhearted. Incredibly sexy. The tempting fulfillment of every woman's fantasy.

When it's time to fight for what they believe in, to win that special woman, our Rebels and Rogues are heroes at heart. Twelve Rebels and Rogues, one each month in 1992, only from Harlequin Temptation.